BLIGHTED

A NOVEL

LISA COURTAWAY

BLIGHTED

A NOVEL

LISA COURTAWAY

ISBN: (ebook): 978-1-7374222-9-7

ISBN: (print): 978-1-7374222-8-0

Editing and Formatting by Two Birds Author Services

www.twobirdsauthorservices.com

Cover Design by Miblart

www.miblart.com

Dedicated to all Oklahomans whose lives were negatively impacted by the 2025 wildfires and in loving memory of my dear, sweet Pita.

PRETERM

April 14, 1978

Dear Diary,

Mother has finally ruined my life forever. She gave me no choice. Break up with Thomas, or she would cut me off after graduation. So it's over. She said she wouldn't pay for college if I didn't end my relationship with him. I told her we were going to prom. I was so excited. To think I believed she'd enjoy shopping for a dress with me. Instead, she asked a million questions about him, and when I told her of his life plans, she lost it. I haven't stopped crying for three weeks since she forbade me to see him. He doesn't understand. Because I could never tell him the truth.

My mother says you're not good enough for me.

How can I tell him that? I can't say something so heartless to someone so kind? I wish I were stronger. Could stand up for myself and defy her wishes. But what else am I supposed to do after graduation? Go to beauty school? As if! Who's going to trust a pimply-faced kid with a stringy mop of mousy brown hair and wafer-thin fingernails with their beauty routine? Should I be a secretary? Maybe, but I barely passed typing class. Daddy always wanted me to attend college. He set up the fund for my education, and now she wants to rob me of the opportunity because she doesn't like my boyfriend! Daddy wouldn't agree with her, I know it. I can't go to school and support myself at the same time. I've never had a job before. Never needed one. Daddy has provided for us well, even after his death. I don't have it in me to be a career woman. Mother made that very clear, pointing out my lack of experience, skill, drive … all true.

Besides, I've never defied her orders. And I don't think I can start now. Maybe she's right, but my heart says she isn't. Thomas is the love of my life. My soulmate.

I tried encouraging him to attend school too. To aim for something more than working in the factory where his father is the foreman. But he idolizes his father. Insists university isn't for him. He'd rather wear a hard hat than carry books. His favorite class has always been shop. He'd never have passed English Lit without my help.

I'll never love anyone like I love Thomas. It is so hard to pass him in the halls and not rush to him, tell him about my day, feel the warmth of his embrace. I'm counting down the days to graduation, when I won't have to face this misery anymore. Only four more weeks and I am done with high school. I had so looked forward to the summer with Thomas. We had big plans.

Mother insists there are plenty of other fish in the sea, but she doesn't get it. I think she's proud of herself for breaking my heart. Like she lives to hurt me. When I told her I had broken up with Thomas, she said I'd thank her someday. She honestly believes she's saved me from a life of poverty and hardship. But his family doesn't live in poverty—far from it. They just don't live up to her standards. She's probably hoping I'll find someone who reminds her of Daniel or maybe Daddy. As wonderful as he is, poor Thomas could never fit that bill. There's nothing wrong with him, of course. He's just not them. No one could ever fill either of their shoes, and I'm not looking to replace them. I just want to feel loved again.

For now,
Alice Quinn

ONE

PUSH

1989

"Slide down, dear," the nurse whispered with a smile.

I clamped my eyes shut against the glaring exam light. Its stark beam bounced off the sterile metal surfaces and gleaming white tile. Why did they keep this room so cold? Conception shouldn't take place in a freezer. While I didn't expect candlelight and soft music, dimmed lights and heat would've been nice. I followed instructions and wiggled my bottom to bring my hips closer to the edge of the table while keeping my feet in the stirrups.

"Move down a bit more, Mrs. White. I don't bite." Dr. Addison peered over the sheet draping my knees. The light caught his teeth, and they gleamed as he coughed up an awkward chuckle, making him seem as if he were hiding something, as if he did bite. Before lowering his head mirror over his eye, he winked, intending to reassure me he truly didn't, I assumed.

I scooted down farther and put my all into softening my rigid legs. It was impossible to loosen up… Shivering in a paper gown, stirrups jabbing into my feet, my womanhood exposed to strangers.

"Relax," the nurse said, grabbing the handle on the light and aiming the beam lower. "Try taking some deep breaths."

I complied, or did my best to comply, but flinched when Dr. Addison touched my thigh.

"Inserting the speculum," he mumbled.

His voice faded away into his concentration. My muscles locked up, any pliancy disappearing in a rush as the speculum pushed inside my body. I'd gritted my teeth through several pelvic exams, adhering to guidelines of having an annual Pap smear since my first six years ago, right after I married Roger. The procedures always left me feeling violated. My family doctor, the man who delivered me twenty-eight years ago and until now handled all my medical care, didn't stop calling me Ms. Quinn and start using my married name until he'd performed my third Pap test.

It was during that visit when I first broached the subject of getting pregnant. I'd never taken birth control, and despite Roger's healthy libido, I still found myself unable to conceive after three years of marriage. My doctor had assured me I was too young to concern myself with such matters. He suggested I drop a few pounds and promised I'd be a mother in no time. That was almost three years ago, and I still hadn't conceived. My doctor insisted there was no need to worry for a few more years, but I pressed the matter and he referred me to Dr. Addison. I wasn't willing to wait on fate any longer.

I clenched my teeth and forced myself to exhale.

"Good, good. You're doing just fine, Mrs. White," Dr. Addison said, his voice now muffled behind the sheet as he leaned further into me, his breath hot on my legs. My hand clamped the edge of the table and squeezed. My nails bored into the exam table vinyl; breath trapped in my throat, I prayed for the procedure to be over.

"You may feel a little pinch as I pass the catheter through your cervix."

I gasped, and a tear slid down the side of my face, catching in my ear in a tiny, cold puddle. Little pinch was an understatement. A searing burn shuddered through me. My pulse rushed in my ears like a sonic vibration, and more tears leaked from my clenched eyes. It would all be worth it, I reminded myself, conjuring up an image of a baby in my arms.

Before I could exhale again, the catheter slithered out of me, and the pressure dissipated as the speculum collapsed.

"And that's it," Dr. Addison said. "Now, you're going to lie here for about twenty minutes with a little gravitational boost. You may have some light spotting." He pushed the small metal table to the side and removed his gloves.

"It's over?" I asked, my voice dreamlike and distant.

The nurse pushed a button on the side of the exam table, lifting the bottom half, hoisting up my lower body. Perhaps it was my imagination, but I could feel things shift inside me, sensed a rush of energy force itself into my womb. I'd never experienced anything like it before and believed it was a sign. This had to work.

"Yes, it is," Dr. Addison replied. "With a bit of luck, we'll see a positive pregnancy test in a couple of weeks. The receptionist will schedule your follow-up." His eyes met mine, and I struggled not to look away. His tongue jutted out and rested on his lower lip, likely a habitual quirk. It made me uncomfortable; seemed snake-like and predatory. My face burned red. I looked away, chiding myself for being coy.

"Any questions?" Dr. Addison asked.

At least a dozen questions circled my brain, but I dismissed them with a shake of my head. Information overload only led to more anxiety. "None come to mind," I lied.

"Aside from strenuous exercise, feel free to return to normal activity, and we'll see you back in a couple of weeks." He left the room.

Normal activity? Nothing had been normal for years as my attempts to become a mother failed month after month. There was nothing normal about this entire process. Surely his words were in jest.

"Can I get you anything while you wait, dear?" the nurse asked as she plucked a tissue from a box on the counter and waved it toward me.

"No," I whispered, accepting the tissue. It was rough and small, but I used it to dab my eyes. My focus shifted to my insides, willing what Roger crassly dubbed his "swimmers" to get to work. Two ripe follicles harbored inside me, and I imagined them sending out beacons, summoning the sperm to my eggs. The idea of twins terrified me. One healthy child was all I needed, but Dr. Addison had outlined the potential risk of having a multiple pregnancy, given the success of the fertility drugs in producing two perfectly sized ova.

"I know it will be tempting, but try to refrain from taking a home pregnancy test. It might help spare you some disappointment. Those sticks are convenient, but the test we administer is much more accurate. Now sit tight. I'll be back soon to let you know you can get dressed."

The nurse left me alone in the sterile room. This wasn't the way it was supposed to happen. It was unnatural to be companionless while creating life. If I did conceive, I'd have been closer to Dr. Addison during the conception than to my husband. I wished Roger had stayed with me, at least sat by my side and held my hand. But he had a big presentation and ducked out after "making a deposit." It took considerable finagling to get him to agree to fertility treatment in the first place, and he could never be convinced that some of our difficulties getting pregnant might lie with him.

"Unexplained infertility. What a crock!" he'd complained after our initial consultation with Dr. Addison. He called the whole thing a scam. "I can't think of any other field where the word unexplained can be used to pry people's wallets open."

I knew he only agreed to the treatment to shut me up. That and his growing discomfort with colleagues questioning why he and his wife were still childless. Dr. Addison could expedite the process. As I inched closer to my thirties, the ticking of my biological clock grew louder. I'd read every magazine article I could find on infertility. According to experts, a woman's fertility plummets in her thirties. Maybe some would say I was too young to go to such lengths as medical intervention, but I could no longer ignore my need to become a mother. My life ached for something more, more than dreaming up new casseroles, bridge club, and housecleaning. I needed a child. A child would change everything, give me purpose, and I couldn't sit by any longer while my body denied me.

"Can't be any more of a chore than the way we've been doing

things, I suppose," Roger said when I told him about the new fertility doctor and his success rate. "Seriously, Alice, who schedules sex? It isn't normal."

I'd been prepared for him to write me off, shut me down, refuse to see Dr. Addison. But he needed a child to round out his image of the perfect life, and I wondered if he'd grown as concerned as I had that getting pregnant wasn't happening as quickly as it had for his coworkers and our friends. I was surprised when he agreed to go along with the procedures.

My face flushed red when, after our arrival for the appointment, the nurse asked if I would like to join my husband in the private collection room. She jokingly called it the Honeymoon Suite, but my husband referred to it as the depository; another of his vulgar colloquialisms. I'd glanced into the dim room, and my breakfast rose in my throat at the sight of the leather-clad daybed and a pile of pornographic magazines stacked on the floor nearby. At the foot of the bed sat a television and VCR. A pile of VHS tapes leaned against the TV stand. It looked more like a seedy motel room than a doctor's office.

"No, thank you," I whispered, catching Roger's expression, one resembling the look of a kid in a candy store. My hands twitched, aching to slap the smug look off his face. How dare he twist the conception of our child into something so tawdry? "I'll wait in the lobby," I said as I retreated down the hall.

"This shouldn't take long," Roger boasted to the nurse, removing his suit jacket and sauntering into the room.

For Roger, becoming a father was another item to check off his list. The obligatory white-collar pageantry of success. Power career: check. Presentable, loyal wife: check. Large home in a prestigious neighborhood: check. Next up was having a child. This check proved more elusive than he expected. Still, he refused to even scan the articles I'd collected on fertility science, denying there was a problem while going along with my requests.

"You sick?" he'd asked when I first started documenting my body temperature before getting out of bed.

"No, I'm feeling fine," I replied, jotting the thermometer

reading in my day planner. "But your temperature drops when you ovulate."

He rolled his eyes but partook when I lit candles and wore his favorite negligée. What he called scheduled sex, I called timed romance.

"Might as well enjoy the fun part," he conceded, as he disrobed and climbed into bed.

Before long, there was no fun part, even for him. "It isn't so easy for a man to perform on demand," he grumbled, rolling over away from me. On those nights when he denied me, when his body wasn't up for the simple task, I lay awake and cried as he snored. Another month lost; another egg shriveling up and wasting away inside me. He didn't get it.

My desire for a child ran deeper than his—it was a chance to right the wrongs of my childhood. It meant having a lifelong companion. Someone I could dote on and help grow into an exemplary woman. Hopefully, it would be a girl. Being a boy-mom wasn't in my makeup. I'd have a chance to prove myself and show that despite a less-than-ideal upbringing, I could be a perfect mother. I'd always believed I was made to love a child. Motherhood would heal my soul. And most importantly, it meant knowing I'd never be left alone as long as I protected that child from the evils of the world.

I never imagined my path to becoming a mother would find me lying by myself in a pasteurized room with exam table paper sticking to my skin, crinkling and tearing under my weight, the sting of the procedure still biting my pelvis. Never dreamed I would be forced to monitor my cycle, inject myself with hormones designed to stimulate my body's production of eggs, and lie in wait for a precisely timed injection to trigger the release of those ripened ova. It was beyond unsavory to track the viscosity of my bodily fluids. Was my discharge stretchy enough? The proper color? I'd even resorted to taking cough medicines when I had no cough, because an article I'd read hinted that over-the-counter expectorants might improve the quality of my cervical mucus. How I envied women who never had to concern themselves with such things.

All Roger had to do was meet his own physical needs, while I suffered. His contribution took place in the privacy of a dark room, during an act he'd no doubt perfected before the first whiskers sprouted on his face. An act which brought him pleasure and release. I shuddered at the thought of him pleasing himself while I endured the discomfort and bloating the injections caused. The pain and humiliation of the procedure itself. He griped endlessly about the process, the cost, the inconvenience. I showed sympathy, stroked his ego, praised him for his efforts, while my insides and mind twisted with pharmaceutical manipulation.

All the planning, expense, and torment culminated in this moment. Here I was. Alone in a procedure room. It had to work. IUI, a clipped, tidy acronym for intrauterine insemination. A mouthful of a term that removed all of nature from a natural act. I'd jumped through so many hoops and subjected my body and mind to such torture to achieve something countless people did daily without thought.

After Roger had submitted his donation—an odd appellation— it was spun and washed. The process sounded more like a laundry chore than the act of banishing undesirable sperm, leaving only the heartiest of cells to be injected via a fine tube into my uterus.

A knock on the door startled me from my thoughts.

"Come in," I said with a girlish giggle that made me cringe.

The nurse entered the room.

"You're good to go, Mrs. White," she said, pushing the button on the table. My lower body sank and my insides clenched. "There's a pantyliner on the countertop next to your purse. You might want to use it in case there's any spotting. Have a good day!" She left me alone again.

I wished I could stay here longer with my hips thrust toward the sky, blood pulsing in my head. Maybe another half hour would ensure success, so I would never have to suffer this indignity again. Instead, I rose and got dressed. I checked my hair in the reflective surface of a paper towel dispenser and made sure my mascara hadn't run.

In the lobby, I got in line to schedule my return visit. As nerve-wracking as this appointment had been, I knew the next would find me climbing the walls. The woman in front of me was engaged in a heated exchange with the receptionist.

"Yes, I know it may be unorthodox, but I want to pick a different donor. I should have some say over the selection of my child's father, don't you think?"

"Yes, of course, Mrs. Ellington, but the contract you signed was for your first selection, donor number eighteen-thirty-three. You can most definitely choose another donor, but I can't make changes without Dr. Addison's review. There are protocols." The young receptionist's face flushed, and she spoke in a hushed tone, glancing around the irate Mrs. Ellington and fixing me with a contrite grin. "I'll just be another moment, ma'am."

I nodded and turned my back, shifting my eyes to the waiting room full of eager but nervous women distracting themselves with back issues of *Better Homes and Gardens* and *Self* magazines. Soft music floated through the bright room from overhead speakers. The tune was calming and sedate, no doubt selected to be so, but the room buzzed with unspoken stories no orchestral piece could compete with … forced relations, broken hearts, empty wombs. Desperation tainted the space despite the efforts made to create warmth and comfort.

"Fine! Talk to Dr. Addison and call me. I don't know what to tell you other than I had a bad feeling after this last treatment failed. There's no point betting on a losing horse. I need a shake-up. I'm not getting any younger."

"Understood, Mrs. Ellington. I'm sure we can work things out. I'll be in touch soon. Have a good day."

Mrs. Ellington was already making her way to the exit. She did not return the sentiment.

"Sorry for the wait, Mrs. White," the receptionist said. "Looks like we need to pick a time for testing."

It took only a moment to seal my fate. In two long weeks, I would find out whether my dream had come true or been dashed. Unfazed by the weight of what was a mundane daily task for her, she jotted the details on a card and handed it to me. I wished her well and left the office.

While I waited for the elevator, Mrs. Ellington exited the lady's room in the hallway. She straightened her skirt and adjusted her handbag before moving toward me.

"Can you believe this place?" she asked, leaning around me to poke at the down button with a long, crimson fingernail, ignoring the fact that the button was already lit. "Acting like I'm being unreasonable for wanting to change things up. Donor eighteen-whatever can't be the only virile medical student in that binder of theirs who looks like my Edward."

I played dumb and ignored her. Why was the elevator taking so long?

"How about you? What number did you pick out of the stud farm lineup? Tell you what, it'd be a lot more fun if we could just meet up with these stallions in a hotel. Bet it'd work faster, too. Never dreamed it'd take more than one stab for me. Forgive the pun. Not like I had a problem getting knocked up before. Hello, I'm not talking to myself." She crossed her arms and tapped her foot.

"Oh, sorry," I stammered, glancing around the hallway. My eyes fell in embarrassment, unable to meet hers, and they landed on her feet. The heels of her shoes had to be six inches tall. She towered above me. As traumatic as the last hour had been, at least I didn't have to make a decision about who I wanted to father my child. Things could always be worse. "I, um, well, I guess I am fortunate in that regard. We aren't using a donor."

"Oh, so it's you with the problem, huh? I guess I should be more grateful. I'm popping out eggs left and right, but I married a man a bit older than me. Turns out he's shooting blanks. The poor old coot wants to be a dad again so bad, and, well, modern medicine and all."

I nodded, overwhelmed by the deluge of personal details the impeccably dressed Mrs. Ellington bombarded me with, and willed the elevator to show while dreading the ride three floors down with the fiery woman. The bell dinged, and I braced myself for the doors to open, hoping to find a car crammed full of people. It was empty.

"Finally," she hissed, pushing past me. As I stepped into the elevator, she jabbed her finger repeatedly at the *L* button. The doors crawled shut.

"I could use a drink. How about you?" she asked, rummaging through her purse. "This place gives me the willies, pun intended this time, if you know what I mean." She chuckled and poked my midsection with her sharp fingernail.

In the confines of the elevator car, a cloying mix of cigarette smoke and a powdery fragrance churned my stomach. My mother would have scoffed at her heavy-handed perfume. And why would a woman in fertility treatment smoke?

"I suppose a cup of tea sounds nice," I said, wondering who uttered those words. Did I just accept an invitation from this brash stranger? It was unlike me, but a voice in the back of my mind told me this was not a time to go home to an empty house where I would likely spend the day wearing a track in the carpet as I paced and fretted over each gas bubble or muscle twinge. I didn't want to be alone, and this woman and I shared at least one thing in common: we were both going to great lengths to become mothers. I'd inferred this would not be her first child, but had to admit her story piqued my curiosity.

"Tea? Honey, please." She hooked her arm in mine as the doors slid open. "I need something stronger than tea."

TWO

IMPLANTATION

A bright sun nudged the chill out of the crisp fall day, so we left our cars in the parking lot at the medical plaza and made small talk as we crossed 21st Street on foot. We dropped the formalities of Mrs. Ellington and Mrs. White while we waited at the corner for the light to change. Her name was Nancy. She talked nonstop, which was fine with me. I've always been a person of few words. I was a shrinking violet to her morning glory … but I've found sometimes that stance can serve me well.

"Polo Grill is right around the corner. Their martinis are divine."

We walked arm in arm, something I hadn't done with another woman since I was a girl and my mother needed to keep me at her side. I struggled to keep up with Nancy as we strolled along the cobblestone pathway of the open-air shopping center. Aside from the teetering height of her heels, her legs were long and lean, as were her angular features. With her arm linked in mine, my fingers brushed against the fine fabric of her suit. Free of the stifling medical office, I got a better look at my new acquaintance. Her blonde hair turned in a glamorous twist at the back of her head. A clip adorned with pearls held the impossible hairdo in place at the nape of her neck. To balance the creamy knit of her jacket, she wore a silky, low-cut blouse, pearl drop earrings, and a gold necklace. The sun danced over a tennis bracelet on her thin wrist, and the large diamond set in the ring she wore on her left hand cast prism auras on the leaves overhead. Every inch of her was put together to perfection.

What did she see in me that had made her strike up a conversation? I was petite, with thick bones. Withdrawn. My fine hair could be described as nothing more fetching than brunette. Freckles dotted my fair skin, and I still struggled with blemishes, making me look younger than I felt. My fashion sense was derived purely from my mother's input and department store mannequins. I was hardly the society woman of certitude Nancy was.

Inside the tiny Tudor-style bistro, I spotted a smartly dressed middle-aged man tucked into a corner near the bar. He sat in a tufted leather high-back, his fingers floating over the strings of a guitar. The notes were subdued and blended with the low murmur of patron's conversations and cutlery clinking on china. Sun filtered through gauzy valances to brighten the room, darkened by a low-hanging ceiling inlaid with heavy wooden beams. We followed the hostess across the tumbled brick floor to a small booth. An ancient lantern sat on the table. A thick candle flickered and melted in its globe; mallets and trophies rested on the aged wood window ledge next to our seats.

"I'll have a martini, and my friend, Alice, here will have…" She looked at me, waiting for a reply.

"Herbal tea for me, please."

"You've a much stronger constitution than I," Nancy said, watching the waitress depart. "I've needed this drink since I woke up, and I'm not the one who's spent the bulk of my day in stirrups with the dreamy Dr. Addison staring at my hoo-ha." She erupted in laughter, drawing stares from other guests.

I blushed, struggling to coalesce Nancy's graceful demeanor with her crass language, and took my napkin from the table, smoothing it in my lap. I'd never looked past Dr. Addison's professional position to consider his appearance. Now that she mentioned it, I considered his chiseled bone structure, athletic build, and icy blue eyes.

"You don't mind if I smoke," Nancy said, pulling a cigarette from a slender case encrusted in crystals. She didn't phrase it as a question, and she didn't wait for my reply before lighting up. I forced my jaw shut. While some people still believed the occasional drink during pregnancy was fine, smoking had been deemed detrimental some time ago. I waved at the hazy tendril as it inched closer to my nose. Nancy didn't take notice of my discomfort.

"How many attempts have you made so far?" she asked as she eyed the red glow at the tip of her cigarette and plucked something invisible from her tongue. "They are hellish, aren't they? The indignity of it all. But my Edward wants an heir, so an heir I shall give him."

"Today was my first—" I began.

"For your sake, I hope it's your last," she interrupted. "My next ride in Dr. Addison's saddle will be my third. Are you taking the hormones?" She didn't wait for my reply but pressed on as if she'd gotten the answer she wanted. "Lord, getting a glimpse of what menopause will be like has me terrified of the future. I've been shooting that stuff into my thigh for months now. The emotional roller coaster is almost unbearable." Her cadence slowed, her words no longer rushing out as if rehearsed. She twirled her finger in her drink before removing it and dabbing it on her napkin.

Words teetered on my lips, but I could not comfort her despite understanding what she meant. The thought of being subjected to IUI for a second or third time shrouded me in discomfort. *Please let me be pregnant.*

"I can hardly stand myself anymore," she continued, lifting her glass to her lips. She took a drink, and her gaze shifted across the room, settling on something or someone outside my line of sight. When she spoke again, her commanding self returned. "I'm a regular Fertile Myrtle, but the good doc says the shots will increase my odds, especially at my age. They act like a woman in her mid-thirties is over the hill. Ha! And my sex drive! Don't get me started. Edward may be shooting blanks, but he's shooting plenty of them these days to keep up with my needs."

"Oh, you already have a child?" I questioned, ignoring the personal details, unable to fathom why any woman would subject herself to fertility treatments if she was already a mother. I needed to know why she would go to such extreme measures when she'd already been given such a gift.

"Yes, two. A son from husband number two and a daughter from husband number three. At least I think she's his. Sometimes you can't be certain, right?" Again she laughed at her own joke, making me question her seriousness. "For all I know, the man who raised me isn't my dad! My mother had quite the roving eye. Did you know, statistically speaking, one in four children is being raised by a man who isn't actually their father? Oftentimes, the poor sap isn't even aware that junior belongs to someone else."

Her eyes bugged at the statistic, and I fought to keep mine from doing the same. She wasn't joking. She believed parenthood was a game and the sanctity of marriage meant nothing. It was shameful. Discomfort lay on me like a wet blanket as I struggled for something to say. I spotted the waitress approaching our table, and a sigh of relief escaped me. A martini glass, small teapot, and cup and saucer balanced on the tray in her hand. She placed the items on our table and asked if we'd like to order food. I hadn't yet looked at the menu, but at the mention of lunch, my stomach stirred. I wondered if I'd soon be eating for two.

"Nothing yet, doll. Check back in a bit, please," Nancy said, dismissing the waitress and smashing her cigarette butt out in the tabletop ashtray.

"Back to kids. My fourth husband, Edward, is a bit older than me. Not quite old enough to be my father, but the age difference has raised an eyebrow or two." She lifted the cocktail stick to her lips and drew an olive into her mouth, chewing it slowly before returning the skewer to the glass and using it to mix her drink.

Lifting the cup to her lips, she drained half the contents with a lengthy pull.

"I see," I said, pouring hot water over the tea bag. She spoke as if we'd known each other for years, freely offering information I hadn't asked for. Perhaps she was this forward with everyone. Unable to think of anything else to say, I took a sip of my tea. It was too soon, and it burned my throat, but allowed enough of a lull to prompt Nancy to continue.

"Edward lost his only son in a boating accident before we met. He was beside himself with grief when I found him. Lonely but rich." She peered at me over her glass and winked as if she'd let me in on inside information. "Our courtship was a whirlwind. As soon as my divorce was final, of course. On our wedding night he asked me to have a child. I didn't imagine myself wearing empire-waist jumpers and those God-awful maternity underwear again. Don't get me started on the sleepless nights and potty training. I thought I was done with all the drudgery of baby-rearing. But I'd do anything for Edward, so here we are."

She leaned back in her seat and regarded her drink. "Enough about me. How'd you find yourself in Dr. Addison's office?"

"Well, Roger, my husband," I stammered, struggling for words. The reason I'd sought Dr. Addison's help paled compared to hers. I pressed on, not wanting to appear rude but reluctant to divulge as much as she did. "We've been trying for some time now."

"Ah, I remember the good old-fashioned way—spontaneous, fun. That's how it should be," she commented before draining her drink. She waved a hand at the waitress and pointed to her empty glass. "You do seem a little younger than the usual Dr. Addison set. You in a hurry for some reason?"

My fingers lifted to a stubborn blemish on my chin as my cheeks flushed. "I'm not as young as I look," I replied, hoping I'd hidden my annoyance. How would she feel if I'd said she was too old to be a new mother again?

"It was meant to be a compliment," she replied, plucking a cocktail onion off the garnish skewer. She popped it in her mouth and spoke while chewing. "Go on."

"After a couple of years of thinking it would happen when it happened, I started taking my temperature, monitoring my cycle. I've never been regular." I shocked myself with my willingness to share such intimate details with a woman I'd just met, but no one had ever asked me about my desire to become a mother. No one knew how difficult it was to buy gifts for other women's baby showers. To congratulate countless acquaintances on their impending births while seething at their good fortune. No one knew how news stories of child abuse and the horrors parents could subject their children to tore through my heart with bitter sadness.

While Nancy and I had little in common, she knew some of what I was going through. In an effort to obtain what women achieved daily, we endured injections, side effects, humiliating treatments, endless blood draws, and intrusions. It was all so unfair, and it felt good to share these confidences with someone who understood at least some of it. I hadn't spoken to anyone about the challenges I'd faced, the despair I'd experienced—it wasn't polite conversation fodder.

"Well, you're in excellent hands now. I have several friends who turned to Dr. Addison as a last resort. I'm happy to report most of them are waddling around on swollen feet, ready to pop any second now. He's the best around. This town is lucky to have him."

The waitress arrived with a fresh drink. Nancy drummed her long fingernails on the table. She peered around the waitress, scanning the bar area. A smile flashed on her face as if she'd recognized someone. She fluttered her fingers in a curt wave, her head held high. Her pupils expanded in the blue ocean of her irises. I considered looking over my shoulder to see who had caught her eye.

"Can you excuse me, please? I need to use the powder room," I said sheepishly.

"Sure thing, hon. Those hormones have me peeing like a racehorse too. Restrooms are that way." She pointed, and I saw she held another cigarette in her slender fingers. I rose and hurried past her before she could light it.

Alone in the bathroom, my mind went to my belly. The doctor had been right. A small pink spot dotted my undergarments. I took it as a good sign. One to be expected, which was promising. Outside the stall, I studied myself in the mirror, certain I would look different soon. That the glow of motherhood would emanate from me in short time. I placed my hands on my stomach and wondered how big it would grow.

An elderly woman entered the bathroom, forcing me out of my thoughts. I washed my hands and smiled at her in the mirror before she disappeared into a stall. As I approached our booth, I saw Nancy was no longer seated. My teacup was gone; the table cleared. Confused, I looked around and spotted her at the bar. She sat close to a man, her hand on his shoulder. Recalling her husband was, according to her, older than she, caused me to pause. This man was at best in his early forties, with a thick head of wavy golden hair and a line-free face. She spotted me and waved me over.

"Alice, meet my friend. What was your name again?"

"Chad, Chad Stopes. Nice to meet you, Alice." He extended his hand, and I shook it. "Can I buy you a drink?" It was the man who'd been playing guitar when we entered.

"I'll take another," Nancy said, snapping her fingers at the bartender.

"Um, no, thank you. I really must go. Errands and all." I had no plans, but felt like a third wheel standing in the flow of foot traffic. The noise in the room grew and the space shrank as the lunch rush poured in. Mr. Stopes did not offer me a seat.

"It was nice gabbing with you, Alice. We should meet up again soon." She was dismissive. Her eyes never left Chad's face. Her hand fell to his knee.

I searched for something else to say but decided to bow out instead. Nancy and Chad didn't appear to remember I was there, as their attention shifted to their drinks and their chemistry. I pushed my way through the growing lunch crowd to the hostess station and questioned the woman about my tab, only to learn Mr. Stopes had taken care of it.

"Oh," I replied, not knowing what else to say. I came up with, "Thank you," and squeezed past a large group who entered the establishment laughing. Outside, I peered back into the cafe through a window. Chad's arm was draped around Nancy's waist and his hand rested on her hip. I stared, not knowing what to think. As I did, I saw her foot inch up his pant leg. Her toe, pointed inside an already impossibly pointy shoe, snaked higher up his calf. A gold ankle bracelet looped around her spindly ankle. Chad leaned in and whispered in her ear, and Nancy threw her head back and laughed. All the while, her foot coiled around his legs, the bracelet gleaming under the lights.

Again I wondered, why would a woman like Nancy subject herself to the indignities of fertility treatment? To me, it seemed she could save herself the trouble and expense of the doctor's office and the procedures. She could find a father right there in an upscale restaurant instead of shelling out countless dollars to be prodded and poked in a sterile exam room. It wasn't like her husband would have a clue. The child wouldn't be his, no matter what. Even Nancy questioned the paternity of one of her existing children. How did it come so easy for some who showed so little respect for such a gift? It wasn't fair.

As I walked back to my car, I did some window shopping. I was in no hurry to return to my quiet home. A quaint children's boutique caught my eye; its window dressed with fluffy white clouds atop a sea of pink, blue, and yellow merchandise, evoking a field of dreamy flowers. Tiny stuffed animals dotted the makeshift meadow of pastel. It pulled me inside. A bell jingled, announcing my entry, and a young woman popped out from a back room.

"Can I help you find something?" she asked.

"I'm just looking, thank you," I replied.

"I'm unpacking some new arrivals in the back. If you need anything, there's a bell by the register. Just give me a ding."

I nodded, and she disappeared behind a curtain. The room smelled like babies. A rotating shelf filled with powders and lotions stood to my right. I plucked each sample from the display and sniffed them all. When I found a particularly pleasing one, I rubbed it on my hands and up my arms, then capped the tube and made my way farther into the enchanting store. As I did so, I kept my wrist to my nose, breathing in the fresh aroma. My baby would wear this lotion.

My fingers brushed over every gown and bunting, the fabric of each cloud-like and downy. I cracked open chunky books; the pages were filled with brightly colored illustrations and sentiments of cherished love. Closing my eyes, I imagined rocking my infant as I whispered the words on the pages.

A basket brimming with stuffed animals lured me even farther into the shop. A little pink rabbit caught my eye. I was powerless. It was coming home with me. I hugged it to my chest as I approached the cash register and tapped the bell. The shopkeeper emerged from the back, tiny blue mittens in hand.

"Oh, isn't this adorable?" she said, taking the rabbit. "Will you need gift wrap?" She swaddled the pink poof in tissue paper.

"No, thank you," I said.

I paid for my purchase, my eyes never wandering from the bag that contained my new talisman. It held so much more than a cute trinket. The adorable stuffed animal was the promise of a child who would seek its comfort in times of upset. It would stoke their imagination. My child would serve it tea, read it stories, and mend its pretend wounds. My child would snuggle it close when drifting off to sleep and tote it everywhere. I could see the bunny in its later life —worn, faded, stained, adored.

"Here you go. It is sure to make some little girl very happy."

"Yes, it will," I said and exited the store. It was the first gift of many I would buy for the life I was certain grew inside me.

At home, I made myself lunch. The rabbit sat on the table as I ate and tidied up. In our bedroom, I tucked the bunny in a drawer with my nightclothes and lay down for a bit, certain my actions would further aid gravity. I nodded off and came to over an hour later, just in time to start dinner. That evening, Roger did not ask me how the procedure went; didn't mention it at all. Rather, he spoke of his presentation and how landing the new account, a small but growing pizza chain, could mean a promotion, a raise, a bonus. He hummed a few bars of the jingle he was working on.

I smiled and nodded at the proper moments, barely registering his words. My mind was busy conjuring up images of the daughter I was certain was budding inside me. I'd read enough pamphlets at Dr. Addison's office to know implantation didn't occur for several days, but it didn't stop me from imagining the life stirring within me. Would she have my eyes? Roger's cleft chin? I went to bed and dreamed of my child, confident a miracle had occurred.

THREE

EFFACEMENT

Roger's cologne still hung in the air the following morning after I saw him off and busied myself in the kitchen, cleaning up breakfast dishes. Satisfied the house was presentable for the cleaning ladies who would arrive later in the day, I prepared to visit my mother at her nursing home. This weekly chore was one of my least favorites, but was expected of a dutiful daughter. Something I did out of obligation, more to save face than anything else. The duty of an obedient child. My mother had no one else.

In the entryway, I reapplied lipstick, smoothed my hair, and was putting my jacket on when the doorbell rang. A list of potential visitors shuffled through my mind. Flowers from Roger lauding yesterday's momentous event? Impossible. A package? Doubtful. Door-to-door salesman? The most likely culprit.

I hurried to the door and peered out the peephole. It was Nancy Ellington. How had she gotten my address? I hadn't even mentioned where I lived. Having only moved into the sprawling ranch home in the historic midtown neighborhood months earlier, I hadn't established a closeness with my neighbors or even a comfortable familiarity with the area. We certainly had no common acquaintances outside the office of Dr. Addison.

Nancy prodded the bell again.

"Coming," I said, removing my jacket, returning it to the coat rack, and opening the door.

"Good morning, doll," she proclaimed, pushing past me.

I stepped back, swinging the door open wider, unable to fathom how and why the woman was on my doorstep. Her scent, the expensive but overpowering perfume, which did nothing to mask the tang of cigarettes, filled the space. She handed me a pink box I recognized from the bakery on Cherry Street.

"There's a cat out there, you know," she said, plucking a tissue from her coat pocket and rubbing her nose with it. "I think it's feral. I'm horribly allergic and practically had to pry the beast from my leg."

"Oh yes, sorry. He isn't feral. He's very sweet." I peered over her shoulder to see if the cat was still nearby. She must have frightened him off. "I suspect the former owners left him behind, the poor dear. Roger is adamant he not be allowed in the house, but I feed him, so he sticks around. I call him Orson."

Before I'd closed the door, she'd removed her jacket. She handed it to me and made her way to the kitchen, giving no indication of how she knew where the sunny eat-in nook sat in my home's layout. I draped her coat over the coat rack and trailed behind her as she marched through the house as if she'd been there previously.

"Well, you should detach yourself. Think of the bugs and parasites that thing is carrying. Filthy animals, in my opinion." She sat at the banquette in the nook and opened the box. The aroma of cherry scones wafted my direction. Despite having already eaten a soft-boiled egg and toast with Roger, I wanted one. My appetite was quite hearty these days. I pulled two coffee mugs and plates from the cabinet and joined her at the table after pouring coffee.

"How did you find me, Nancy?" I questioned, taking a scone. My mouth was watering. Perhaps my body was reacting to the strain of creating life. "I'm certain I didn't give you my address."

"Yes, well, I know everyone in this town—everyone who matters, anyway." She surveyed the room with a raised brow. "Claire from my tennis club lives across the street from you. We met for drinks yesterday evening, and I rehashed the run-in you and I had. She swore you had to be her new neighbor. Our dear friend Sharon Denton and her husband used to live here. He took a job in Chicago. The Dentons did not own a cat, by the way. Anyway, Claire described you to a T. I took a chance. When I got here, I saw your car in the drive and knew she was right. I thought the new owners might have refreshed the place prior to moving in, but you've given it a homey touch without any renovations. No small feat!" She brushed her hand across the back of the banquette seat and rubbed her fingers together, and I wished the cleaning ladies had come yesterday. "You probably don't allow smoking in your home?"

"Um, no!" I barked sharply. "Well, Roger enjoys a cigar now and again in his office, but I'd rather…" I trailed off and cast a scrutinizing eye about my kitchen. Roger had nixed my suggestions to put in new floors and countertops. The wallpaper, with its marigold and orange flowers I'd come to ignore, had begun to peel at the ceiling and now it screamed at me.

"Understood, say no more." She retracted her hand, which had been reaching for her purse. "Thanks for the coffee." She raised the cup and blew on it, pushing the cloud of steam in my direction. "So, how are you this morning? Any cramping? You must listen to your body, especially while on hormones. Overstimulation and such. Ghastly, but of concern." She lifted the edge of the curtain and inspected the hem.

"Oh, I'm aware. I think I've read every pamphlet a dozen times. I feel fine. Hopeful." I was still off-balance, shell-shocked by her unannounced visit, but did my best to be polite.

"That's the spirit." She took another sip of coffee, then reached for the sugar, adding two spoonfuls. The remaining scone sat untouched. I nibbled at mine, attempting to hide my keen hunger.

"I hope you don't consider it rude of me to stop by."

I choked down the bite of pastry, eager to give her my undivided attention, sensing I might soon understand what prompted such an unexpected drop-in, but she was silent. I brushed the crumbs off my fingers and took a drink of my coffee as quiet hung in the air. Just when the lull prompted me to search for some reply, she continued.

"After we parted ways yesterday, I felt bad about ditching you." As she spoke, she stared at her coffee, pausing before looking up and locking eyes with me. "It may be forward of me, but I sensed a burgeoning kinship between us. You and I clicked."

The air grew heavy, and I inched forward in my seat, nudging the half-eaten scone away. I anticipated something emotional coming and searched for words to lighten the mood. I couldn't deny I'd sensed a connection too, but after she'd displayed such a flippant attitude toward the gift of motherhood, I knew we could never be close. We were two very different people. She ended my search for the proper response with a laugh.

"And who knows, maybe we'll get knocked up at the same time. We can be pregnancy buddies." She winked and then surprised me further by taking my hand. "There are so few women who know what we're going through, you know? It'd be nice to have someone to commiserate with."

Her hand was warm, calling my attention to the fact that mine were icy. Before the warmth of her fingers could penetrate mine, she pulled away from me. "Plus, I didn't want you to get the wrong idea about my marriage. My Edward is very open to my—" She paused for a moment. "Dalliances, shall we say? He just wants me to be happy. Your discomfort with the situation at the bar was apparent, and I wanted to defend myself."

The real reason for her visit hit me in the face. This wasn't about connecting with a fellow woman struggling to achieve the basic goal we were created for. She herself said she had a slew of friends who passed through Dr. Addison's office. She didn't need me to commiserate with over the procedures. Her intent was pure self-preservation. What did she think I was going to do, track down her husband and fill him in on his wife's extramarital activities? None of it was my business. The scone rose in my throat, and I forced it down with a sip of coffee.

"No need to explain." I picked at the pastry as my mind raced to find the words. Yes, I found her lack of morals disturbing. No, there was no connection between us, aside from the obvious. And I had no intention of being pregnancy buddies with a woman with no regard for her vows, nor the harm she could do to her unborn child by drinking and smoking. While I'd thought of little else than the excitement of possibly being pregnant since parting ways with Nancy yesterday, I was sure a friendship with her wasn't in the cards, because now it hit me… She reminded me of my mother.

"I hate to be rude," I said, rising and gathering my dishes. "The scone was delicious, but I was on my way out the door to visit my mother at Coventry Springs."

She was up before I finished the sentence.

"Say no more. I've got a full day myself," she said, pulling a card from her purse. "Here's my number. Call me and we can have a proper lunch. My third insemination is next week. Wish me luck." She closed the bakery box and left it on the table.

I walked her to the door and handed her jacket to her, noticing the rich fabric and detail. I wanted to hurl it out the door and give her a shove behind it, but I smiled.

"Thank you for the scones. It was lovely seeing you again," I chirped.

She leaned in and brushed her cheek against mine, and the hair raised on my arm. Closing the door behind her, I looked at the card. I had never known a housewife with her own business cards. It listed a slew of her club memberships and chairmanships. Nancy Ellington was quite the philanthropist, according to the three-by-two resumé I held in my hand. My only charitable cause was helping at Mother's nursing home from time to time. I tossed the card in the drawer of the entry table, grabbed my purse and jacket, and exited the house. Orson greeted me as I walked to my car.

"Oh, dear. I forgot to fill your bowl," I cooed. "Why don't you make yourself useful and catch a mouse to snack on? You need to pull your weight around here, mister. I'll reward you with a proper meal when I come home." I bent to scratch his ears, and he flopped onto the ground, twisting his body in the grass. His purr was loud and strong. I considered going back inside to get him a snack, but I was already running late. Nancy's visit had thrown me, and I knew

Mother would be waiting for me and my delivery. With a guilty heart, I left Orson behind. How I wished I could bring him inside to keep me company.

The car ahead of me kicked up a confetti of leaves in all the colors of flint corn as I drove the wide, tree-lined streets out of the neighborhood. The withered foliage swirled and chittered over my car in a chaotic dance. I loved the fall. The dramatic shift of air, colors, and smells soothed me. Even the sun agreeing to shorter stints in the sky created an ambiance that suited me. It was a season free of ghosts. The brief time between September and early November held no remnants of pain. No birthdays or anniversaries to reflect upon with sadness. No reminders of life given, nor of life snatched away.

My mother and I had never been close. Even before my brother, Daniel, died, my mother treated me as if I were a burden. I hadn't been expected. Always quick to point out she didn't think she could still have a child, she referred to me as an accident and chalked the early signs of a pregnancy up to 'the change.' My father softened the word *accident* to *pleasant surprise*. By the time I understood the meaning of these monikers and the polarizing sentiments regarding my brother's birth versus mine, I adored my brother too deeply to notice the divide. Daniel was ten years my senior.

Every moment spent with my mother served as a reminder of all we'd lost. She'd never moved past that horrible time. Her mourning hadn't transitioned. She was mired in disillusionment. My potential failed to impart hope.

Every parent dreamed of a child like Daniel: chiseled good looks, immense intelligence, athletic skill. And those were just his obvious traits. He was kind, a respectful young man, and he treated me like a princess. I hung on his every word. He was the star of the family.

His loss shattered our family. While other boys his age were drafted and sent off to foreign lands to fight a war I knew nothing about, Daniel's intellect afforded him a pass, and instead of going to war, he went to college. My parent's relief was palpable. Even at my young age, I sensed their welcome deliverance from the fate of their friends and neighbors. I overheard their conversations from my bedroom when they thought I was asleep. Terms like *educational deferment*, *draft dodging*, *duty to country* stormed through their exchanges. Daniel complied with my mother's tearful pleas and instead of shipping out for basic training, he shipped out to university.

My parents were at peace with my brother safely ensconced on a bucolic college campus, far away from the bloody jungle battlefields. As a sophomore preparing for premed, he was due to come home from university for the holidays. Daniel never made it home for Thanksgiving. With finals ensuing, he and his friends went to a campus bar—one last hurrah before hunkering down for their studies. Daniel stepped in to defend a young woman being berated by her boyfriend. The man, just back from a tour in Vietnam, didn't take kindly to the interference. He waited outside for Daniel to leave. While my brother walked to his dorm, the man confronted him, slit his throat, and left him on the sidewalk to bleed out. Although not a war hero, my brother still died a hero.

Daniel's passing sucked the life out of our home. The loss was overwhelming. The death of one stole the hearts of three others. We never recovered. My mother would rather have died on those campus grounds with her beloved son. My father, buckling under his own sadness, was tasked with keeping his wife afloat. I vanished beneath their grief. We buried my father less than three years after we put Daniel to rest. For my mother and me, the second loss sealed our fate. I was witness to his death. Try as I might, I could never shake the horrible memory, and every visit I made to Mother brought it all crashing back.

That day, I'd awoken to a heart-stopping noise. The weekend morning's customary sounds at the soulless house faded into the background: the begging call from new life growing in the nest outside my window ceased; the *tick-tick-tick* of the neighbor's sprinkler fell silent; the heavy toll of the bells from Holy Family Cathedral withered. All was drowned out by a thump. Unyielding but wavering, almost spasmodic, the deep thwack rumbled against the wall, rattling the contents of my bookshelf.

I grappled with the possible source of the noise. As a thought forced its way into my head, my cheeks bloomed hot and red. I rolled away from the sound, clamping a pillow over my head. Often intermingled with father's moans or mother's girlish giggles, I recognized the sound. How long had it been since I'd heard this noise? It was definitely before my brother died, back when I was too young to know what I was hearing.

Despite my red-faced chagrin, I wondered if the act could mark a turning point. A reawakening. My mind drifted to my mother's eyes. Once bright, my brother's murder extinguished their light. Could the act taking place in the next room reignite a spark? Drive away the icy gloom that shrouded our existence?

My mother's voice called me back to the moment. The banging on the wall continued, but grew weak, capricious. I bolted upright, tossed the pillow aside, and pricked my ears.

Mother called again. "Breakfast," her empty voice repeated. "It's getting cold."

My eyes darted from the bedroom door to the wall. The bookshelf quivered. I threw back the covers and ran into the hall. My parents' bedroom door was closed. I bolted into the room without knocking. My eyes struggled to adjust to the dim room. I snapped the switch on the wall. As light filled the space, I saw his feet on the floor between the far side of the bed and the wall. His body twitched inside his plaid pajamas. The spasms made it appear as if he were being electrocuted. The wall tremored. I scrambled over the bed on hands and knees. Bile rose in my throat, silencing a scream. His eyes were wide and scared. A soapy foam flowed from his mouth, pooling on the wood floor. He shuddered again before falling still. A heavy wind escaped his mouth and caused his body to deflate.

"Daddy!" I shrieked into his face as I swiped the frothy spittle from his mouth. His eyes were on me now, empty and unseeing. The little life that had remained after Daniel's painful departure was snuffed out forever.

Before the ambulance arrived, our neighbor, Mrs. Brennan, ushered me to her house. A widow, she was the only sitter I knew throughout my childhood, aside from Daniel. While I was old enough now to stay home on my own, I was grateful to be in her home and not alone in the house where images of my father flopping like a fish out of water played in a loop inside my head.

There was so much to love about Mrs. Brennan and her home. Tom and Jerry, her two house cats, provided endless entertainment. Whether they chased a dangling string, darted at shadows, or curled up on your lap, the felines' presence added to the coziness. A fire burned in her fireplace as soon as the outside temperature dropped below fifty degrees, and mouthwatering aromas emanated from her kitchen no matter what the time of year. A study lined with book-shelves teeming with novels ranging from children's stories to leather-bound encyclopedias fueled my curiosities. Photos of the beaming faces of her children, now grown, graced every inch of her sitting room and hallway walls. She squeezed new frames in the gaps as her family grew; grandchildren were now the center of her life.

Nothing else in her home had changed since her husband's passing five years earlier. Her house was a respite, but I longed to know what was happening to my father as the ambulance departed silently down our street.

Hours later, my Aunt Elizabeth woke me from where I slept on Mrs. Brennan's sofa. As I gathered my belongings and put my shoes on, I heard my aunt and Mrs. Brennen speaking in hushed tones. Cerebral hemorrhage. A tongue-twisty mouthful of a term. It's what doctors said took my father, but I knew better. He died of a broken heart. The pain of a bright future snatched away by a drunken stranger. The pain of losing a son. Of losing a wife. Of losing everything. All those things conspired to burst a blood vessel in his head.

As I lay in the black of my bedroom that night, I listened to my mother and my aunt speaking. My mother didn't cry. I'd believed she'd shed so many tears her well had run dry. I went to my bedroom door and pressed my ear to the crack, desperate to learn more about my father's fate and my own.

"Can I make you a cup of tea?" my aunt asked.

"Pour me a drink, Elizabeth," my mother replied.

"Margaret, I'm not sure..."

"Elizabeth, my husband died today," she said, her voice dry. "I need a drink."

I heard the clink of ice cubes in a glass. In my mind's eye I could see Aunt Elizabeth reluctantly hand the tumbler to my mother, my aunt's eyes filled with doubt and fear and remorse.

I'd grown used to my mother's drinking. Countless times I'd opened my bedroom door to unknown noises in the night only to find my father carrying her to their room.

"Go back to bed, Alice. Your mother just fell asleep on the couch," he'd whisper.

I wondered who would carry her to bed now.

"You have to be strong," my aunt pleaded with my mother. "Keep yourself together. Put on a brave face."

There was a long silence. No doubt my mother was draining her glass. When her words came, they hit me like a punch.

"Why, Elizabeth? What more do I have to live for?" she asked.

Apparently I didn't count. If she had to pose such a tormented question, then she believed there was nothing more. No breath was more important than those she'd lost. I was insignificant. The wrong child died. How had the accidental pleasant surprise been the one she was burdened with now? Cruel.

"Margaret!" my aunt gasped. "Don't say those kinds of things. You're still a mother. She is your child, and she needs you. You've both been through so much, this loss on top of everything else … As if losing…"

My aunt caught herself before she said something that would drag Mother deeper into her grief. I could see Mother's expression in my mind. The same warning glare she'd shot me when Daniel's name escaped my lips. *Don't say it.* My aunt refreshed my mother's drink instead of finishing her sentence. The rattle of ice cubes in glass filled the silence.

"She'll get over it," Mother said. "She's young." The words slid out as one, eliding and drawn. She paused, likely accepting her fresh drink before she said five words. Five words that would shatter my already fractured world and leave me questioning my entire existence. "Besides, she wasn't even his."

The world spun, knocking me to my knees. I clung to my door-knob to keep me attached to reality as the floor shook beneath me. I must have heard her wrong. What did my mother mean? Not even his. She was right about some of it; I was young, but old enough for comprehension to seep into my heart. My father, the man I adored more than anyone since Daniel's passing, wasn't my father? I wasn't his daughter? Nothing made sense.

"Margaret!" my aunt exclaimed. "What are you talking about?" Again, I heard the chatter of ice in the glass and envisioned Aunt Margaret wrestling the cup away from Mother, as if Mother's vile declaration came from the drink itself. "Maybe you've had too much to drink. Stop saying such horrible things."

"It's the truth, Elizabeth," my mother continued with her confession. "Alan knew. Well, he should have known. Unless he believed in immaculate conception." She chuckled, a heartless simper that chilled my soul.

"Please stop," my aunt implored. Mother disregarded her wishes. From the floor behind my bedroom door, I screamed inside, also wishing my mother to be silent, but she pressed on.

"It was a one-night stand," she said. "Meant nothing, but I had needs. Needs Alan hadn't fulfilled for some time, so I went in search of some companionship. Why do you think there was such an age gap between them? Like I would have planned it that way. I was content with Daniel; I didn't need another child. Talk about a shock! My period was two months late before it occurred to me I could be pregnant. I even considered ending it."

"Margaret, please stop."

"Oh now," my mother said, her tone cold and detached, just like her. "A little confession does the soul good, don't you think? I've been holding on to this secret for so long now. It feels good to finally be able to let it go."

A river of tears streamed down my face as I listened. My ears rang, and I struggled to hear anything beyond the sirens sounding in my mind.

"So here it is, my disclosure." Her words were wavy now, rounded, each one connected to the next as her tongue grew lazy. "I have a bastard child, and I have no one to blame but myself. Guess she's my punishment, but Alan should have accepted some of the blame. He forced my hand. He hadn't touched me in months. It was a rough patch in the marriage. These things happen. He even believed me when I told him we'd had an encounter on his birthday. He was too sloshed to remember, so he fell for it, but I think he knew. Deep inside him, he knew she wasn't his."

"Well, as far as I'm concerned, Alan is—was her father. She was the apple of his eye."

"She was, wasn't she," Mother conceded. "I always wondered about that, but I think it was just his way of convincing himself. He was a good father to her. Now be a dear and pour me another."

I chose not to believe my mother. She was wrong, had to be mistaken. My father and I had the same laugh. We both loved animals and comedies and crossword puzzles. I sat on the floor and counted all the things my father and I had in common. They were too vast to be denied. My mother was wrong.

When I saw my father for the last time, I scanned his face, looking for similarities. I stood over the coffin and examined him. His hands were like mine—short fingers, stubby nails. Our hair was the same drab brown, wavy bordering on frizzy. Deeply enthralled in the task, I forgot to say goodbye. I wasted my last moments with my beloved father, convincing myself my mother was a liar.

———

I tucked two bottles of gin underneath the other items in the bag I'd brought for Mother, wrapping them in some new housecoats I'd purchased for her, to keep the glass from clinking together. She wouldn't be grateful for the new clothes, even though she'd complained about the tattered appearance of her favorite garments. My visits were more about what she needed, not what she wanted.

She sat at the window in her room, the shades lifted just enough to offer her a glimpse of the patch of grass and small tree outside. I'd placed a feeder and a birdbath in the alcove beyond her window when she first moved in. She was content to listen to the hum of her game shows and watch the wrens and finches flit about. Mother wasn't one to mingle much with the other residents.

I flipped the light on and walked to her dresser to unload her goods. She didn't seem to notice me at first, even with the change of lighting. It wasn't until I grabbed the remote and punched the volume down on her television that she acknowledged my arrival.

"You're late," she grumbled, shuffling her feet to turn her wheelchair away from the TV and toward me. There was nothing wrong with her legs. Well, nothing but the same affliction that plagued her heart: atrophy. She'd given up on physical therapy after her fall a year ago and had grown more attached to the ease of the wheelchair. Now she rarely attempted to stand on her own or walk even short distances. Hopelessness trickled through her, weakening her spirit and body.

"Well, I'm here now," I said cheerfully, trying to lighten the mood.

"You bring supplies?"

"Yes, of course," I replied, removing items from the box. I loaded her groceries into the fridge and stacked her pantry goods on top of it, noting that the supply of Ensure drinks and Snackwell bars was almost untouched. She didn't bother joining others in the cafeteria for meals. I knew I should speak to her doctor about her appetite, but every time I mentioned her health, her drinking came up. Some caretakers at Coventry Springs believed we should intervene, see if Mother would agree to AA. Others knew the battle wasn't worth fighting. I saw little point in her cleaning up this late in the game and dodged the pressure.

"Scoot over," she said, almost rolling onto my foot. She retrieved the small ice tray from the tiny fridge and tossed some cubes into a cup. Her unsteady hands made the task nearly impossible. She snatched one of the gin bottles from me before I had a chance to secret it away in the only sliver of cupboard the tight room allowed for.

"Mom, it's not even noon yet," I admonished, watching her splash the clear liquid over ice. She couldn't get the lid back on the plastic cup and passed it all to me without a word. If I were a better daughter, I'd have refused to assist her. But the fear of a tirade forced me to secure the lid and add a new straw before handing it back to her.

She used her feet to shuffle the chair closer to the television, where she adjusted the dial. The volume soared.

"So, I had my first procedure yesterday," I said, amplifying my voice to be heard over the closing music to the game show on the TV. The afternoon news cued up, and she leaned forward, snapping the television off before the bubbly anchorwoman offered her greeting.

"Procedure?" she grumbled.

"Yes, remember I told you? Roger and I are seeing the new fertility doctor in town. I know I'm jumping the gun, but I think I might finally be pregnant." My hands fell to my lower belly, dancing over my skirt fabric. "We're so excited."

"I don't know about all that. You're getting a little long in the tooth, don't you think? I mean really, Alice, by the time I was your age Daniel was almost eight, and I'd had a miscarriage." She stopped speaking long enough to take a pull on the straw and catch her breath.

I stood with my back to her, wishing I'd said nothing and hoping she was done. But I knew better.

She adjusted the straw in her cup and continued. "Of course, I was older when I had you, but that was a complete mishap. If you and Roger haven't had a child by now, maybe it's not in the cards. You certainly don't need to concern yourself with my feelings; I gave up on being a grandmother a long time ago."

I tried to deflect her words, let them roll off me. The idea of her being supportive or encouraging was laughable. I should have known better. Tears welled in my eyes, and I pulled the housecoats out of the bag.

"What do you think of these? There was a sale at Miss Jackson's." I held the dresses up one by one. She glanced my direction. "I thought you would like them. They're washed and ready to wear. Want me to help you into one?"

"That won't be necessary. I'm already dressed for the day."

"Okay, well, I'll just hang them up for you." I went to the wardrobe and hung each dress. When I turned back to her, she was asleep. The cup dangled precariously in her loosened grip. I rescued the drink before it fell to the floor and placed it on the side table next to her. She didn't stir.

I grabbed my purse, turned the light out, and closed the door behind me. On the way back to my car, I imagined returning in a couple of weeks with the news she would be a grandmother. Maybe the promise of a new life would perk her up.

FOUR

FALSE POSITIVE

Two weeks crawled by. As the days passed, my body and its inner workings became an obsession. Convinced of a rapid metamorphosis inside me, I sat in Dr. Addison's waiting room, wringing my hands, back straight. My feet had a life of their own, shuffling anxiously. The soft overhead music did nothing to calm me. The tiny stuffed bunny—my new good luck charm—was nestled safely in my purse. After I stopped in the lab for a blood draw, they sent me back to the lobby, where I watched patients and nurses come and go through the glass door leading to the heart of the doctor's practice. I'd hoped Roger would join me, but he was on a plane traveling to meet a new client.

Dr. Addison's nurse appeared in the hallway. Her hand held a box of tissues, and her face held a look I couldn't interpret.

"Mrs. White," she called. Her eyes settled on me. What was her expression? Excitement? Pity? She was unreadable.

I rose on shaking legs and walked toward her. She held the door, pulled several tissues from the box, and passed them to me. Preparing me for what? Tears of joy? Devastation?

"Right this way, Mrs. White. Let's step into my office."

Inside the small but cheery space, she pointed to the only other chair besides hers and took a seat behind her desk. I sat and clutched my purse in my hands.

"I'm so sorry, Mrs. White," she said, folding her hands on her desktop. "This cycle did not result in pregnancy."

My mind struggled with her words. I played them back in my head, stealing them out of her mouth as she spoke. She said *not*. How could that be? I'd felt so many solid signs: fatigue, hunger, irritability. I was bloated and nauseous, and my breasts were tender and swollen. It made no sense. How had my body betrayed me so? Was my mother right? Had I waited too long?

The nurse stared at me, her smile unchanged but somehow now conveyed sympathy. I'd gone so far as to insist Roger take a handful of daily vitamins to boost his chances. I'd done everything right. There was no reason why I shouldn't be pregnant.

"But I…"

"I know, dear. It is such a disappointment." Her face fell slack for a beat before a smile spread across it, and her tone changed when she added, "But we put this behind us and try again."

"I…" I wanted to ask her to give me another test. Maybe wait a day or two. She needed to know how certain I was. I wanted her to explain how I could have so many symptoms. I hadn't gotten my period yet. There still had to be hope. But I had no words.

"I've got the schedule for your next IUI here with your prescriptions. It will be easier this time, now that you are familiar with the process and know what to expect. Don't lose faith, Mrs. White. Success on the first try isn't a given. There is absolutely nothing to worry about at this point."

At this point? What did she mean? I balled the tissues in my hand, rose, and took the folder she held out to me. I turned to leave.

"I've already scheduled the appointments. If your husband can't supply a sample in person, there are guidelines for properly collecting and delivering his contribution in the folder."

I stopped, my hand on the doorknob, my back to the nurse; unable to face her again.

"Please don't feel too discouraged, Mrs. White. While this is a disappointing setback, we push forward. Dr. Addison is a wonderful doctor. We'll have better luck next time."

I exited her office without a word and sleepwalked out of the building. In the underground parking lot, I sat in the car and the world surrounding me ceased to exist. My forehead fell to the steering wheel, and I waited for my shock to find emotion. A tear fell, leaving a dark spot on the fabric of my skirt. I don't know how long I sat there before a noise shattered the silence. A jarring, harsh sound shook my body. I didn't recognize it as my voice, for it was a timbre I did not know lived inside me. It reflected a pain so deep it transcended mourning.

I wailed until there was no breath left in my chest. Once I'd released the grief, my mind quieted. My resolve amplified. Roger and I had not spoken of what-ifs. Had not discussed a course of action in the case of failure. He would be angry, would likely refuse another attempt, but I couldn't let him deny me. It would take delicate suasion, but I could do it, had to do it. I used the balled-up tissues to wipe my face and tucked the disintegrating wad into my purse. My good luck charm stared back at me from the passenger seat. I stroked its ears and absolved it of blame. On the drive home, I prepared my arguments and promised my future child I would not give up on her.

———

"How long are we going to keep this up, Alice?" Roger asked before taking a bite of pot roast. He continued with his mouth full of food, his words barely intelligible. "Have you seen how much this one attempt cost us?"

I shook my head. The untouched food on my plate had grown cold. I forced back tears and told myself to be strong. Roger saw emotion as weakness. I couldn't let him think I was willing to give in. It wasn't about the money. It was just about what I wanted to do with the funds we had. If seeking assistance to conceive a child had been Roger's idea, money wouldn't enter the picture.

"We're so lucky. You're such a good provider," I gushed. "Your career is growing by leaps and bounds, along with your paycheck. I mean, look at this house! I never dreamed of living in something so big in a neighborhood like this." I lifted my hands and twisted from side-to-side, eyes wide, smile broad, like one of the models on my mother's game shows. Dropping my hands to the table and lowering my voice to a whisper, I continued. "As wonderful as it is, it needs the patter of tiny feet."

I watched his face, but couldn't read it, so I changed my course and addressed his bogus excuse. "Sure, it might be a bit of a financial blow in the short term, but I can help out—clip coupons, budget better. It will be so worth it in the end. Think of a tiny little guy following you around singing along to your jingles. Can you picture it?" Roger believed he would father a son just as surely as I believed I would have a girl. "I can see you two now, tossing a ball in the backyard. Building a treehouse. We deserve that, Roger. We'll be great parents."

He was quiet, chewing a bite of food. He put his fork down, took a drink, and wiped his mouth. I fixed a dreamy smile on my face, hoping he shared my vision.

"I say we give it one more go. Two at the most."

I held my breath, disbelieving his words. I took his hand. I only needed one more try; I knew it would work next time. It had to.

"Thank you," I uttered. "Your support means so much."

He pulled his hand from mine. "You're welcome. Of course, I'm going to support you," he said, picking up his fork and poking at his salad. "But I won't make any promises regarding my attitude. Don't expect more. I still think we're being scammed. There's something shifty about that doctor. Can't put my finger on it."

I pushed the food around my plate. My stomach was too full of butterflies to hold anything else. I put the anguish of the morning behind me. The next time, things would go differently.

"I'm not going back into that shyster's office," he said. "I'll opt for the at-home method next time. The depository room gave me the creeps, and my schedule really doesn't allow for such ridiculousness." He pushed back from the table, rose, and tossed his napkin on his plate before retreating to his office.

I would take it. Sentiment was gone from my life. However I needed to make it happen was fine. A baby would bring us closer together.

———

I returned to Dr. Addison's office the following week, visiting every other day for blood draws and ultrasounds. I watched the follicles grow almost imperceptibly and prepared my body and mind for the next insemination. Twenty-four hours after receiving my trigger shot, I walked into the medical plaza with a container of my husband's sperm tucked into my bra. He'd insisted I help him with his part of the process, and I tried. I'd never done anything like it before, and Roger had to guide my hand. I was so worried I'd mess up and the sample wouldn't end up in the tube that he grew frustrated with my efforts and finished on his own. I closed my eyes until I heard his zipper and couldn't look him in the eye for the rest of the morning. Even though we weren't in the same space when his sperm met my egg, we had come together that morning. It had to count for something.

As I made my way through the corridor and into the elevator, I focused on the vial pressed against me, terrified it would slip from my clothing and destroy our chances. It felt as if every person eyed me. As if they knew of the secret I carried between my breasts. I was being ridiculous, but I couldn't help it and refused to make eye contact with any passersby.

The second procedure was identical to the first, but I forced myself to relax and try not to cry or flinch or complain, even silently, about the temperature of the room or the pain of the procedure. My mindset was strong, positive. This was the time. I would soon be rewarded for my efforts.

Two weeks later, my blood in a vial somewhere in the belly of Dr. Addison's office, a test revealed the outcome. I sat in the waiting room again and waited for the nurse to appear in the hallway. When she did, she held a tissue box. Her expression was the same as the one she wore a month before. Her words were too. Again, I had failed. There was no baby.

I suffered through Roger's rants that evening and let him complain. His words bounced off me. I had shed my tears and was moving on one more time. It had to work.

"Don't forget to take your vitamins, dear," I reminded him as he got up from the dinner table.

"Third time's the charm, right?" he conceded, popping the pills in his mouth. "But if it doesn't work this time, we're done."

Once more, I dedicated myself wholly to the process. When doubts crept in, I shoved them down. During the insemination, I didn't allow negative thoughts, ignored the goosebumps that erupted on my naked legs, welcomed the bite of the catheter as it pierced my womb. The morning of my scheduled pregnancy test, I woke to find a spot of blood in my underwear.

Rather than believe my period had started, I convinced myself it was a sign of implantation. I refused to use a pad, had given up on tampons, fearing they might impede the process for no other reason than unjustified bias. It was one of the many superstitions I'd developed. By the time the nurse had consoled me and I was ready to leave the office, my flow had increased, and I asked her for a pad. She handed me a bulky feminine napkin along with the schedule she'd created for the next procedure. Unable to bear the devastation, I didn't tell her there would not be another insemination.

That evening, I asked Roger to pick up dinner at Pennington's, and I took to bed complaining of menstrual cramps. They were intense, and I couldn't endure conversation. Could not listen to him dismiss another failure as if it were the loss of a golf match or a new account. The shrimp basket he ordered for me sat untouched on my bedside table. I didn't see the point in nourishing my body, a body so useless it couldn't create life.

Through the night, as Roger slept beside me, I played out conversations in my mind. From every imaginable angle, I grappled with tactics that might convince him to go for one more round of IUI. How could I sway him? I could think of nothing. Nothing more than my intense longing for a child.

Consumed by the need to be a mother pushed me to consider alternatives. We'd discussed adoption, and he'd scoffed at the idea. I thought about our numerous conversations and how adamant he was that we either have our own baby, or none at all.

"Out of the question! I'm not interested in raising another man's child, Alice."

"You know Bob's wife, Cindy? She couldn't get pregnant. They tried for years and finally adopted a baby girl. Within four months of that adoption, they found out Cindy was with child. She'd taken the pressure off herself, you know, and *bam!*"

"Remember my cousin Judy? She gave up after years of trying. She brought it up at every family gathering; prattled on endlessly about her dream of becoming a mother. Well, what do you know? When she finally shut up about it all, she got knocked up."

"You should get a hobby. Maybe join a women's club. Do something to take your mind off it."

"We need to move on with our lives. If it's meant to be, it will be."

His message was always clear. I just needed to surrender, abandon the dream of becoming a mother. Desperation writhed inside me. I still believed in Dr. Addison and knew he could give me a child.

As the sun peeked through the curtains that morning, and my mind still swam with ideas of how to sway Roger, I settled on a plan, a strategy to address his financial concerns. He obviously hadn't considered his bonus. While it was still a few months away, he was expecting a bonus from his boss in the summer. He'd earmarked the funds for a cruise. I'd lost count of the number of times he'd gushed about his client's vacation on the sea. As he exited the bathroom, I broached the subject of using the bonus money to cover the costs of a few more rounds of IUI.

"Please, Roger. I know it will work—just one more try. If it's about the money—"

"It isn't about the money! I mean, yes, it is ridiculous how much he charges to toy with Mother Nature, but there's more to it. Look at what you've become. You're obsessed, and it's getting annoying."

Annoying? My needs were annoying. I absorbed the word but couldn't relent.

"Well, I'm sorry if I'm not all you hoped for. That I can't bat my eyes and become pregnant."

"Oh, stop!" He stood in the mirror, looping his tie.

"Honey, please," I pleaded, reaching for his shoulders and turning him to face me. I straightened the knot as I spoke. "It's just I feel like we're close. So close that we can't abandon our efforts. We tried unsuccessfully for years before we saw Dr. Addison. Why would you think going back to that would work? He can help us."

"You need a break from the hormones, from all of it. We tried it your way." He checked his watch. "Went from a normal sex life to scheduled, routine intercourse, and now this. The shots, the vials… It's all too much."

He stepped around me and made his way to the bedroom door. I chased after him.

"One more try couldn't hurt," I begged.

"Alice," he said, turning to look at me. "We've done enough. Maybe if we stop stressing about it, it'll just happen on its own."

———

Roger's stance devastated me. I couldn't accept it. All my life I'd given in to the wants of others. Maybe if I hadn't given in when Mother forced me to break up with Thomas, I wouldn't be in this boat. Thomas likely had a slew of kids by now. Maybe they didn't live in an enviable neighborhood. Maybe his wife scrubbed her own floors and worked outside the home, but I bet she knew the joys of motherhood.

If I could eliminate the financial burden of further treatments with Dr. Addison, I could definitely suppress the emotional tidal wave the fertility drugs slammed me with. I could stave off the anxiety and quiet the whine of desperation. If I could promise Roger those two things, he'd have to allow it. Most frustrating to me was that we had the money. He made a good living, and his income increased with each new client he landed. The bonuses grew with each clap on his back. While I loathed the idea of asking my mother for help, I had to try. She was my only other financial resource.

Later in the week, I bought two bottles of top-shelf gin and smuggled them into the nursing home. I also brought a bouquet of pink roses and a heart-shaped box of her favorite chocolates. Valentine's offerings and little soft-soaping.

"You'll have to find a vase for those," she said as she eyed me unloading the flowers. "And you know I can't stomach chocolate anymore."

"Mother, I spoke with your financial advisor," I began.

"Really?" she asked. Her eyes sparked when I pulled the bottles from my bag. "How is James? I haven't heard from him in quite some time. Is there anything to be concerned about?"

I poured her a cup before she had the chance to shuffle her wheelchair into the claustrophobic kitchenette.

"No, nothing too concerning. He's well. We discussed the idea of selling the house, maybe using the proceeds to invest in something with a higher return." I delivered her drink to her and sat in the high-back near the window. "The house is just sitting empty. The upkeep is getting to be a challenge."

"Well, I had intended for you and your family to take the house. Of course, it is a bit large for just the two of you." I tried to conceal the wince as she landed her blow. She wiggled in her chair, proud of herself for the jab. "It wasn't good enough for Roger, eh? Wrong neighborhood, I suppose."

"Oh, I don't know, Mother. He's always had an affinity for midtown. It's closer to his office downtown. Guess he's just not one for the 'burbs." I tried my best to keep the conversation light, my tone steady as I masked my desperation.

"Hmph!" she replied, downing half the cup in one long swallow.

"It's a seller's market, they say," I prodded.

"I'm just not ready to let it go. Too many memories." Her voice quivered, and she dropped her head. The ghosts were stirring in her mind.

"Mom," I began, searching for the right words, the sentiment that might sway her. She hadn't visited our family home in over a year; hadn't left Coventry grounds since she took to the wheelchair. Knowing the house was there, was still hers, was enough, I supposed.

"No, Alice, I just can't sell it. Maybe we could look into renting it out. At the very least, hire a property manager if you're too busy to tend to the upkeep."

"I don't know, Mom. Renters might do more harm than good." My heart crept into the pit of my stomach. If I could convince her to sell, there would be a cash influx I could use to my advantage; secrete some away for my own purposes. Mother's financial advisor kept a tight grasp on her purse strings. He'd notice any suspicious withdrawals. Even so, selling the house would grant me some freedoms.

"I'm just not ready," she said, holding her cup out to me. Tears shimmered in her cloudy eyes.

Hope left my body in a rush. Mother was as stubborn as Roger. There would be no convincing her. I refilled her cup and returned it to her, gathering up my purse and coat as I approached.

"Don't look so disappointed. I'm not long for this earth. Once I'm gone, you can have your way with my belongings."

I leaned in and kissed her on her head, her wiry hair rough against my lips.

"I'll see you next week, Mother. Take care." I closed her door behind me.

FIVE

LIGHTENING

1990

Winter took its time leaving. Emptiness surged in me with each passing week as Roger held strong to the notion that we relax, eliminate the pressure. It was impossible for me to subdue my yearning when the world around me conspired to remind me I was missing out on some of life's greatest gifts. The barrage of television ads for baby products, invitations to baby showers, conversations that inevitably migrated to children ... constant noise driving home my childless state. Everyone was pregnant except me. I continued to track my cycle and read anything I could get my hands on regarding fertility to increase my chances of becoming pregnant, all the while knowing it was pointless. My body, Roger's body—both refused to comply.

I faked spontaneity and devised ways to clue Roger in to my fertility window without scheduling intercourse or using terms like *fertility window*. My cycle had always been an enigma to me; belligerent, refusing to be tracked on a calendar. Twenty-eight days meant nothing to my biology. My period came at random, sometimes absent for months. Other times my flow ceased, only to break through again a week later. I never knew when it would arrive, but when I felt the window might be opening, I lit a candle on the dresser as Roger readied himself for bed. Each time we made love, after Roger drifted off to sleep, I tucked pillows under my hips or slid off the bed and lay on the floor, my legs hooked onto the side of the mattress. Often I awoke shivering on the ground with an aching back and stiff knees, my bladder throbbing. It was worth it, I reminded myself as I felt the gush between my legs—the sticky mess from Roger fleeing my insides when I climbed back in bed, pleading with my bladder to be silent.

Once, I developed a UTI and was forced to sit through a lecture from my new family practitioner on the importance of urinating after sex. She sat in front of the exam table, her round belly mocking me, her tone condescending. Her words drifted in one ear and fled from the other. She didn't understand. I didn't ask about her due date, and she didn't comment on my weight loss.

As the months passed and I pretended to relax, working hard to convince Roger we were of the same mindset, I kept a journal. I documented each time we made love, highlighting how long I'd remained on the floor with hips up, hopeful that one day I could recall the night we'd been successful, perhaps romanticize it in the aftermath. It would be there in writing, my commitment reinforced. Each time I jotted down the details, I thumbed forward forty weeks and scratched a star on the potential due date. I'd lost count of how many stars I'd scribbled over.

In the spring, my mother's health took a turn. Pneumonia, the doctors said. The poison from her tortured heart had leached its way into her lungs. I marveled at her body's perseverance. Her spirit had long ago given up, but her flesh kept going, despite her efforts to prevent it from doing so. She'd been killing herself slowly for almost twenty years.

Alcohol was her constant and proven companion, the one thing to quiet the silence left by Daniel's murder. I tried my best to fashion a normal life for us after Father died, but never succeeded.

Her condition now required frequent visits, and each day I arrived at Coventry Springs to find her sleeping, her breathing labored. Often, if it weren't for her ragged intakes of air and the rasping deflation of her lungs, I'd have believed her to be gone already. As I sat with her, voices from the past wormed their way into my mind. It was impossible for me to feel anything for the woman. And as the hours crawled past, I couldn't help but dwell on how different our story could have been if only she'd loved me. I hated her for throwing away the life she was given. She was just as oblivious to my presence now as she had been all those years ago.

On the first Mother's Day following my father's death, I made my mother breakfast in bed—a tradition I was born into; one established when Daniel was little and one I attempted to fulfill on my own at the age of fourteen. I tiptoed toward her room with a plate of scrambled eggs, a side of French toast, and a glass of orange juice balanced on a tray, along with a flawless pink rose in a crystal bud vase. I'd clipped it from one of Mrs. Brennan's bushes.

This morning, I had news to share. I'd started my period the night before, something I knew would bring her relief. She'd warned of taking me to the doctor to discuss the absence of my monthly, insisting there must be something wrong with me since she'd gotten her period when she was twelve. Maybe she would take me to the drugstore for supplies after breakfast.

The juice sloshed onto the plate as I knocked on her door. She didn't reply. Echoes from Mother's Days past crowded the hallway as I stood balancing the tray. My father booming down the hall, singing, "Oh, What a Beautiful Mornin'," his voice bursting with humor as he sang most of the words wrong. Daniel hurling himself across the room and jumping on the bed. We barged into the room without knocking, but my mother never complained. She feigned surprise, already sitting up in bed with the lights on and curtains open, her hair smoothed.

Suffocating on nostalgia and emboldened by the recollection, I opened the door. Her room was dark: lights off, blinds drawn. She snored softly. I set the tray on her dresser and lifted the window shades.

"Happy Mother's Day!" I exclaimed. Unable to remember any of the song's lyrics past the title, I improvised. "It's a beautiful spring morning!"

She didn't stir. I stood over her and watched her sleep, hoping she'd wake and enjoy my gesture, or at least eat the breakfast. I imagined her fawning over the homemade card I placed on her nightstand, then closed my eyes and tried to remember how it felt to be hugged by her. To be hugged by anyone.

I'd avoided her room since that horrible day when Father abandoned me. Now, as I stood alone beside my snoring mother, ghosts stirred. The closet door stood ajar, and it called to me. I went in. My father's belongings still hung alongside my mother's. I buried my face in his coat. The smell of his cologne overwhelmed my senses, and I fled the room, unable to stifle my sobs.

I rode my bike to the drugstore and bought sanitary napkins. When I returned, I found the tray in the kitchen. The food was untouched, but the juice glass was empty. I lifted it to my nose and took a whiff—citrus and gin. There was a note from my mother under the bud vase.

I hope you asked Mrs. Brennan for permission before clipping this flower.

I never knew what became of the card I'd drawn, but it was the last I ever made for my mother.

Later that year, I taught myself to carve a turkey. I was terrified of the electric knife my father used for the task, but leading up to the big day, I cooked chicken once a week and taught myself. It was a skill Father passed to Daniel and one he insisted was an art.

"Margaret, will you look at this?" Aunt Elizabeth swooned. "Alice prepared the turkey herself!"

"Beautiful bird, Alice," my mother agreed with a raised glass. I stood at the entrance of the dining room, smiling shyly at the compliment, pride reddening my cheeks, my finger tracing the chipped paint where my father's handwriting documented mine and Daniel's growth. Daniel's last recording was before he left for college. It towered over the last marking by my name. According to the scrawled history on the doorframe, I'd stopped growing when my father passed.

"But will you look at this," Mother said, interrupting my thoughts. "You spilled cranberry sauce on my mother's tablecloth. Thanks a million. That stain will never come out. It has survived decades, and now it's ruined."

At Christmas, I borrowed Mother's checkbook and bought gifts, wrapping them and placing them under the tree I decorated. For Easter, I cooked a ham and deviled the eggs. We never made a fuss over birthdays. And so new traditions were born. Ones that couldn't touch their predecessors, but became a mainstay of my childhood while never impressing my mother. We existed in a world of no emotion. Voices were never raised. There was no pride, no anger, no laughter, no excitement. Flatline. Void of conflict. Tears were muffled behind closed doors.

I remained in town to attend college, unable to leave my mother alone. I met Roger my freshman year. I'd hoped he would take my mind off Thomas. At least he took my mother's mind off Thomas, so it was the polarization I needed.

Roger was different from Thomas. A college boy from a good family, he resembled my father. Had the same chiseled cheeks and cleft chin. His blond hair was lighter than my father's but similarly tousled with unruly waves. He was tall and slender and carried himself in a way that exuded confidence. I was instantly captivated by him, as if drawn to a familiar tenor.

He was smitten with me from first glance. Everyone said so. Everyone but Mother, who insisted the attraction was inevitable because I resembled his mother. And so it was. We got married. There was no argument from my small camp, nor from his. I fit the mold: respectable family, educated but not career-driven, congenial, attractive enough. He filled a space. I believed him to be almost a revenant of the man I'd loved more than any other—his looks, his presence, the way he carried himself. He had been cherished as a child. That love seeped into his demeanor, making him confident and commanding.

Leaving school shy of earning a degree didn't bother me. I'd never dreamed of becoming a teacher or a nurse; my only intent was to be a wife and a mother. It was all I'd ever known. Mother insisted women went to college for their MRS. In my case, she was right. Roger offered me a way out of the stifling existence of caring for my mother. My sorority sisters and his fraternity brothers made up the wedding party. The day I left my childhood home, I felt remorse instead of joy. I'd never been given a chance to be a good daughter. Maybe I'd be better at being a good wife and mother.

Pregnancy out of wedlock was a fate worse than death, according to Mother. She was relieved I'd been taken off her hands in respectable form. Courtship, brief engagement, storybook wedding… Everyone knew what came next. My mother never questioned when she would become a grandmother. She never envisioned herself as being someone's Nana. She'd concerned herself only with the first critical steps. Safely betrothed, she couldn't care less what happened within her daughter's marital walls.

Even now, now that I had my own home, had created a life out of the vapor I was, I still believed that little girl was stuck in that sad house. The mire of the girl's existence couldn't penetrate the world beyond those walls. She remained trapped. The person I was now had peeled away from the girl like a snake shedding its skin. That snake still groveled through the halls of my youth where, according to etchings on the kitchen door, I'd never aged past thirteen years.

She shouldn't have been so eager to get rid of me. Without my assistance, she managed on her own for less than five years before a fall prompted my aunt and me to place her in a nursing home. We toured countless centers, ushering her from facility to facility, until she settled on Coventry Springs. She didn't put up any resistance as long as we brought her gin on our visits and never spoke of the past. Before long, Aunt Elizabeth moved to Florida. I remained to make sure Mother had what she needed.

All I wanted was to have the chance to create happy memories in my own home. To silence those hurtful voices by breathing new life into a family—one I created. My Mother's Days would be different, even better than the ones we celebrated before Daniel died. My home would be filled with cherished holiday traditions. All I needed was the chance. My child wouldn't see my final years as a clock ticking down to relished finality. I would be well tended to and mourned when I finally passed on.

For eighteen years, from the very moment officers arrived on her doorstep to deliver the news of Daniel's murder, Mother had longed to die. To have the burden of grief lifted. When her time drew near, she was too sick and drunk to revel in the realization that her wish would soon come to be. And true to form, she was stubborn about it; too stubborn to concede to her own wants. She wouldn't just die. Instead, the days dragged into weeks as she languished between life and death. It was just like her to waste my days while she denied me.

"We're doing what we can to keep her comfortable, Mrs. White," the nurse said, standing over my mother's withering form.

"I understand," I murmured, fussing about, tucking bedsheets and smoothing an errant strand of her silver hair. "Thank you so much for caring for her these past years."

The changing of game shows on the television registered the hours as she clung to existence. Time had a way of bending among the sick and dying. Each day, I used the dinner hour as my excuse to flee. My heels clicked through the quiet halls as I exited the nursing home. Well-rehearsed pity flashed in the eyes of staff and residents as I passed. If only they knew my mother's death would be a long-awaited release—she was steadfast in her belief that in spite of a faithless life, she would join her beloved son and cherished husband upon her departure from this hell.

One day, as the walls pressed in on me, I left the death watch early and stopped at the grocery store on the way home. As I waited at the deli counter for my number to be called, someone said my name.

"Alice? Is that you?"

I recognized the voice immediately and turned. Nancy moved toward me. She looked different. It wasn't until she stepped from behind her grocery-laden shopping cart that I saw why. Her face was full, her cheeks bright. She approached with outstretched arms, leaning into me for a hug. Her belly collided with me before her arms embraced me.

"Well, what a sight you are. How have you been?" she gushed, pulling back from the embrace but still holding my shoulders. Her grasp burned my skin.

She didn't wait for a reply. I couldn't take my eyes off her stomach.

"Will you look at this?" She gestured to her belly, her eyes wide.

"I didn't think it'd ever happen, but here I am … the size of a house. Get a load of these ankles," she said, awkwardly balancing on one foot, pointing down to modest, but still high, heels.

"Nancy." I waited for words to come to me, but none did. My mind was as empty as my body.

"I still have months to go, too! Not that you could tell by looking at me. One day I found out I was pregnant; the next day I couldn't fit into a single thing in my closet. I don't know how I'll ever make it another five months. And look at you! Are you"—she dropped her voice to a whisper, the motion of her lips exaggerated—"losing weight?"

"Well, I…" I intended to use worry over my mother's illness as the source of a decreased appetite. In reality, eating had become something of a chore since abandoning fertility drugs.

"I'll need your secret as soon as I pop. I'm not so sure I'll bounce back from this one like I did with my first two. Oh, to be twenty-something again!"

Somewhere outside the bubble I found myself in with Nancy, a bell dinged and the number fourteen was called. I glanced down at the queue ticket in my hand.

"Oh, that's me. It was great seeing you, Nancy. Congratulations." I choked out the salutation and approached the counter. My order slipped from my mind. The harried man behind the counter looked at me impatiently. There was a block of Swiss cheese on ice under the glass in front of my eyes. I pointed to it and whispered, "Half a pound." A scent hit me from behind, overpowering the tangy aroma of herbed cheeses and cured meats. She still wore the same perfume, and it was obvious she still smoked.

"I'm having a baby shower in August. Of course, you are on the guest list. Promise me you'll attend."

I turned to face her. A sea of blinding fluorescent beams eclipsed her blossoming form. The chatter of every occupant in the supermarket exploded in my ears. Laughter, murmurs, humming. Powdery perfume and smoke invaded my nose, crushing my senses. I needed to run. I closed my eyes and forced myself into the moment. I wanted to scream at her, at the world. How could she be pregnant? She didn't deserve another baby. She already had children, and here I was still barren, still hopeless. It was so unfair. The world was cruel.

"Wouldn't miss it. Count me in." I tried to smile politely, but my face wouldn't cooperate.

Behind me, a bell rang. "Order!"

I snatched the wax paper bundle from the man's gloved hand.

"It was wonderful seeing you, Nancy." I tossed the words over my shoulder as I hurried away with my cart.

———

The following morning, as I readied myself to visit my mother, the night nurse at Coventry Springs phoned.

"Good morning, Mrs. White. We think time is drawing near."

"I understand," I said, snubbing relief from my tone. "I'm on my way."

When I arrived, the head nurse greeted me at the reception desk. She was the same woman who had welcomed my mother to the facility almost five years before. She wore a smile, not one of concern or commiseration, but of hope. Her eyes danced with excitement.

"Now, we've seen this before," she said, moving toward me. "But I wanted to warn you before you got the wrong impression. I mean, in my business, yes, we witness the occasional miracle, but…"

She spoke as we moved down the corridor to my mother's room.

"I'm sorry, Nurse Gladstone, I'm not sure I understand."

"Well, your mother seems to have turned a corner."

"Oh, am I too late?" I asked, insinuating shock and concern by clutching her wrist.

"No, dear, nothing like that." She eased her arm out of my grip. "Quite the opposite, actually. When I checked on her at the beginning of my shift, she was sitting up in bed. Asked for breakfast even."

"Really? The night nurse thought time was short."

"And she was right. It's hard to explain. There are some who rebound. It's sometimes referred to as rallying. It happens from time to time, and it's unexpected, miraculous even, especially when some of those few go on to make a recovery. They are on the brink of death when something happens and they improve."

We stopped outside my mother's door. Beyond, I could hear applause and laughter, and the bells and whistles of her favorite game show. Nurse Gladstone placed her hand on my shoulder.

"More often than not, this unexplained turnabout is only a temporary reprieve from the inevitable. Though promising, I don't want you to get your hopes up. Sometimes the dying have episodes of clarity. Like they need to say goodbye, perhaps."

My mother said goodbye to me many years ago. But this was just like her. It was almost as if she were in my head, aware of what her death could mean to me and depriving me of the reward. Typical.

"At any rate," the nurse continued, "I didn't want you to be shocked when you saw her this morning. Just enjoy what she has to offer. Having said all that, maybe I'm wrong. She could surprise us all and pull through. Such are the mysteries of life."

"Of course," I whispered as her words soaked into me like heavy rain permeates parched earth. But her words did not bring relief; they brought bitterness. The muscles of my neck quivered as they fought to keep my shoulders from slumping under the weight of her words. "Thank you, Nurse Gladstone."

She pushed the door open.

"Look who's here, Margaret."

"Good morning, Alice," my mother whispered. Her focus was on the television, where a woman crossed her fingers after spinning a giant wheel with lit-up numbers.

"Mother!" I gushed as I approached the bed. "Don't you look wonderful today!"

She ignored me.

"You let us know if you ladies need anything at all," the nurse said before exiting the room.

I filled a tumbler with gin and delivered it to her outstretched hand. She took it without a word and put the straw to her mouth.

When I heard the sucking sound of air over ice, I took the cup, filled it again and handed it to her. She drank half of the contents before passing it back to me. I set it on the table next to her and remained close, ready to hand it back. I couldn't let her die sober.

Mother remained alert for another hour. Her eyes never wandered from the television. Her body wracked with coughing spats every ten minutes or so, drowning out the din of game shows. After each spell, I stood and guided the straw to her mouth. She drank readily. Her favorite elixir healed everything; even the deep, rasping cough dissipated with each sip. I pretended to watch the programs with her. But nothing registered until I heard her snoring. I lowered the head of her bed and removed the extra pillow that had been propping her up, clutching it to my chest, twisting it in my hands. The minutes dragged by.

I considered turning the television off. The shrill contestants and garish music grated on me, but I left it on. Despite her giving no signs, perhaps she could hear it. Who was I to deny her the comfort? She never opened her eyes again.

I remained with her for hours as she slept. I called Aunt Elizabeth. She would be on the next flight. My mother's breath was paper thin, but perhaps she just needed rest and would rebound again, refreshed, hungry, no doubt thirsty. What kept her here? Was it to torment me further? What had I done to inspire her perpetual spite? Her end would mark a new beginning for me.

Before clocking out, Nurse Gladstone stopped in.

"I've instructed the nurses to leave you and your mother alone," she whispered, her voice steeped with pity. "They won't bother you in case you need a nap. You should try to rest. It could be a long night. Don't hesitate to ring for them if you need anything. Good night, dear."

It was almost as if she was giving me permission.

As the sun faded, something slammed into the window, startling me. I left Mother's bedside, loosening my grip on the pillow. I dropped it at the foot of the bed and moved to see what caused the noise. A dazed finch lay on the window ledge, its wings twitching helplessly, providing the creature no lift. Its cries penetrated the glass as it called for the others in its charm. Its blood-red face stared at me, eyes pleading, yellow wings spasming, black chest rising and falling sharply. If the window could be opened, I would have lifted it and given the bird a nudge, a helping hand to allow it to regain flight or ease its suffering. Instead, I watched as it clambered, the waning sun casting shadows on its shuddering form. I grew weary watching the poor creature die slowly and exited the room.

"She's gone," I told the nurse whose shift was just beginning. She squeezed my hand as she passed me and went to mother's room to confirm what I knew to be true.

The following morning, before leaving for the airport to pick up Aunt Elizabeth, I called my mother's advisor, James, instructing him to secure a realtor and put the house on the market. Next, I called Dr. Addison's office and made an appointment for his first available opening.

SIX

VIABLE

"Alice?"

I stood at the reception desk at Dr. Addison's office, waiting to check in, when I heard the familiar voice. All morning, while preparing for the appointment, I reassured myself that the chances of anyone seeing me at the fertility clinic were low. How many times had I been invisible inside Dr. Addison's office? And yet, her she was. The one person I never wanted to see again.

"Fancy seeing you here!" Nancy said. She rose slowly and waddled toward me, arms outstretched. Her belly had grown in the weeks since I'd seen her last at the grocery store.

"Nancy," I said, my voice barely a whisper as shock washed over me. I allowed her to embrace me. Her perfume churned my stomach, and I felt my breakfast rising in my throat. I wasn't sure if it was the cigarettes and perfume that caused the reaction or if it was the sight of her and her full womb.

"Where's your husband?" she asked, looking over my shoulder. "Is he parking the car?"

"Um, no, actually he couldn't make it today."

"Oh, I see. What a shame. I'd hoped to finally meet him. But men hate this place, don't they? I swear they see it as an affront to their masculinity or some such nonsense." She lowered her voice a bit, but still drew glances. A couple of women lowered their magazines and eyeballed the woman who dared to give voice to an undeniable reality. The only man in the waiting room rattled his newspaper and cleared his throat. Leave it to Nancy to make the stress of this visit even more arduous.

"Well, I'm just here for my check-up," she said, rubbing her rotund midsection slowly. "This little one is growing like a weed!"

Envy pounded me as I watched her caress her stomach. She didn't deserve another child. What a selfish woman! Emptiness pulsed in my womb, and I wanted nothing more than to get away from her. I didn't need this negative energy invading what should be a liberating but terrifying day for me.

"What brings you into the handsome Dr. Addison's office today? Ultrasound? Blood draw?" Her eyes widened. "Pregnancy test? Is that it? Oh, how I hope it is and you get a positive result. You've been at this too long. My goodness, how many treatments have you had at this point? I'm so very sorry you are having to suffer like this. What does this make? If I do some quick math," Nancy said, clicking her long nails together as she counted on her fingers. "You must be on your sixth or seventh attempt. Ugh, how dreadful. You deserve a trophy for enduring all this torment. I simply hate it for you."

I was lost for words. I couldn't tell her the truth. Wouldn't tell her the truth. It was none of her business. She could never know I was embarking on a fertility journey solo, against my husband's wishes. I tried to formulate a response, or better yet an escape plan, but was rescued by Dr. Addison's nurse.

"Nancy Ellington," the nurse's voice rang out, freeing me from the excruciating conversation.

"Here I am," Nancy said, turning to the nurse. "Excuse me, I'll just be a moment."

The nurse didn't conceal her eye roll and let out an exasperated sigh. She checked her watch.

"We should get together soon. Let's do lunch," Nancy said to me. "Best of luck with whatever Dr. Addison has in store for you today. I know your time is coming soon. Dr. Addison is a miracle worker!"

She didn't give me a chance to reply, which I was grateful for. Hopefully she'd forget this run-in and wouldn't discuss it with anyone else. The last thing I needed was for someone to find out. If word got back to Roger, I couldn't imagine how he'd react.

I watched Nancy greet the nurse and didn't turn away until she'd lumbered to the scale in the hallway. She slipped out of her shoes and jacket and put her purse on the floor, all the while making conversation with Dr. Addison's nurse. Nancy got on the scales, but stood backwards on the platform so she couldn't see what she weighed. Again, envy reared its tortuous head. I wanted to bolt. To run from the office and cry it out in my car. Why did fate despise me so? I wasn't asking for much, and still here I was. Meanwhile, Nancy was more concerned with her weight gain than the health of her unborn child.

I took a deep breath and shook off the pain. This had to work, and it had to be kept top secret. Everything, my whole life, my marriage, all my hopes and dreams hinged on this visit. I couldn't let Nancy shake my resolve.

"Good morning, Mrs. White. It's so good to see you again," the receptionist said when I approached her desk. "You're all checked in. Have a seat and someone will be with you momentarily. Within minutes, the nurse appeared again and ushered me to Dr. Addison's office where I waited anxiously, unsure of how he would react to my requests.

"Mrs. White, welcome back. It's been a while, yes?" Dr. Addison addressed me as he entered his office. He shook my hand and held on to it, clasping his other hand over our entwined fingers. His hands were warm and soft.

I was grateful for his arrival, as the walls felt like they were closing in on me. In that room, there was nothing else to do but stare at the collage on his office wall, made up of countless birth announcements. The images, his successes on full display in clouds of pink and blue, should have given me hope and lightened my spirits. Instead, I felt more isolated, fearing I'd never order a birth announcement myself. I wondered if I would be denied the one thing I wanted most in life. I'd been bracing myself for the conversation, certain he'd send me away, tell me to come back with my husband. Or at the very least, eye me with suspicion. But my concerns remained unfounded so far. He unbuttoned his lab coat before sitting on the edge of his desk.

"Yes, it's been a few months," I said, shifting in my seat. I'd sat in the same chair almost a year ago, absorbing Dr. Addison's words while Roger sat next to me, disbelieving the doctor's claims, at times scoffing out loud. If our first IUI had been successful, I would be holding a newborn right now instead of being here alone. Roger believed I was touring the hospital to become a volunteer in the auxiliary, certain the charity work would give me an outlet for my anxiety. We hadn't discussed my return to fertility treatment. The financial windfall from my mother's passing allowed me the opportunity to finance another attempt or two. He insisted we use my inheritance to pay off our mortgage, but I'd managed to squirrel some funds away.

"I'd hoped, as I do with all my clients, that the fertility gods had smiled upon you."

The warmth of his smile enveloped me like an embrace. He used the word clients instead of patients. I'd always considered myself a patient, but client seemed somehow more intimate, connected, not so clinical.

"No, I'm afraid not," I replied, crossing my legs and fidgeting with my wedding ring.

"Well, I'm sorry to hear it." His tone divulged sincerity, sorrow. "I understand how challenging this can be emotionally, physically, and the financial burden of treatments can be taxing. Was there a change of heart? Perhaps you're pursuing adoption?" He rose and moved to the chair behind his desk. As he sat, he pulled a thick file from a stack on his desk and folded his hands atop it. My last name was branded on its spine. His eyes bore into me.

"No, nothing of the sort." I shifted again in my seat and smoothed an absent wrinkle in my skirt, plucking at a piece of lint that wasn't there. "Mr. White, well, he grew impatient with the process."

"I see. Fertility treatment can be a polarizing subject for couples. But you're here now. Alone."

He let the word hang, drawing it out, then dropping it without a hint of the direction he intended for me to take it. Was it a question? The silence was stifling, forcing me to fill it.

"I'd like to explore my options. My desire for a child is as intense as ever." Even to my own ears, the words sounded flat.

"Yes, it never truly fades without fulfillment. I understand."

He did get it. For the first time in a long time, I felt heard.

"What were you thinking?" he continued. His gaze never released me. He reached inside me. Knew what I needed to feel whole. Understood my longing. My only want.

"I'd like to try again."

"Will Mr. White be a participant when we resume?"

"No, I don't believe so." I dropped my eyes. "I was thinking of using… I'm considering alternative measures."

I couldn't bring myself to use the word; I was too consumed with guilt. My mind waged an internal war. After my mother's passing, I'd broached the subject of returning to Dr. Addison with Roger. He was adamant we continue to try on our own and was sure we'd be successful eventually without medical intervention. He'd dug his heels in, leaving me no choice.

"You're speaking of using a donor?"

"Yes, I think a donor would be my, rather our, best option at this point." The words tumbled out in a rush, and my muscles softened once I'd released them.

"Well, it wouldn't be unheard of." He opened the thick folder and flipped through the pages, pausing on one and running his fingers over the text as he spoke. "I see from a quick glance at your husband's test results his morphology is normal, but his count and motility aren't optimal. I didn't believe those factors insurmountable, but we could increase the odds with a more hearty donor. It looks like you've got a somewhat irregular cycle, which can present its own problems. Again, not ideal, but not impossible to overcome. If everything was perfect, well, you wouldn't need me."

He flipped through the heavy file. As he did, I glimpsed the scan sheets—shiny, curled paper clipped to each section. They held gray, grainy images of the eggs my body shed after their hope had perished. He looked at me and smiled.

"Let's get you set up in an examination room. I'll take a few minutes to reacquaint myself with your medical history and be in shortly. From there, we can assess where you are in your cycle and come up with a schedule." As he spoke, he pushed a button on his phone. The nurse entered the room. That smile.

"Come with me, Mrs. White."

Sitting in the icy room, I braced myself for more injections and blood draws. The ultrasound machine stood in the corner, its intrusive wand a stark reminder of what lay ahead, taunting me with its familiar knowledge of my insides. How would the process differ without Roger's illusory support? Would I be able to hide my indiscretion from him, and if so, for how long? I wasn't sure I'd make it through one round. What if it too was unsuccessful? Did I have the strength to deceive Roger over and over until it worked? He'd always insisted I was a different person when I was taking hormones. Could I hide those changes I'd never even recognized in myself?

I was spiraling when a voice came from deep inside me.

Your destiny is to be a mother.

Mothers can handle anything.

You are strong.

Stop doubting yourself.

Was it the voice of my future child? Wherever the words came from, they calmed me. I breathed deeply. Inhaling soundness. Exhaling doubt.

The nurse tapped on the door and entered.

"I almost forgot," she said with a laugh, clutching a heavy blue binder to her chest. "There's no rush. You have all the time you need to make a decision, but while you wait, you can look through our catalog. I think you'll be very impressed with our donor list."

She held the book out to me. I took it from her with trembling hands.

All the courage and calm I'd mustered evaporated. I did not know what to expect. I'd never thought past the potential of having to convince Dr. Addison to allow me to use a donor, to proceed without my husband at my side. With that behind me, the reality of hand-picking the father of my child hit me. How could I be tasked with such a monumental decision? I couldn't. It was too big a burden. The ramifications were too immense. I couldn't breathe.

Could I raise another man's child alongside Roger and be at peace? Or would the deception eat away at me? What if he sensed something? Didn't believe the child to be his?

In my mind, I called out to the voice, and it came, reassuring me again I could manage. The answer was inside me, and I would make the right choice. Calm washed over me. My fate was in my hands, and I was capable. I was beholden to the life I was meant to create. With one more deep breath, I cracked open the binder.

———

Dear Lauren,

I learned the news today. You are growing inside me. Finally, after all these years of false hopes, near misses, tears, emptiness … I am full. Your tiny spark burst to life. The days until your arrival stretch before me, and I am overwhelmed with anticipation; beside myself with happiness.

I've barely absorbed the reality and already you are all I can think of. What will you look like? How will your voice sound? I dream of the day when I push you forth into the world, lay my eyes on your precious face, hear the raw sound of your first cries. You are beautiful, of course you are. No matter if you have Daniel's upturned nose and golden curls, my mother's emerald eyes, and my thin lips, you will be the most exquisite child ever born. My daughter. The one I've waited my whole life for. I'm certain you are a girl. Of that, I have no doubt. Mother's intuition.

You are the center of my world. My reason for existence. My purpose. Please forgive me for resting such weight on your tiny shoulders. I ask nothing of you. Your mere presence will fulfill my longings. You will be the only one. Not just because of the challenges faced breathing life into my womb—even if I'd been fruitful from the first try, I would need only one. There will be nothing to overshadow the wonder of you.

We are in this together, sweet Lauren. I will do my part to give you the best start. I'll get plenty of rest and exercise, fresh air and sun, take my vitamins and eat a healthy diet. I will follow the advice of my doctor without fail. Your vessel will remain pure. I'm entirely dedicated to securing the best outcome for you.

You will be born to a mother who wants nothing more than you. Wants nothing more than to give you life. A life she can share with you. You're not an accident and are so much more than a pleasant surprise. You are the reason I ever took breath.

You are cherished, little one. I can't wait to meet you!

Your loving mother

I capped my pen—one bought especially for this purpose on my way home from what I hoped would be my last visit to Dr. Addison's clinic. Aside from the sheer joy of finally being pregnant, I felt overwhelming happiness in the realization I'd never again be subjected to the tortures of fertility treatments. That journey, with its indignities and pain, was over. My decisions made. My secrets safe. I traced my fingers over the words I'd written, the significance of their meaning vibrating through me.

I closed the journal, which I'd purchased at Vandevers when I bought thank-you cards for the few who had sent condolences after my mother's passing. I hadn't sent them yet, although her voice taunted me daily, letting me know the proper timeframe for expressing the sentiments was nearly expired. I vowed to get the pesky task out of the way so I could enjoy my pregnancy.

A pink sky marbled with feathery clouds parting for a beam of golden light adorned the journal's cover. I'd no intention of buying a motherhood journal, but the image spoke to me. I snapped it up and added it to my purchases without hesitation. My baby, my Lauren, would likely never read my musings. Although I'd written the letter to her, it was really for me. I was bursting with such an abundance of elation. I needed an outlet to express the emotions. I hadn't yet told Roger the news. For a while longer at least, I'd keep it to myself, give myself time to cherish each moment in solitude. The world would know soon enough.

I would write in the journal throughout my pregnancy. Well, almost. Near the middle of my third trimester, I had to tuck it away. By that time my emotions were so difficult to manage. I cried at the drop of a hat. I did my best to laugh them off as tears of joy. Most of them were.

I tucked the journal into my keepsake box and wondered if I would know what was happening when I felt the first stirrings inside me? All I did know was I couldn't wait to feel her moving. Not a single hint of fear tinged my excitement. There should be a healthy amount of trepidation, I told myself. But just as I was sure the life inside me was a girl, I knew all would be well. While I longed to hold my child in my arms, I vowed to relish every moment. Look forward to experiencing each symptom my body gave. This was my one chance to embrace all I was made to do.

I did share my secret with Orson. He could be trusted with confidences. Each day when I took his food to the deep recesses of the yard, in a spot hidden behind a row of juniper trees, I whispered my thoughts to him. He was a good listener as he lapped up the cream I saved from breakfast and gobbled fat cut from evening meals. We met in the sanctuary I maintained for him, where he took refuge from the perils an independent tomcat faced in the wilderness of an urban neighborhood. He showed his gratitude by dropping slain mice at the back door and by winding his body through my legs as I weeded the flower beds. He was my confidante. Before Lauren was born, he shared a secret of his own with me. Orson wasn't a Tom, and like me, Orson was also expecting.

SEVEN

CROWNING

I rang the bell and hid from the blazing summer sun under the portico as I simmered in the late summer swelter. The air itself was a weighty brume. I shifted the gift wrapped in sky-blue paper between my hands, afraid my sweaty palms would mar the delicate covering. The invitation, boldly announcing *It's a Boy* on thick, icy blue card stock, protruded from my purse.

When the invitation arrived in the mail, I considered throwing it away. Part of me hoped to never come face-to-face with Nancy again, but now I didn't have to hide from baby showers, not even Nancy's. At long last I was one of them, the lucky women who knew the joy of growing life within them. Even though I didn't plan on sharing the news with anyone yet, especially not Nancy, carrying the secret made me want to be out in the world. To enjoy a party celebrating new life. Maybe I'd get some ideas for my own baby shower.

The growing Ellington family lived only blocks from my home in a more stately area of the neighborhood that bragged of older money and richer history. As I navigated the roads from my home to hers, the houses grew in grandeur and size, their facades giving face to their occupants. Old money. More money. Money.

A maid in a powder-blue smock opened the door. A wave of cold air washed over me, and I readily accepted the bracing chill. Another attendant took the gift and added it to a pyramid of offerings in a lavish dining room that opened to the expansive foyer.

Grand French doors led to the yard, where children dashed about. The air rang with their laughter and shouts, punctuated by splashes as they jumped into a glittering in-ground pool.

Blue touched every spot of the grand room. Forget-me-not, lavender thistle, and eucalyptus bouquets burst from vases, filling the space with musky sweetness. Shimmery balloons bobbed in each corner. A table covered in silk cloth held an array of finger foods dotted with blue cakes and cookies. All the offerings perched on fine china the color of robin's eggs.

"Alice! You came!" Nancy's voice echoed across the room. A jowly man helped her out of her chair, the girth of his midsection in close competition with Nancy's. She rose with great effort, pressing her hand to her lower back as she waddled over to me.

"Everyone, this is Alice White. Alice, everyone." She waved an arm around the room, which was filled with women of all ages. The guests paused their conversations and looked my way, nodding and smiling. The man who helped her out of her chair trailed behind her, unable to match pace with the heavily pregnant woman. He landed next to Nancy and placed one hand on her belly.

"Alice, this is Edward," Nancy said. "I tried to tell him this was no place for menfolk, but he insisted on attending."

Edward peeled his hand off Nancy's stomach and shook mine. As soon as he'd released my grip, his hand perched again on her midsection, rubbing it in slow circles. He was squat with blunt features. The size of bushy eyebrows vied with his twitchy, white mustache.

"Call me a fool," he said. "But at my age, I'm beyond caring." The stir of his hand on her swollen stomach was hypnotizing. I forced myself to look away. "Wouldn't miss this for the world. Nice to meet you, Alice, and thank you for joining us in celebrating the anticipated arrival of our son."

"Edward, be a dear and get me a refill," Nancy said, passing her empty flute to her husband. "Alice, would you like a mimosa?"

"No, thank you. I shouldn't," I replied. Words teetered on my tongue, longing to leap out. I choked them back. It wouldn't be proper for me to announce my pregnancy at a baby shower. It would be akin to announcing an engagement at a wedding, only more inappropriate.

"Bring Alice a glass of punch, please. There's no booze in it, I promise," she said with a wink.

Edward took her glass and shuffled across the room, stopping to chat with several of the women. Nancy's gaze followed him, her eyes ardent.

"You look wonderful," she said, turning her attention to me. "Almost glowing, I'd say."

The words pushed against my teeth.

"Speaking of glowing…" I gestured to her stomach. She took my hand and pressed it to her belly. I snapped it from her grasp as if I'd palmed a hot iron and glanced at my fingers, expecting them to show red.

Bewilderment flashed across her face before she brushed off my reaction. "Oh, stop," she said, and laughed. "Lying doesn't become you, Alice." Her hands settled on the mound of her belly, and she locked her fingers together, shielding the life within her. "It's okay. I'm a whale, I know it. Shouldn't even be hosting this party. Doctor wants me on bed rest… My blood pressure, of all things. Bed rest! Can you imagine? Me, chained to a bed twenty-four-seven? Not going to happen. Besides, I haven't even found a nanny yet! I'm certainly not taking interviews from my boudoir."

She lifted her napkin to catch a bead of sweat as it seeped from her temple. "Aside from a few headaches and not fitting into my shoes, I'm basically fine. He warned me that ignoring his advice could result in an early delivery. As if that's some kind of threat. Sounds more like a godsend. Stick a fork in me."

"You can't rush perfection," I replied, knowing the futility of suggesting she heed the advice of her doctor. I'd be wasting my breath. My eyes were drawn to her feet. Flesh pushed out of the top of her modest shoes like rising bread. Her lower legs were thick like tree trunks, and lacy blue lines trailed her calves, peeking through silky stockings. Her ankle bracelet was as absent as her ankles. "The baby will know when the time is right."

"Oh, I don't know—there is a race afoot! Have you met Monica Gilbert?" I followed Nancy as she plodded to a nearby chair, where a woman sat devouring a plate of canapés. Her stomach rested on her lap, almost touching her knees.

Monica looked up, her face flushed, a crumb trapped in the corner of her mouth.

"Nice to meet you," she said. She rested the plate on her belly and held out her hand. "Sorry to meet you while I am stuffing my face, but these babies are hungry."

"She is eating for three," Nancy chimed in, bending stiffly to rub the woman's stomach. "You should give that belly a rub too, Alice, for good luck. Go ahead. She doesn't mind."

My hands seized the handles of my purse, refusing to budge. My cheeks flared, and I coughed out an awkward chuckle. "That's all right, really."

"Monica is having twins!" Nancy continued, shrugging off the misstep. "Can you imagine? She is another lucky patient of Dr. Addison's. Our treatments were what, a month apart, Monica? But I think you just might beat me to the delivery room."

"Oh, who knows? I feel like I've been pregnant for years, and all I am really sure of is that I'm as big as a house and ready to pop!" She laughed, but then tears welled in her eyes. "But I will be forever grateful to Dr. Addison. I can't wait for these little miracles to arrive." She made a show of rubbing her entire belly; the plate barely shifted as she did. A tear broke free and slid down her face.

Edward reappeared with a full champagne flute and punch glass.

"Maybe you should rest a spell, dear," he suggested.

Nancy kissed him on the cheek and waved him off. She took a pull on her drink and turned to the room. "I think we're all here now, ladies," she sang out. "Follow me for a tour of the nursery!"

Excitement rippled through the room. Edward helped Monica up, then rushed to Nancy's side and held her hand as the group followed them out of the room. We ascended the wide staircase slowly as Edward held fast to Nancy's hand. She paused at the top to catch her breath before straightening her back and proceeding down a vast hallway.

The room was something from a magazine, saturated with silvery-white decor accented by dreamy touches of dusty blue. The crib was round, something I'd never seen before. I circled it, admiring the fine wood with my fingertips, wondering where she purchased sheets for such an impractical item. A mural of a sunny sky adorned the ceiling. Clouds and birds floated overhead. I was taken in by the scene. A stork, complete with a bundle in its beak, glided above, and a whimsical hot-air balloon swam in the imagined sky. A cursive *J* embellished the balloon, perhaps hinting at the new heir's name. While it struck me as a tad garish, it was painted with a delicate hand and oozed refinement.

Nancy sat in a plush rocker, her ancient husband at her side. She rubbed her belly in slow, lazy circles as she rattled off the names of the designers who helped bring her "dream nursery to life," pointed out details in the mural, and spoke about the origins of the wallpaper.

"Look at this rug!" she gushed. "Isn't it sumptuous?"

As Nancy denoted the pedigree of the flooring, a flood of saliva filled my mouth. The sensation was choking, and I struggled to remain composed. Sweat erupted on my forehead, and my stomach lifted into my throat. I tried to push through the crowd discreetly, but the punch I'd sipped moments ago made its return, filling my mouth with a taste that was more pleasant going down than coming up. It threatened to spill out of me, and the urgency to escape the room tightened. I choked it down and ran for the door.

As I fled, I wanted to whisper apologies to excuse my disruptive behavior, but didn't dare open my mouth. In the hallway, I cupped my hand to my face and bolted for the first door I saw. I threw it open, and relief washed over me. I'd happened upon a bathroom. The consolation was erased as my insides lurched. I tossed the toilet seat up, dropped to my knees and spilled the contents of my stomach into the bowl. My hair clung to my face in sweaty tendrils as I heaved.

Someone knocked on the door.

"Alice, dear," Nancy called. "Are you all right? Can I get you anything?"

I slumped against the wall and grabbed at the toilet paper, curling it into a ball I used to wipe my mouth. The relief was instantaneous, but my recovery wasn't as swift. The bitter remnants burned my mouth. My vision was blurry, focus slow to return.

"I'm okay. Just need a moment," I reported as I rose on shaky legs and flushed. Fragments of the toast I'd eaten for breakfast swirled in the brightly colored punch. It should have induced another wave of nausea, but I stared at the mess in wonder as it was siphoned away. I'd just experienced my first bout of morning sickness. It was something I'd been awaiting, for it was the first outward sign that my body was working to create a child. What I'd read was right. Morning sickness didn't have to come at the first light of day.

The person staring back at me in the mirror, though disheveled, radiated. My cheeks and lips were full and red. I splashed cold water on my face and cupped it into my mouth, swishing it about and spitting. Before leaving, I checked the bowl to make sure nothing had floated back up, then stopped in the mirror again to admire my new look, smooth my hair, and wipe my mouth once more. Another wave of nausea slopped in my stomach, and I rested my head against the cool marble of the countertop until it passed. Once it had, I admired my glow one more time and stepped into the hall.

Nancy stood outside the bathroom door.

"I knew it," she declared, looping her arm in mine. "I could tell the moment I laid eyes on you." She squeezed me close and breathed into my ear, "You're pregnant!"

I pulled back. A smile spread across my face. I couldn't contain the news any longer. "I am!"

"Another Dr. Addison miracle baby," Nancy squealed as we made our way down the hall. She clung to my arm, her other hand gripping the rail as we returned to the party.

Having announced my state to Nancy, I could no longer keep the news from Roger. That evening at dinner, after he wiped his mouth with his napkin and pushed his plate away, I took his hand.

"I've got the best news," I said, my heart bursting.

"Let me guess." He paused, his eyes glancing up. "You were promoted to gift shop attendant at the hospital auxiliary? I know you weren't fond of making flower deliveries."

I propped myself up, unwilling to deflate, and brushed his nonsensical words aside, reminding myself of the alibi I'd used to conceal the time spent with Dr. Addison. His words stung, though. Didn't he realize nothing but motherhood mattered to me? Certainly not a volunteer gig at the hospital.

"No, better." It suddenly became important to me he guess. I couldn't understand how something so monumental wouldn't be the first idea to touch his mind.

"Come on. It's been a long day. George insisted we go through the course, the whole eighteen holes. Let's not play games." He took his vitamins from his coaster and washed them down with his beer, then continued. "Spill it."

"I'm pregnant," I said, hoping the announcement would garner a response that drowned out his lackluster complicity. My other hand fell to his, and I squeezed.

He was silent.

The moments slipped by, and I searched his face for any sign of emotion. What was he thinking?

"Really?" A whisper of a smile touched his face. His cheeks flushed.

"Really!"

He stood and laughed, pulling me up in an embrace, lifting me off my feet. I buried my face in his neck. My body tingled.

He put me down and held me at arm's length, his eyes roving over me before drawing me back in. As he held me, he spoke.

"I knew it would happen. I was right all along. We just needed to stop trying so damn hard."

No one held a baby shower for me, but Roger's secretary collected gifts, which he brought home in dribs and drabs near the end of my pregnancy. Each present was beautifully wrapped, a treasure for me and my Lauren.

EIGHT

LABOR

1990-2001

My daughter entered the world in a sea of screams and blood and sweat. My body tore open, heaving her into existence. I felt something of mine pass to her as she left the sanctuary of my womb. A part of my soul detached when the umbilical cord was severed. A bit of me that was suppressed and unused. An essence I'd squandered, but she took to use for herself. I hoped it would allow her to manifest independence, self-acceptance, and worthiness. It would empower her to recognize her potential. I passed that seed to Lauren and I vowed to spend every breath nurturing it. She would bloom in my love.

As she sucked in her first breath and expelled her first wail, I knew her voice was already louder than mine ever could be. My tears dropped onto her red face as she squirmed in my arms. Rooting. Seeking my life force. I'd never felt so important, and never would again.

The moment we brought her home from the hospital was the first time our house felt like home. Perhaps it was a self-fulfilling prophecy, or maybe she was simply a needy child, but that tiny person was demanding. Over the next months, she slept little and cried often. I was incapable of deciphering her cries. Many times, I bawled along with her as I pored over books and tried everything imaginable to soothe her.

We sat on the bathroom floor near the tub, tap open, water flowing. Some days, the rushing sound calmed her. Other times it didn't, so I bound her to my body and bounced, jostling her up and down in a dance choreographed by instinct and exhaustion, while running the vacuum cleaner over the same one-foot tract. Often, the motion and noise from the sweeper quieted her. Sometimes not, and I drove through the dark streets with the windows cracked, radio tuned to static, silently urging her to sleep. I learned to massage her belly, rubbing lotion between my palms until warm, and manipulating her tiny body to free a gas bubble and ease her discomfort. I never left her in her crib to cry—something the books insisted was a viable option that wouldn't harm an infant. But how could it not? How could one listen to the cries of their baby and turn a deaf ear? This advice angered me, for it railed against nature.

After hours of writhing and crying and burping and spitting up, she would settle and nurse as if half starved. I marveled at my body's ability to sustain and grow this lively little being.

She grew. Fast. Much too fast for my liking and despite getting little sleep. Lauren didn't sleep through the night until she was almost two years old. Many women complained of their child's lack of sleep, but I embraced those times when it was just she and I and my only goal was to comfort her. Even in the black of night, when the peace of slumber was a fading memory and I walked around the house with my child silently imploring her to sleep, I gave thanks and I prayed to a god I wasn't sure I believed in.

Perhaps my mother never did so. Maybe she never called out to the universe to watch over my brother. To protect him from illness, accident, evil. Was that why fate fell upon him and stole his life? Of course, if she hadn't prayed for Daniel, she certainly hadn't prayed for me, and I was still here. But to be safe, I'd not make the same mistake. I looked upon the precious face of my nursing infant and cried out to whatever power determined our destiny.

Keep her safe. Keep her alive. Please let her bury me. Without her breath, I am nothing.

I held her while she napped, defying the guidelines established by every pediatric board and harried mother. I was spoiling her. I should sleep-train. The amount of propaganda spewed regarding proper sleep structure for an infant was staggering. But I loved to hold her while she slept. I was enthralled by her face reacting to visions I could not see. Her quickening breath and curled smile, a furrowed brow and a whimper left me imagining what she saw in her dreams. I could watch her sleep all day. She was mesmerizing.

I knew I'd be sad when naps weren't required to get her through the day. But not for the same reasons as other mothers. It wasn't about a loss of freedom or infringement upon my time. I wasn't concerned with the housework I neglected while Lauren napped. No, I would mourn the closeness, the hours spent together.

Aunt Elizabeth came to visit when Lauren was only days old. Although I'd trusted her my whole life, I couldn't relinquish care of Lauren to her. My aunt never had any children of her own. Her advice was outdated and lacked soul. Each suggestion battered my instincts and made me doubt myself. I'd not prepared myself for judgments.

"You should establish a strict feeding and nap routine as quickly as possible, Alice. Babies thrive on such things. And put her in her crib. You're spoiling her."

"She would sleep better if you fed her formula. They say it's just as good as breast milk. Add some rice cereal to it, thicken it up. She will sleep better, and the feeding won't be entirely your burden."

"Cloth diapers are much better for her than disposable ones. I jotted down a list of diaper services that come highly recommended. You should give them a call."

"In my day, babies slept on their stomachs. She isn't comfortable on her back; that's why she cries so much."

"She should get a bath every day. It's good for her skin."

Something as simple as handing Lauren over to Aunt Elizabeth so I could shower triggered panic that consumed me. When she held Lauren, horrible visions invaded my mind—images of my aunt tripping and dropping the baby. Aberrations of Lauren's head crashing against a counter's edge or the hearth flooded my thoughts. All attempts at forcing the notions out failed, and I rushed through my tasks, returning to Lauren, overwrought and shaking. Even with Lauren safely back in my arms, the nightmare impressions plagued me.

I was relieved when Aunt Elizabeth went back to Florida, but the visions continued. I was powerless not to snatch Lauren away from Roger when he held her. He was never careful enough with her weak neck and manhandled her when changing a diaper. He scoffed when I insisted he wash his hands before picking her up.

"Germs build immunity. Children can't live in bubbles."

"Your way isn't the only way, Alice."

"Relax, she's not as fragile as you think."

"Maybe if you focused some of your energy on your husband and your home, you wouldn't be so uptight all the time."

His words hit me with force. Each offhanded jab got absorbed like a malicious affront. My skills were questioned, my abilities doubted, my instincts disparaged. Aside from a smattering of burp cloths in various places, I kept the house tidy. Surely he understood that Lauren was my priority. I hadn't been in the mood, had shunned his advances, but he knew how many times I was up with her at night. He rolled over at her cries, if he even stirred at all. I was too tired for sex, and besides, my breasts dripped like faucets. Lauren's needs superseded mine and would until she didn't depend on me for life, no matter what Roger thought.

Despite my angst, Lauren thrived. By the time she began to toddle on wobbly legs, the flood of my hormones had surged, peaked, and petered out, allowing me to exhale. The sleepless nights were forgotten, and colicky cries were replaced by peals of laughter. Problems were resolvable, seemingly catastrophic issues manageable, tears easily soothed, illnesses and injuries treatable. I was a good mother. She was inquisitive, loving, and strong-willed. I saw Daniel in her eyes. Heard my father in her laugh.

I crafted a perfect childhood for Lauren. We spent our days exploring parks and zoos. We brought home armfuls of books from the library and enjoyed afternoons at birthday parties, children's theatre, and museums. Our summer days were spent at the community pool, and winter days we sledded on nearby hills and built snowmen. Rainy days found us splashing in puddles and digging up worms in the garden, while on sunny days we made flower tiaras for Orson. We sipped from tiny cups, our pinkies held high in our garden tea parties. There were playdates and tumbling classes, swimming lessons, and blanket forts.

They were the best days of my life. Just me and my child. Often, I experienced the wonder of discovery along with her. A new world unfurled around me, and Lauren guided me through this awakening with her chubby fingers curled around mine. Colors were brighter. Emotions, long dulled, pulsed like electrified nerve endings.

I'd never spent ten minutes allowing a ladybug to tickle its way up and down my arm as I counted its spots. Had never asked for the same book to be read night after night so I could absorb it to memory and recall its wonder as I drifted to sleep. Had never created whole villages in sidewalk chalk and explored their dusty streets as the sun fell from the sky, dipping into the river. But now I lived those moments with Lauren. It was she and I exploring and learning and feeling. It was more than I ever dreamed it would be. I didn't need anyone or anything besides my child. She was my sun, my moon, and the air I breathed.

On her first day of kindergarten, while I gripped her tiny hand on the way to the door of her classroom, wishing I didn't have to let it go, she broke free of my grasp and joined her classmates without so much as a glance over her shoulder. Other children clung to their mothers, tearful and timid.

Within two months, a lice outbreak found me braiding and wrapping her long locks in elaborate plaits and buns, something I continued throughout her elementary years. People, even strangers, fawned over her beautiful hair. Thick and long, wavy, the color of spun gold. I beamed with pride at the compliments, knowing she carried a piece of me with her every day—my love woven into the intricate twists. Sometimes, when I cleaned her brush, I kept the fallen strands in my pocket, so I too would have a piece of her with me while she was away learning to read and write.

She lost her first tooth at school and brought the tiny pearl to me in an envelope printed with a heart-shattering apology for losing it away from home, depriving me of the experience. I kept each subsequent little jewel in a baby food jar tucked inside my keepsake trunk.

Eustachian tubes went in, and tonsils came out. There were broken bones and stitches, illnesses and hurt feelings. Each time pain reached for her, she turned to me. A hug, a kiss—comfort was always within reach. I ended every day standing in her bedroom doorway, listening to her breath. I lost track of time and purpose while soaking in her presence.

When she was in second grade, we said goodbye to Orson. The two of us spent that Saturday morning digging a hole and burying our beloved cat. Lauren placed flowers on the mound of dirt and made a promise to Orson's only surviving kitten, Rosy.

"Daddy has to let you move into the house now," Lauren cooed to the cat, hoisting it off the ground and into her arms. "No kitty should have to sleep outside, especially alone. It isn't fair."

Roger refused.

Rosy lived in the yard, and when Lauren was in the fourth grade, the cat had her own litter. This time, two survived. My garden never looked better, as I spent more time pruning just to watch Rosy raise her young. I spent hours playing with them as they grew, my forearms pocked with pinprick scabs from their tiny claws. Rosy's ability to rein her babies in and keep them on course was admirable. She was so in tune to their needs, and they followed her like shadows, hanging on her every action as she guided them. Under her innate nurturing, the kittens transitioned from squirming, whimpering little balls, helpless and vulnerable, to independent hunters. They responded without hesitation to her every chirp and mew, never wandering beyond the boundaries she set. She flaunted her skill; her mastery of raising young was enviable.

When it came time to relinquish her young to the world, Rosy did so with confidence. She'd fulfilled her obligation and was ready to reestablish her independence, refusing their efforts to nurse by settling on the garden bench, out of reach of their needling claws and prickling teeth. One kitten remained among the junipers in our garden; the other went to live in a home with Lauren's best friend,

Sadie. Roger stonewalled against his daughter's pleas to allow the kitten in her room. She was stalwart. He was unflappable. I wondered how he could deny her something she was so passionate about. I thought he only reserved that stance for me.

One morning, as Lauren prepared for a field trip on the last day of her fifth-grade year, I retrieved the newspaper off the front porch. Over coffee, I flipped through the pages, searching for camps or clubs to fill her summer days when a photo caught my eye.

It was a picture of Roger in the business section. His face beamed in the grainy black-and-white image, wearing an expression I'd long recognized. One that said he'd had one or two too many. His eyes were wide with something I couldn't identify: pride, surprise, exultation? He sat at a table in a ballroom, a small trophy raised in his hand. Underneath was the headline:

Local Ad Man Awarded American Advertising Federation Silver Medal Award

The awards ceremony took place two weeks earlier, and I'd almost forgotten about it. He'd received dozens of ADDY awards, but this was the highlight of his career. On the night of the event, I dressed in an evening gown selected for the occasion with Lauren's help. As I sat at my vanity putting on earrings, Lauren appeared at my door. Her cheeks were flushed, her color off, and dark circles draped her eyes.

"Mommy, I don't feel good," she whimpered before vomiting at the threshold of the bedroom.

Without a moment's hesitation, I called the sitter and apologized for the late cancellation. I couldn't leave Lauren in her state. Roger went to the ceremony without me. He returned long after I'd gone to bed, smelling of whiskey and a scent that rose from the recesses of my tired mind—familiar and haunting, yet out of my reach. A heady blend of cigarette smoke and cloying perfume. I shrugged it off as remnants from the party. He'd leaned in for a kiss, which I reproached, too sleepy from a long evening of tending to Lauren's bout of food poisoning to be roused fully.

The next morning, he detailed the night's events. Lauren and I pulled together an impromptu congratulatory party that evening, inviting some neighbors and making a cake. Roger was in his element as he flipped steaks for the adults and served burgers to the children, all the while pointing to the trophy and relaying how he came up with an acceptance speech on the fly. I ordered a trophy stand for his office.

I finished reading the article and rose, excited to show it to Roger, but paused as something at the bottom of the photo caught my eye. I slid back down in my chair and pulled the image close. Now, as I reflected on that night, it hit me. I realized how I knew the scent clinging to him when he crawled into bed.

Just inside the frame, at Roger's feet, was another foot. A woman's foot. Stiletto heels, toenails darkened in the gray-scale image, a familiar anklet wound around her leg. A woman's foot entwined with Roger's. Cropped just so by the photographer, no doubt overlooked by the typesetter. A woman's foot, used as a tool to seduce a drunken man.

NINE

CONTRACTIONS

2001-2005

"You're making a mountain out of a molehill, Alice," Roger fumed, tossing the newspaper onto the bed. He moved to the mirror, tying his tie. "I've got enough on my plate already. There's no room on my calendar for your delusional paranoia. The Bell account is breathing down my neck for their jingle. My creative director is on another bender, so he's producing crap when he manages to produce anything at all, and somehow it's my problem. Do you know how hard it is to keep a grown man away from hookers and coke? Well, no, you wouldn't, but it's harder than you'd think."

He turned to me. I expected to see fire in his eyes but saw apathy.

"This is just like you to ruin what was supposed to be my big day. You couldn't just let me enjoy it, could you? You had to make it about you. Typical."

His words hit their mark. Maybe I was overreacting, but I'd seen Nancy in action all those years ago. How she could bridge the gap from complete strangers to romantic prospect in minutes. How she could manipulate a target in record time and become a couple in the blink of an eye. She was a master at extramarital affairs and sought her fulfillment recklessly, never considering other people. But it took two to shift overt flirtation into something improper.

Still, the image gnawed at me. I retrieved the paper from the bed and studied it again. The day before, I'd let the picture and its implications stew, and I lost sleep, reaching the decision to confront him in the small hours of the morning. Now I doubted my instincts. Felt foolish. Roger had a way of twisting my thoughts.

"Listen, it was an innocent flirtation. Inappropriate, maybe. But that's all it was. I'd had too much to drink. I was celebrating. What else do you want me to say?"

"There's nothing innocent about that woman." Despite his attempts to squash my feelings before exploring them, I had to uncover the extent of their encounter.

"What are you talking about?" He sat on the bed bench and used a shoehorn to slip on his wingtips.

"Do you remember her name?" I asked.

He slumped his shoulders and forced an exaggerated sigh that stirred the air.

"No, I don't remember her name. She was there with her husband. The man was old as dirt. I think he fell asleep during my acceptance speech. She congratulated me. We talked and had a drink. That was it. It never would have happened if you'd been there. Have you ever thought about that?"

"Our child was sick, Roger." My cheeks burned red, and I turned away from him, fixating again on the black-and-white image. Now who was making things about themselves? My duty was to our child.

"Oh, I know, Alice. It's all about our child," he said, rising and adjusting his belt. "That's all it's been about since before she was born. Before you go blaming this on me, take a look in the mirror. You aren't just a mother. You're also a wife, in case you forgot." He snatched his pillbox off the dresser, opened a tab, and shook the pills into his mouth, washing them down with a swig of coffee before exiting the room.

Indignation threw me, snatched my voice away. Who had

divvied out a week's worth of blood pressure pills and vitamins into the pillbox? Who brought him the cup of coffee he drank on his way out of the bedroom? Who brought his suits and ties to and from the cleaners? Who returned the shoehorn to the closet and put his pajamas in the hamper? I was silent, my mind racing as I stared at the photo.

Down the hall, I heard the front door slam. He'd left. Next, I heard Lauren's feet hit the floor in her bedroom. She'd be eager to start the first day of summer. I swiped a tear from my eye and went to the hall to greet her.

"What should we do today?" I asked, pushing a tangle of hair from her face.

"Everyone is going to the pool after lunch," she replied. She yawned, gripping the air with tiny fists, stretching tall. "Can I have waffles for breakfast?"

If she'd heard our raised voices or noticed my red eyes, she gave no indication. Her complacency served to spur Roger's assertions. I was reading too much into it. I wished I could hush the insistent voice in my head warning there was more to the story.

Summers whipped by quicker with each passing year, and this one was no different. Once the Fourth of July celebrations ended, the other moms at the pool started counting down to the first day of school. Not me. I wished the season never ended and dreaded Lauren's return to school. We baked in the sun by the pool, our coppery skin dotted white with waning mosquito bites. I sipped sweet tea and nosed in on her and her friends, my eyes concealed behind dark shades to cloak my curiosity. Their conversations ranged from training bras and makeup to MTV and boy bands. They traded in their American Girl dolls for Spice Girls posters and stuffed animals for telephones in their bedrooms.

I wasn't ready for Lauren to start middle school. I tried not to dwell on the empty hours I'd face in the fall. My only solace regarding the coming school year was being on the PTA board and volunteering as homeroom mom.

"Mom, I'm too old for braids," Lauren said when I joined her in the bathroom the morning of middle school schedule pickup. "All the girls wear their hair down. I can't wait to get these braces off." Lauren leaned toward the mirror, baring her teeth. She'd chosen pink bands.

I imagined what she'd look like free of the metal brackets as I tidied her bathroom counter, placing her hair bows back in the drawer.

"Are we going to the mall after schedule pickup? I have to find the perfect first-day outfit! Can I get some butterfly clips?"

Her confidence grew with the rest of her. She was so much more than I was as she transitioned from child to preteen; she became self-assured and commanding. My love fed that growth.

We walked the unfamiliar halls of the middle school, pausing frequently for Lauren to swap schedules with her friends. Their laughter echoed through the corridors of the building. The school was enormous. While I worried about Lauren being overwhelmed, she forged ahead in search of her homeroom class. When we found the right room, I entered and made a beeline for the teacher, eager to put my name in the hat for homeroom mom before others had the chance.

"Mr. Parker, nice to meet you. I'm Lauren White's mother, Alice," I said, shaking the teacher's hand. He was impossibly young. Lauren remained in the hallway, chattering with a group of girls.

"Glad to meet you, Mrs. White. I teach U.S. history. I look forward to getting to know your daughter."

"I was wondering if you've selected a homeroom mom yet?" I asked, lowering my voice as Lauren approached.

"Um, well, no, actually. We don't really have homeroom moms in middle school," he replied.

Lauren joined us as he continued.

"Technically, I am Lauren's homeroom teacher, but it's really just a moniker. This is her first class of the day, so it's considered homeroom. The office just designates us to hand out take-home materials and such."

"Oh, right. Of course, it's silly. I've just been homeroom mom every year since, well, since she started school." I ran my fingers through a lock of Lauren's hair, and she batted my hand away. "This whole middle school thing is going to take some getting used to."

"It is a big change," he said, holding out a hand to Lauren. "You must be Lauren. Welcome to Mr. Parker's U.S. History class. Happy to have you here."

Lauren blushed.

"Mom," she hissed as we exited Mr. Parker's classroom. "How could you embarrass me like that? There are no homeroom moms in middle school. Ugh!" She didn't offer me the chance to apologize. "Let's go to the cafeteria next. They have club sign-ups. I want to join theatre club. Oh, there's Claire. I heard she got her belly button pierced! So rad!"

She ran ahead and joined her friend, who pulled her shirt up and stuck her stomach out. I trailed behind them.

The school mascot, a giant eagle dressed in green and gold, greeted us at the entrance to the cafeteria. The room buzzed with exuberance. Parents and kids rambled through the cavernous space, and a cacophony of excitement echoed off the high ceiling. A woman shoved a piece of paper into my hand.

"You'll need to fill this out. You can buy spirit wear over there," she said, pointing to her right. "And don't forget to pick up the student handbook. Follow the signs around the room," she said with a shiny smile and quick shoulder shrug.

I'd lost sight of Lauren in the sea of spiked hair and baggy jeans. I strolled past the tables, spotted one for PTA sign-ups, and joined the line. Maybe I'd run for PTA president. I'd served two years as president at the elementary school and had the spare time. Looking around the room, brimming with anticipation for the new year, I wondered how stiff the competition would be.

"Next," a familiar voice said.

I scanned the room in the direction the voice came from, and my eyes fell on a pair of impractical heels jutting out from the table at the head of the line. Her ankle bracelet grabbed my attention. My eyes traced up her long legs and fell on Nancy Ellington's face. She sat behind the table, waving at me.

"Alice White! Oh, my goodness! Get your little tush on over here!"

I wanted to walk away, to fade into the swarms of mothers and kids. Disappear. Run. I fixed a smile on my face and stepped forward.

"Nancy, I didn't know your son went to public school." I tried to remain composed and considered commenting about her hair, which was now a faded shade of molasses. I decided it would be better not to, unsure if the look was new or not as I realized how long it'd been since I'd seen her face-to-face. The only time I'd seen a hint of the woman in over ten years was in Roger's newspaper photograph.

I'd spent the entire summer watching Roger closely for signs of infidelity. I was quick to smell his jacket when he returned from happy hour and inspected his collars for traces of makeup before dropping them at the cleaners. He'd become so reclusive, only heightening my suspicions. He insisted he had to work, build his clientele list, stay on top of his game. While he'd spent the summer hidden in his home office, he didn't seem to be hiding anything from me other than contempt when I tried to convince him to spend more time with us. Lauren's childhood was rushing past at a disquieting pace, and he chose to miss so much of it, using his job to avoid his family. Then again, maybe guilt forced him to further distance himself.

"Well, Jennings insisted he wouldn't attend the all-boys' school another minute." Nancy's response pulled me back into the conversation. "Threatened to run away if we made him." She laughed, batting the arm of the woman sitting next to her.

"Oh, I see," I muttered, not getting the humor.

"So here we are, Eagles now. I've got to admit, this place looks like way more of a hoot than that fuddy-duddy Catholic school." She crossed herself halfheartedly. "Please say you'll be joining me on the PTA board? I'm running for president this year. I know it's our first year in the district, but I thought it'd be a great way to get to know the other moms. I hope to get your vote."

"How ambitious of you," I said, willing the blow not to register on my face. I smiled, completely aware it looked forced.

"I don't know about ambitious. It's not rocket science, Alice. Unless you know nothing about rockets. Or science. Am I right?"

The woman sitting next to Nancy laughed.

"How hard can it be throwing together some bake sales and planning a few field trips? It'd be a blast working with you. Here's the sign-up info. Drop it back by after filling it out. Maybe the kids will have some classes together. It's going to be a great year!"

Her positivity only soured my already bleak expectations for the shift from elementary to secondary school. There was no homeroom mom gig, and now PTA was out of the question too.

"Mom," Lauren called, waving at me from two tables over. Relief filled me. Without glancing back, I joined my daughter at the spirit wear booth. She threw her items down on the table: T-shirts, a jacket, a ball cap, and bumper stickers. I pulled my pocketbook out. Lauren grabbed a pennant and some pompoms, adding them to the pile. As I paid for her purchases, I let the PTA form slip from my hands. It floated to the floor, and I nudged it under the tablecloth with my foot.

The following Monday, Lauren insisted on taking the school bus instead of having me drop her off, as I was accustomed to doing on the first day of school. She paused in the front yard for me to take her picture. Rosy and her kitten Bud chased a bug in the background.

That year was full of many firsts. School dances, slumber parties, even a school trip. Lauren got the lead in the spring musical, playing opposite Jennings Ellington. The two shared an on-stage kiss, their faces hidden from the audience by his hat.

"We don't really kiss, Mom. That'd just be gross," she informed us over dinner the night of dress rehearsal. Despite her comments, I noted a faint tint to her cheeks when she spoke, a lift in her voice. I brushed it off. A schoolgirl crush. Jennings Ellington was a handsome boy.

Jennings took Lauren's hand and walked her to the front of the stage for their curtain call on opening night, raising their arms before diving into a bow. He held her hand as she curtsied, and they hugged. Roger was away on business for their first show. Nancy was there. Her husband clung to her arm, hunched over and shuffling as they inched to their seats. I sat three rows behind them. Nancy led the standing ovation at the end.

Roger traveled more that year, a trend which continued. His client list and the agency were expanding their reach to surrounding states. He bought a sleeper sofa for his office, so we often slept apart. I got better rest than I had since before Lauren was born on the nights he opted not to join me in bed. His snoring had become impossible to ignore, so I enjoyed the solitude. Bud made a habit of leaping onto my windowsill every night. as if he came to wish me sweet dreams before he departed on his nightly prowls.

During school shopping the following year, Lauren broke away from me at the stores. We'd reconnect near the dressing rooms, but she didn't invite me in or ask for my opinion. I followed her to the register and made the purchases. The year after that, she asked Roger for his credit card and got a ride to the mall.

"No one goes to the mall with their parents anymore, Mom."

Despite the sting of accepting her need to pull away, I found ways to spend time with Lauren. By the time she entered high school, I'd been relegated to chauffeur, and I embraced the new role. We filled hours in the car, just the two of us. Lauren sang my praises as I ushered her to and from voice coaching, dance lessons, and rehearsals. But I didn't need any more thanks than her time. Mostly I listened to her run lines. By showtime, I could recite the script from my seat in the audience. I felt such a part of it all, sewing her costumes, styling her hair, making sure she was fed and had everything she needed so she could put her all into musical theater, her passion.

"Mom, can I ask you a question?" Lauren asked one day as the clouds burst and heavy rain pelted our car. We crawled along Utica Avenue with the other commuters, traffic at a near standstill due to an accident. I looked at her and was struck by her beauty, admiring the turn of her nose and the creamy river of blonde hair that hung below her shoulders. Lightning cracked, and shadows danced over her knotted brow; her expression solemn. She was becoming a young woman, and the absence of braces on her teeth snatched away any lingering remnants of childhood.

Turning my eyes back to the motionless traffic, I tried to remember what I was like at that age. We were so different. My early teenage years were about survival and mourning a life that never came to be. I took such pride in knowing I'd spared Lauren from such grief; her childhood wouldn't be stained with sadness and pain. I'd do anything to protect her and the life she lived. She was free to pursue her dreams, and I hoped she felt loved.

"Earth to Mom," she said, reaching across the console, snapping a finger in my face to draw back into the moment. "You in there?" She laughed.

"Sorry, guess my mind was wandering," I replied. "What's up?"

"How do you know if a boy is in love with you?" she asked, her voice dipping to a murmur.

Heat rose in my chest, edging its way through my arms and up my neck, igniting my cheeks. I didn't know what to say; her words felt like an ambush. She was too young to be asking about love, wasn't she? We'd never spoken of boys beyond boy-band crushes. A horn blared behind me, and I shook my head, focusing on the road now as traffic lurched forward. I closed the gap in front of me and attempted to peer around the car ahead to see if the jam was breaking up as I clamored for words. Lauren pressed.

"Mom?"

"Well, honey… Hmm. In love," I said, turning to her and forcing a smile. I shrugged, the heat still burning crimson on my face, and wondered if she sensed my discomfort with the subject. "Those are big words for someone your age."

"I'm not a kid anymore, Mom," she said, causing me to flinch.

"Sweetie." I drew the word out, making sure to strike the right tone: apologetic, understanding, aware. I scoffed and tried to collect my thoughts. "I know you're not a kid anymore. Who's the lucky guy?"

She bounced in her seat and clapped her hands together while her feet fluttered on the floorboard. I silently congratulated myself for getting it right.

"Just a boy." She giggled. "I don't want to jinx anything, but, like, when you feel different about someone, like, ugh, I don't know how to describe it. Sometimes I catch him just looking at me."

I glanced her way as traffic resumed a normal speed, the rain waning to a misty drizzle. Now her cheeks matched mine, and her energy shifted. Her words echoed through my mind, calling up images of Thomas. For a moment, I considered telling her about him. I knew the answer to her question but didn't want to encourage her, so I shook the notion away. There were plenty of fish in the sea. A girlhood crush would be a thing of the past in a couple of weeks.

"It's silly," she said, breaking me free from my thoughts again. "Forget I said anything."

Silence filled the car for a few minutes as I turned down a side street. It was a heavy and unfulfilled silence, but she'd grown quiet and I couldn't find words. When we approached the parking lot of her dance studio, she spoke.

"Don't tell anyone, okay, Mom? Not even Dad," she said, collecting her bag. She got out of the car and paused. "Promise!"

"I promise," I said with a wink. "Now get out of the rain! I'll watch from out here this evening. See you in a couple of hours. Love you!"

"Love you too," she called, slamming the door, hopping over puddles to join a group of friends near the entrance.

Later in the evening, I stopped at Roger's office on the way to bed. I knocked, and he opened the door, drink in hand, tugging on his tie.

"I'm working on a tight deadline here, Alice," he said, not welcoming me in. "Can this wait?"

"No, actually," I whispered, glancing down the hallway. I heard the shower still running in the bathroom and pushed past Roger. "I need to talk to you about something serious, right now."

"Please make it quick." He closed the door behind me with an eye roll.

"You need to talk to Lauren about dating," I hissed.

"Dating?" he asked, his voice booming.

"Yes." I held my finger to my lips and leaned against the door. "Lower your voice."

"Can't we talk about this tomorrow?" He sat back down at his desk, clasped his hands behind his neck and dropped his chin to his chest.

"No, it can't wait. I think she may have a boyfriend," I began.

"Think? May? Do you hear yourself, Alice?" He looked up at me. He didn't hide his exasperation. "Fine, what do you want me to say?"

"Well, keep it casual but firm. Don't mention this." I wagged my finger between us. "Or any boy or anything along those lines. Just let her know what our stance is on dating."

"What is our stance on dating, Alice?" He picked up a folder and shuffled through the pages. "I think yours might differ from mine."

"Oh, really?" I said, unable to keep my voice quiet. I could hear Lauren in the bathroom now. The shower was off, and she was brushing her teeth. "She's not old enough to date. I didn't start dating until I was sixteen. She's only fourteen, and she's already asking about being in love. It's absurd! We need to discourage this type of behavior and let her know it won't be tolerated."

"Right," he said, reaching for a storyboard. "Sixteen, got it. I'll talk to her over breakfast because I really have to get this presentation together before I go to bed. I've got hours ahead of me."

I moved to the door and pressed my ear against the crack. Lauren shuffled by outside and I waited for her to close her bedroom door, then turned back to Roger. "You're her father. I'd hoped you'd show a little more concern." I didn't allow him the chance to reply, slipping out of his office and down the hall.

The next morning, I prepared waffles and set the table in the breakfast nook and waited. They were both running late, and Roger rushed in with his tie draped over his shoulder. He plucked a piece of bacon from the platter, washing it down with a swig of now-tepid coffee.

"Have you seen Lauren yet?" I asked, crossing the room. Steam swirled from the plate of waffles I held. I skirted him and peered down the hall.

"No, and I don't have time to wait for her." He grabbed a waffle and rolled it in a napkin as Lauren bounded out of her room.

"But…" I stepped in front of him, cutting off his escape route. "You said you would—"

"Mom," Lauren said, hopping into the kitchen, finger looped inside the heel of a tennis shoe. She struggled to get it on as she jumped toward the table. "Can you wrap some of that up for me? My ride is already here. I gotta run."

"Well, honey," I started, wrapping her food in a paper towel so she could take it with her.

"Laur," Roger interrupted. "Your mom says you've got yourself a beau."

Lauren dropped her foot, abandoning her effort to get her shoe on. Her bag slipped from her arm. I fought for words, desperate to change the direction of Roger's thoughtless attempts to be a good father. There was nothing I could say. Her eyes found mine.

"A beau? What? Wait. Mom!" Emotions shifted across her face. She settled on anger, and it simmered in her eyes, singeing me.

Roger ignored the heat and pressed on.

"No dating until you're sixteen," he said, and rubbed her head and nabbed two more strips of bacon from the plate. "Your mom and I agreed. All right then, have a great day, ladies."

A horn blasted outside as Roger opened the front door.

"I can't believe you," Lauren said, rejecting my offering of a bacon strip rolled in a waffle. "You promised," she simpered before taking her shoe from the floor and running outside.

Soon after, Lauren's friends got their driver's licenses. She no longer needed me to shuffle her from place to place. Neither she nor Roger had found time in their busy schedules for driving lessons, and I didn't press the issue. I really didn't like the thought of her out there on her own with a flat tire or worse, getting into an accident. More and more, I took meals alone, leaving a plate covered in cling wrap in the refrigerator for when she returned from rehearsals. Roger ate in his office.

One morning while I worked in the garden, a new kitten approached. Rosy and Bud threw their obligatory fits, but soon the little yellow cat was part of the family of felines I cared for. Before this cat, whom I named Kane, entered her first heat cycle, Rosy vanished. She was there one morning and gone the next. I tried putting tuna out for her to lure her home, but it was eaten by Bud and Kane. I never saw Rosy again.

TEN

TRANSITION

2007

Once I was no longer needed at Lauren's school, I found my days empty, and I struggled to find purpose. I spent more time at Coventry Springs, giving the hours previously spent on bake sales and book fairs to the residents of the nursing home. When my gig as Lauren's taxi driver ended, I had even more time on my hands. I filled the emptiness at the facility, where I felt wanted. As Lauren grew up and Roger grew increasingly distant, I spent more days at the nursing home than not. They needed me.

It wasn't always easy. Caring for those in their waning years didn't lend itself to joy and hope. But it offered a window to appreciation and meaning. I'd like to believe what I gave the residents of Coventry Springs was valuable, immeasurable even. And while I am certain it was to many, what I gained from my hours with the elderly and staff was far greater than I could ever convey.

Even the sadness of losing Betty, an eighty-nine-year-old former schoolteacher who loved reading the classics, was softened by the memory of her stories of a life fully lived. She had many books she still wanted to devour, but ran out of time when macular degeneration stole her sight. I enjoyed listening to her insights into the stories when we closed each chapter and learned things I had been too busy or too distracted to learn while in school. She insisted books on tape were nothing compared to the "music" of my voice. I couldn't help but wonder if I'd have been a different person had my own mother been more like Betty.

Filling in crosswords for Diego, a retired railway conductor, opened a treasury of words to me. While I'd always considered myself well-spoken, Diego expounded upon language, revealing origins, context and layers I'd never known or considered. Parkinson's took his ability to fill in the squares, even ones enlarged to aid those with deteriorating eyesight. He imparted to me words of wisdom my father might have offered if given the chance. He passed away in his sleep one evening at seventy-eight.

Threading needles for Maisy brought joy to the eighty-four-year-old, allowing her to create incredible needlepoint pieces on her scroll frame. Her mottled and coriaceous hands flicked and pulled as she shared her stories of motherhood. The whisper of thread drawn through canvas invoked a rhythm as her history spilled from her mouth. When she really got on a roll, she removed her dentures, insisting her words were clearer without her "falsies" in.

"Sounds like you are a wonderful mother," I told her one day.

"Most of us think we're good moms," she said, pausing with her needle high above the canvas. A sad laugh escaped her lips, and her gaze grew distant. "Then we have daughters."

I laughed, but saw a tear slip down her cheek. Her eyes settled on me with an expression that reached inside me and touched my heart. One of sadness and loss.

"The boys are easy. They dote on their mothers. You've seen mine here every week, haven't you?" she asked.

I nodded, recalling the brood I'd spotted in her room and in the dining hall, and the gallery of colorful drawings she had taped to the wall in her room. Maisy had several grandchildren and at least four great-grandchildren.

"But daughters. They're different. Sure, they let it slide while you braid their hair and do their makeup. Buy them prom dresses and the best of everything you can afford. They wait. Wait until you feel like you've done everything right. Then, just when you think you can relax, pat yourself on the back, they hit you with a power you never knew existed. If you're lucky, they come back around and help you up. Forgive you for all the wrongs you didn't know you'd put upon them."

Maisy fell silent. Her hands halted their work. Her gaze drifted off. She seemed to have traveled back in time, her face reflecting a scene being relived in her mind. With a shaky, gnarled hand, she brushed away tears and looked at me as if she'd forgotten I was there.

"Mine hasn't forgiven me, hasn't come back," she said, gathering her thread and tucking it into her ancient craft basket. She closed the lid and rested her hands on top of the worn wood. "We mothers tend to think we know what's best for our kids. To think my daughter isn't in my life because of a man. I should have just lied and pretended to like him. Maybe things would be different."

Maisy sat quietly for some time. The emotions of a lifetime flashed by, a wave of expressions passing in her gaze as she visited a history I knew nothing about. Another tear slipped down her face, and a trail of sadness settled in the deep lines, flowing on a current of grief. "If you'll excuse me, dear, I think I'll lie down before supper."

We left the community room, and I helped her down the hall to her suite where she got into bed and was snoring softly within moments. Although identical in layout to my mother's space, Maisy's room was warm and inviting, nothing like the place my mother had resided in before her passing. Maybe it was my fault for not giving her grandchildren.

Feeling like an interloper, I explored what was now Maisy's home, moving to the display on her dresser. Framed photos crowded its top. There was only one of Maisy with a woman who, though many years younger, held the same light in her eyes, same turn of mouth, and large, white teeth contrasted by the same shade of ebony skin. Only one image of her daughter. I longed to know where her daughter was now. Why she didn't visit. Who was this man who came between them? But I dared not inquire. Whatever had occurred was obviously a source of great pain for Maisy.

Two years after our conversation about sons and daughters, I sat at Maisy's funeral and surveyed the gathering mourners. I recognized her sons and their wives and marveled at how her grandchildren had grown. Her daughter's name had been mentioned as one of her survivors, but I did not see the woman who held such a close resemblance to her mother. My tears that day were more for the absence of Maisy's daughter than for the loss of Maisy. She left a solander box of her needlework pieces for me. It sat in my closet for many years, a hidden treasure.

Aside from my duties of assisting residents with their meals, calling bingo, helping with puzzles, reading and cross-wording, I attended their funerals. Even if said funeral was the interment of a box of ashes into a family plot. Even if I was the only attendee. Even if there was no service and I had no knowledge of a final resting place, I marshaled in my mind. I laid them to rest in my heart.

"You should get a job here, Miss Alice," Roberta, one of the housekeepers, suggested as she mopped the floors of the community hall and I gathered cards and daubers one afternoon. Maisy's absence was still fresh at Coventry Springs. "No one should spend this much time in a place without getting paid for it."

I'd never had a job. I couldn't speak those words out loud to Roberta. I'd never been ashamed of my jobless status. My efforts had always been better spent raising Lauren. But confessing this to Roberta was unthinkable. The woman had started cleaning alongside her mother when she was younger than Lauren. Shame teemed within me, and I fumbled for a response.

"Oh, Roberta, what would anyone want with me? I never even graduated college." I wanted to grab the words and choke them back down as soon as they rushed out of my mouth.

"College? Who says you need college? I didn't even make it past the fourth grade. Those ladies in the back office haven't stepped foot in a college classroom. Give yourself more credit, ma'am."

I tucked Roberta's words inside me and considered them often. Lauren was a senior now, and almost at an age where she would need me even less. Maybe it was time to consider doing something more than just volunteering. Roger would protest, but maybe Roberta was right. Maybe I'd talk to Roger soon and see if he could be convinced to let me go back to school or get something part-time.

For now, I wanted to relish every day of Lauren's last year of high school. There would be plenty of time for me to carve a new path once she graduated. Not wanting anything to overshadow the most exciting year of Lauren's life, I vowed to keep the idea to myself for a while.

———

"Yum, Mom. This looks delicious, but I won't be home for dinner tomorrow," Lauren said that night, joining Roger and me at the table. "I really need my curfew lifted. I'm running lines with a friend. This is my senior year, and if I don't get the lead, I'll die."

"Is this friend a boy?" Roger jabbed.

"Lame, Dad. But for your information, yes, it is a boy."

"The Ellington boy?" I asked, knowing the answer. Lauren and Jennings had been co-stars in nearly every school performance since middle school. After Roger's bumbling attempt at laying down the dating laws, Lauren hadn't spoken of the boy—of any boy—again. I was grateful she listened to her father.

"As you know, his name is Jennings, and yes, Mom, I'll be with him."

"You two seem pretty close these days. Maybe you should ask him to the winter semi-formal," Roger continued.

"Whatever," Lauren replied, not concealing a dramatic eye roll. "Yes, we are close, but it's like brother and sister close. And you know, maybe we should go to the dance together, if we go at all. Who needs that distraction? It's not like it's prom. We really have to nail this audition. If we get the parts we want, we'll have so much work to do we might as well move in together."

My fork slipped from my hand and clattered onto my plate. I picked it up and tried to steer the conversation away from the Ellington home. This dinner—one I'd pushed for when I realized everyone would be home that evening—was veering in a direction I hadn't seen coming.

"Why can't you practice over here? Jennings could join us for dinner," I said before taking a bite of salad, an act I believed would render my interest casual.

"Right, because you're such a huge fan of his. I don't know what you have against him. He's just a boy, but honestly, Mom, you're like an ice princess when he's around."

By now, our run-ins with the Ellingtons had become unavoidable as Lauren and Jennings co-starred in school plays and community theatre performances. The encounters were nothing short of insulting. Roger and Nancy behaved as if they'd never met. Of course, by then her precious Edward wasn't likely to remember what he ate for breakfast, so he gave no hints of familiarity. Though our meetings were brief, I sensed the conspiratorial connection between Nancy and Roger, and was certain I spied a knowing glance, a blushing cheek.

"Ice princess, good one, Laur," Roger said, laughing.

"Well, I just think it would be a nice gesture to have him over. It isn't polite to expect Nancy to host all your sessions." I struggled to steady my tone.

"His house is way bigger. No one bothers us. Like, we don't even see anyone when I'm there. And they have way better snacks. Plus, they have a baby grand. It's boss!"

"Speaking of senior year, how many college applications have you submitted so far?" Roger said, steering the conversation in a baffling but welcome direction.

My response was simple. "Roger, we've discussed this. She's already been offered a scholarship to TU. They have an excellent theater program and are right here in town. Think of how much we'll save on room and board since she won't need to live in a dorm."

"Actually, I've been thinking of taking a gap year," Lauren said, suddenly interested in her dinner roll. She didn't look up. The words hovered in the air. Roger set his silverware down. My stomach knotted, and I tossed my napkin on the table.

"A gap year? What kind of nonsense is that?" Roger asked, leaning back in his chair.

"It's not nonsense, Dad. I was thinking of going to New York City, auditioning, checking out schools there."

"New York City?" I meant to convey shock, outrage even, but the words slipped out with no conviction and were just a squeal. My lungs refused to accept air. Lauren's path had been decided long ago. She would go to college in town. The suggestion she divert from this course left me reeling. The ground beneath me was crumbling. I was slipping.

"It's out of the question," Roger's voice boomed. "You'll go to school, and once you've earned a degree, you can flit about wherever you want and take a stab at auditions and such. You'll need something to fall back on once you've come to your senses."

"Thanks for the vote of confidence, Dad."

"Sweetie," I began. It was the only word I could find. I was grateful for Roger's stance.

"Lauren, you are very talented, but let's be realistic," Roger said, trying to backpedal.

"It's so far away." I wasn't sure if I'd uttered the words out loud. Neither of them seemed to hear me.

"I'm seventeen, Dad. Reality will bite me soon enough. I owe it to myself to explore my talent. Why else have you and Mom dedicated so much money and time to my lessons all these years?"

"You can't go to New York alone, honey. It's such a big city. And so far away." I still struggled to find a voice in the conversation.

"I won't be alone, Mom."

I was grateful she replied to me, as I was uncertain the words were coming out.

"Oh, really?" Roger barked. "Who's moving to the Big Apple with you, Lauren? And better yet, who is paying for this little adventure? You have a college fund that is to be used for college, not for gallivanting around Shakespeare in the Park festivals."

"If you must know," she began, placing both palms on the table and taking a deep breath, "Jennings and I want to go together. His parents support his creativity and his decisions!" Her voice trembled. Until now, she'd dammed her tears, but one slipped free. As soon as it slid off her chin, more chased after it, cutting soggy lines down her face.

I wanted to rescue her. But more than rescuing her, I wanted this all to end. I blurted out the first thing I could think of to bury the conversation. To obliterate the mere thought of Lauren leaving home.

"I'm thinking about getting a job."

There was a pause. Lauren wiped her face; her sniffles poked at the heavy silence.

"That makes about as much sense as Lauren moving to New York City," Roger replied, pushing his chair back and disappearing down the hall to his office.

Later that night, I knocked on Roger's office door. I heard his heavy sigh as he shuffled across the room. The lock clicked, and he cracked the door.

"Can I come in? I think we need to talk."

His body slumped, and he glanced over his shoulder before stepping back and allowing me in. This room in my own house was foreign to me. I rarely entered, as it made me uncomfortable, like I didn't belong. It had all the warmth of a dank cavern. Heavy curtains concealed the window and held fast the cigar smoke and stale cologne. His garment bag hung on a hook near the door. Below the hook, his attaché case sat open, mock-up boards and papers spilling onto the floor. The sofa was pulled out into a bed, shrinking the room; sheets twisted, unmade. Each time I crossed the threshold into his office, the room looked as if it deteriorated more. Roger had begun locking the door even to the cleaning ladies some-time in the past year. It needed a deep clean and some airing out. He grabbed his toiletry bag off the guest chair and gestured for me to sit.

"I need you to make it quick. This presentation is due tomorrow morning," he said, returning to his seat behind his desk. I'd heard the words so many times they were like one of Lauren's scripts. His computer screen hid his face, and he rolled his chair to the side, allowing me to see him. A small mirror covered with crumbs of white powder sat on the edge of his desk. He palmed it, sliding it out of my view.

"I'm sorry to bother you, but I really think we need to discuss this New York City thing. We can't possibly let her move there. And with a boy. It's out of the question, Roger. What are we going to do?"

"Oh, Lord, Alice. It's a pipe dream. I say we let it lie. She'll forget all about it." His eyes shifted back to his computer screen.

"I don't think she will forget about it. This has been her life since she was ten years old. It doesn't seem like some kind of pie-in-the-sky musing." I inched forward in my seat, hands gripping the ledge of his desk. My body pushed toward him, urging him to hear me, see me. "We need to get on the same page. She can't move so far away. She's too young."

"I don't know. Maybe she should go out and experience the world some. She's a smart kid. She'll come to her senses." He didn't try to hide his disinterest in the conversation, picking up a story-board as he spoke. "I bet she won't even last a couple of months."

"That's not acceptable. She can't leave." A drop of sweat snaked down my back.

"She'll be eighteen soon." He put the storyboard down and punched a key on his keyboard before continuing, "We won't have any say. If we forbid her from doing something, she'll just pull further away."

"You're her father! Tell her no!" I rose from the seat, wishing I could pace, but the cluttered room made it impossible, so I fell back into the chair.

"Whoa! Chill out." He rubbed his nose and leaned back in his chair.

"No, you don't understand. We have to put a stop to these notions immediately. She can't go so far away. Roger, please." My hands were beyond my control. To stop them from shaking, I raked my fingers through my hair. It didn't work, so I shoved them under my legs. My legs picked up the tension and started bouncing. Why was this room so hot? One hand worked its way out from under me. My finger was in my mouth. I gnawed on a hangnail.

"Calm down! Not every kid who moves away gets knifed in a barroom brawl."

His words landed like a slap. The sting worked through my entire body. My hand dropped to my lap. I had no reply.

"Now, I really need to get back to work." He stood and walked toward me. If he believed a hug and an apology would calm me, he was wrong. The thought of his hands on me brought new beads of sweat to my temples. He sidestepped around the chair and bent to retrieve a storyboard from the floor behind me before returning to his seat. He rolled back behind the computer, hiding his face, and sniffed.

I rose and turned to leave when he leaned back out.

"You need to drop this getting a job idea too. It's ludicrous. I can't have people thinking my wife needs to work. If you need more spending money, just say so."

I left his den but remained outside the door, having no concept of what to do next. His chair squeaked, and he inhaled deeply before returning to his keyboard. His feverish tapping echoed through the hall. I didn't want to know more. Didn't care what he was doing to keep himself alert or awaken his creativity. I didn't even care that he disapproved of me getting a job. The only thing that mattered was keeping Lauren close.

I stopped at her door. On the other side, she laughed softly, then I could only hear faint murmurs. I couldn't decipher her words. I lifted my hand to knock but didn't complete the action. There was no point in speaking to her now. I hadn't conjured a rational thought since she announced her desire to move away. If I spoke to her in my current state, I would only lose ground.

Feeling like a castoff in my own home, I fled to the garden. The air was crisp, falling cold on my skin. I pulled my sweater tight and walked to the junipers. Bud and Kane hadn't yet left on their nocturnal prowls. They lay curled together on a pile of straw. I sat on the ground nearby, and they approached slowly, stretching their limbs and arching their backs. Bud climbed into my lap, his purr loud. They likely believed I'd brought them food. I stroked Bud's fur and attempted to knit my thoughts into a plan of action. There had to be some way to convince Lauren to stay. Just as there had to be some way to get Roger on my side. If I pushed him further, he'd side with her just to keep from saying I was right.

I'm not sure how long I sat outside. The cats lost interest and meandered away, slipping into the darkness. A light drizzle began to fall, and I rose. The mist clung to my sweater and dampened my hair. As I walked to the house, Lauren's bedroom light dimmed. Stopping outside Roger's office, I heard his chair squeak and his fingers tapping his keyboard. I turned the hall light out and retreated to my bedroom.

ELEVEN

QUICKENING

"Alice? Hello? Alice? I hope you can hear me."

Roger's voice bellowed through the kitchen, tinny and full of static on the answering machine. He was away on business, but was due back that night. Weeks had passed since Lauren announced her revised life plan, and none of us had brought it up since. My confusion over whether Lauren took our words to heart or if Roger even backed me in denying her the chance to go to New York made it a topic I was happy to avoid. Tension sat in every room like dust gathering on furniture, but his absence, no matter how brief, had allowed me to relax a bit, so I wasn't upset by the news he shared in his message he'd left me while I was out that afternoon.

"This place is a zoo. I can hardly hear myself speak. I'm stuck in Boise because my flight home got canceled. No flights allowed in for the rest of the night. Look, I'll call you later. I need to find a hotel room before they're all—" The machine cut him off.

I'd doubted he would make his flight, having heard on the radio that our airport was closed as a massive winter storm cut a swath across the middle of the country. Ice and plummeting temperatures —record breaking, the radio announcer said—had descended on the state just a week before Christmas. A sheen of sleet blanketed my car when I left the grocery store. By the time I made it home, my car struggled up the drive.

"Lauren," I called down the hall. I was sure she wasn't home yet. The house was dark. I dialed her pager, leaving a message for her to get home now. I was glad I'd talked Roger into purchasing a cell phone for her for Christmas. The box was wrapped, ready to be placed under the Christmas tree I left half decorated when I decided a trip to the store was warranted.

I flipped on the small television in the kitchen to learn more about the storm as I unpacked groceries. I'd bought extra milk, eggs, and bread, items I really didn't need, but had used as an excuse to purchase kitty litter and a box. I'd corralled Kane and Bud into the garage before I left for the store. If temperatures dropped as low as the meteorologist warned, the cats might not survive outside. While I knew Roger would be fuming about being stuck out of state another night, I was grateful that the cats would be safe and warm and I wouldn't have to plead with him to allow them to stay in the garage. I made a mental note to plug the space heater in for them when I delivered their evening meal and set up the litter box.

"Let's go now to our reporter in the field." The news anchor's voice caught my attention. I moved to the television, nudging the volume up. On screen, a winding row of cars sat at a standstill. A river of red lights in one direction, white in the other. "Lori, that's quite a traffic jam. I understand law enforcement is busy cleaning up a pretty serious accident."

A woman stood braving the elements. The fur of her lined coat hood whipped at her face. A gloved hand held fast to her ear; the other gripped the microphone. Her shoulders were hunched to ward off the wind. She nodded and spoke.

"That's right, Leann. We are on State Highway 66, where the highway patrol is still busy clearing a single-car accident. A process hindered by the weather and reports of multiple fatalities."

Red and blue lights flickered across an icy field as the camera zoomed in on a twisted SUV off the highway.

The door slammed in the entryway, and I turned the television off.

"Lauren, honey, is that you? I'm glad you're home. It's getting ugly out there."

She didn't reply. The only response was the sound of the bathroom door closing and the shower being turned on.

———

Early the next morning, I woke to a ringing telephone. Certain it was Roger, I picked it up, expecting to be greeted by an onslaught of anger and frustration.

"Roger?"

"No, this is Nancy. We need to talk."

I sat up in bed. The room was dark because of the murky sky. I flipped on the bedside lamp.

"Nancy?"

"Yes. When can I come over?"

"Come over? Well, I hardly think—"

"I don't care about the weather, Alice. We need to talk. I'm leaving in a half an hour. I'll see you soon."

She hung up. I pulled the phone from my ear and stared at it. It wasn't even eight o'clock. Why would she need to speak to me so urgently? I hastened my morning routine, all the while creating sequences in my head. Were she and Roger having an outright affair? Had they been entwined since they'd met all those years ago at the awards ceremony? Had I missed the clues? Did she want to come clean?

As soon as I'd chased that notion from my head, another scenario popped up. Was it Lauren? Had my daughter done something dangerous? Illegal? Something to upset Nancy so much she'd drive over in unsafe conditions? The what-ifs plagued me as I moved to the family room, turning on the Christmas tree lights and heading to the kitchen to put a pot of coffee on.

I pressed my ear against the garage door and heard nothing. The cats had probably settled into their five-star accommodations nicely and were in no hurry to go back out into the cold. I'd purchased some Danishes the night before, grocery store bakery, but they'd have to do. I took them from the pantry and placed them on the kitchen table. Then I grabbed an extra mug for Nancy.

The doorbell rang, and I rushed to the foyer. A blast of cold air beat Nancy into the house. She hurried in and removed her hat, exposing a shock of unnatural red hair; it reminded me of black cherries. She didn't allow me time to contemplate her new look.

"Please tell me you have coffee. I tried to stop for some on the way over, but nothing is open. Really, people, it's a little cold air and ice, not the end of the world." She took off her coat and handed it to me.

"Yes, I've got coffee, but Nancy, I don't understand." I hung her coat on a hook. Perhaps it was the early hour, or maybe it was the lighting, but she'd aged since I'd last seen her; now she looked unpolished. A strand of hair jutted up from her hair clip. A shadow of gray crept through her hairline. I'd never seen her in jeans and boots. She was more human. From the first day I'd met her, I'd never known her to appear so… The first word that jumped into my mind was vulnerable.

She cupped her hands, blew into them, and rubbed them together. "Pretty tree. You should really throw some logs in the fireplace," she commented, moving past me to the kitchen.

I trailed behind her as she went straight to the coffeepot and stood there. I clambered after her and poured her a cup, which she promptly took to the table. I poured one for myself and sat.

"Did you see anything about the accident last night?" she asked.

"The accident? No. What? Who?" I'd forgotten about the news story I'd seen on television the night before, and my mind burst into high alert. Had Lauren snuck out of the house? Certainly not. She was too smart for that kind of behavior and had never done anything of the sort. Still, I berated myself for not peeking in on her this morning.

"It was Dr. Addison," she hissed conspiratorially, her eyes shifting about the room.

"Dr. Addison?" I now noticed dark rings under her eyes. Flecks of mascara settled in fine lines. Her lipstick was smeared at one corner of her mouth.

"Yes, Dr. Addison, our Dr. Addison. Are we alone?"

"Well, yes. Roger is stuck in Boise. Lauren is asleep."

"Good," she said, relaxing a bit. She poured sugar into her cup. "You got anything stronger? Never mind, it's early. I'm trying to cut back."

"Nancy, what is this about? What accident? What does Dr. Addison have to do with anything?"

"Sorry, right." She took a long drink from her cup. "There was an accident last night."

My mind now flashed to the news story. I never considered it being someone I knew.

"Oh yes, I saw something on TV. It looked bad. Is he all right?"

"No, he's dead."

"Dead?" My heart dropped into my stomach. "Oh, dear, that's just…"

"His whole family. Well, I guess one kid survived, but they aren't holding out much hope for them. He had boy/girl twins. Not sure which one is still clinging to life."

"That's horrible." I took a drink and struggled to gulp it down, a knot twisting in my throat.

"Yeah, it's tragic, but some are saying it was no accident." She fiddled with her spoon, spinning it on the tabletop. Her nail polish was chipped.

"What?"

"Word is he killed himself and tried to take his whole family with him."

"What? Why would he do such a thing? Right before Christmas?" I grasped my mug, warming my hands as a chill shivered through me.

"I didn't want to be the one to tell you this." Her lips quivered, and she reached for her cup. Her hands were trembling. A tear slipped from her eye, dragging more mascara into the crevices below her lashes.

"Nancy," I whispered. Instinct told me to take her hand, comfort her. But history wouldn't allow me to. I leaned back in my chair, distancing myself.

She waved her hand in front of her face. "Alice, it's just terrible."

"Nancy, please, you're worrying me. What is going on?"

She drank the remainder of her coffee and held the cup out to me with shaking hands, never making eye contact. I took her mug and mine to the pot and poured fresh cups. I grabbed a box of tissues from the counter, tucked it under my arm, and returned to the table. I set them in front of her, then returned to the kitchen. I stood on tiptoes and opened a cabinet above the refrigerator, pulling a bottle of whiskey down. Aside from what he kept on his office bar cart, it was the place we'd moved all the alcohol to when Lauren turned fourteen.

Nancy took the bottle from me, and a weak smile flashed on her face. She poured some into her coffee and added more sugar.

"Thank you. I'm sorry, really. I'm just such a mess. I'd heard rumors a couple of weeks ago but didn't give them any credence until I saw what he'd done. Now it is starting to make sense."

"I'm sorry, Nancy, but none of this is making sense to me."

"Right, right. I just don't know where to start." She took another swig of her coffee, swallowed, and inhaled deeply, her eyes fluttering closed as if gathering visions into cohesive thoughts. "Okay, a few weeks ago, I got a call from Dr. Addison's nurse. You remember her, right? Always standing at the ready, tissues in hand." She pulled a tissue from the box on the table. A sardonic laugh escaped her. "Thanks for these, by the way," she said as she dabbed at her eyes, further smearing her mascara.

"Sure. Yes, I remember the nurse," I replied, hoping to prod her along.

"She called me. Completely out of the blue. It was weird."

"I can imagine."

Nancy took another deep breath and another pull from her coffee. The tremor in her hands subsided a bit.

"She said she had evidence that Dr. Addison had done some very bad things." She turned the corner of her napkin up, folding it and unfolding it as she spoke.

"Bad things? Like what?"

Her eyes met mine. Her expression was unreadable, as if she felt too many emotions to convey. I struggled to stay in my seat. I wanted to grab her face and squeeze the words out. Why was she tormenting me like this?

"Horrible things." Her head collapsed into her hands, and she sobbed loudly.

I glanced down the hall, fearing her cries would wake Lauren. Needing something to do, I pulled two Danishes from the box and placed them on plates, pushing one toward Nancy and taking a bite from mine.

"He used his own sperm." Her body deflated.

The words wormed into my mind but made no sense.

"What are you talking about?"

"Carol—the nurse, that's her name. Carol said Dr. Addison used his own sperm to impregnate some of his patients."

We sat in silence as I chased her words around my head, urging them to come together into something logical.

"He tricked us, Alice. All this time I've believed donor number eighteen-forty-seven, a tall, blond cardiology resident who played lacrosse, was the father of my Jennings. But cardiology-lacrosse guy is not the father of my son. His father is Dr. Addison." Her words were halting as she fought to stay composed. Once she'd spoken, she broke down.

I let her cry, as I could find nothing to impart. I rose, still working to understand what she was saying. Without thinking, I added another nip to her coffee cup when I refreshed it. She didn't add sugar this time and took the cup as she wiped her nose with her other hand. I sat.

"I don't understand what you're saying. How did his nurse find out? Why did she turn to you?"

"Oh, it's a mess of a story," she began, having collected herself a bit with a swig of her coffee. "It seems she'd always had suspicions about Dr. Addison, but never had a grasp on how to prove it. That was until her own daughter found herself in a predicament. Carol's daughter wasn't sure who the father of her child was and had to resort to paternity tests. Apparently, that experience gave Carol a lightbulb moment. She did some digging and started contacting Dr.

Addison's patients. Actually, she believed he was having affairs with some of his patients. Turns out his methods were even more diabolical."

"More diabolical than sleeping with his patients?"

"Yes! He wasn't sleeping with his patients; he was abusing them, without their consent, without their knowledge."

"But why? Why would he do something so barbaric?"

"Who knows? Evil man. Now we'll never get answers to those questions." She finished her coffee and took the bottle, adding a healthy splash of liquor to the empty mug. "Carol had no idea just how many victims Dr. Addison claimed until things started to snowball. First, she reached out to a few former patients, ones she suspected of having improper relations with him. Some dismissed her and refused to speak to her. But others had nagging misgivings themselves."

"Like what?" I asked, wondering how anyone could have such doubts.

"Oh, I don't know. Little things that gnawed on them. Many of them were like me. They knew their own husbands weren't the fathers; they'd used donors. Anyway, a few of these women had their children tested against the doctor. Carol secured a sample of the doctor's blood. You won't believe the lengths she went to." She nudged her mug toward me, and I went to the coffee pot, topping my cup off as well.

"What did she do?" I asked, returning to the table, steam wafting from the cups.

"She stabbed him with a scalpel!" She added another splash of whiskey to her coffee, her eyes wide. She was so consumed with the telling of the story that her tears dried.

"Stabbed him?"

"Well, cut him, but still. She just knew it was something she needed to prove or disprove. She'd convinced herself by checking blood types of some of the women she suspected had affairs with him. But blood typing isn't definitive. Of course, she hoped she was wrong, but obviously she wasn't. It started with three women, three who agreed to test their children when presented with the blood type discrepancies. And she was right about all of them. She confronted all three of them, and they denied having affairs with the doctor. They insisted they hadn't, and she believed them. Word got out. Those three told their other friends, and before she knew it, she had a slew of women lined up to have their children's paternity tested. It's ghastly!"

Down the hall, Lauren's door creaked open, and I glimpsed her as she shuffled into the hall bathroom.

"Oh dear, is that Lauren? I can't let her see me like this," Nancy whispered. She did her best to smooth her hair, discovering the errant piece, licking her fingers and flattening it. Her sudden concern about her appearance confused me. I searched for an explanation for her being at my home, in her state, even worse at this hour and with the weather. Nancy's focus seemed to be on herself.

"How's my makeup?" she asked.

"You've got a smudge under your left eye." I reached out as if to wipe it but withdrew my hand.

She blew her nose and rose, tucking the tissues into her purse.

"Look, there's a lot we need to talk about, but not with Lauren around. Does she have plans today?"

"These days, all she ever plans to do is go to your house, but I don't want her out in this. Surely, you don't want Jennings driving over to pick her up."

"When are you going to let that child get her license, Alice, really? How about I stick around until she's ready to go and drive her over myself? Jennings can bring her back home later. Things are supposed to thaw out this afternoon."

"Nancy, you've been—"

Her eyes tracked mine as they fell on the bottle sitting on the table with the lid off.

"Nonsense. Think of it as performance-enhancing, like I do."

"Well, um…" I didn't have time to form a response. Lauren was out of the bathroom, making her way down the hall. I hurried to tuck the bottle back into the cabinet.

"Hey, Mrs. E, what are you doing here?" Lauren said, giving the woman a hug.

The embrace startled me. Envy lit a fire inside my body as I watched.

"Oh, you know, just discussing a little graduation party business with your mom. I thought I'd give you a lift to my place. Jennings isn't experienced driving on ice."

"Sweet! I'm almost ready." She grabbed a Danish from the table and wrapped it in a napkin. "Mind if I drink a cup of coffee in your car?"

"Of course not! I'll go warm the car up. Be careful out on the sidewalk. It's pretty slippery." Nancy wrapped her hand around Lauren's thick ponytail and let the strands of hair run through her fingers as she walked by.

"Cool, I'll just grab my bag," Lauren said, pouring coffee into her travel mug.

"You want any cream or sugar with that?" I asked.

"Nope, I like mine straight up. Who needs all those extra calories?"

I watched Nancy exit the house and turned back to Lauren.

"I really don't think you should be out in this weather."

"Chill, Mom. I'll be fine. Jennings and I have a lot of new blocking to work through."

I approached her, arms out for an embrace, but my fingers glanced off her shoulder as she bent to retrieve her bag from the floor where she'd dropped it. I followed her to the entryway, where she shrugged her coat on, putting the Danish in her mouth while she zipped it up. She left without saying goodbye.

TWELVE

INVASIVE

An hour later, the phone rang.

"Listen, Alice," Nancy began before I could say hello. "Carol is coming to my house next week to collect a buccal swab from Jennings. She's already confirmed that his blood type matches Dr. Addison and doesn't match the donor nor mine, so she's pretty confident Dr. Addison—"

"Wait," I said. "I thought you said you knew he'd used his semen. You mean to tell me this could all just be nothing? You have no proof? Jennings may not be his? Nancy, come on."

"That's what the test is for. But I know what it will say. I feel it in my gut. I haven't figured out how I'm going to explain any of it to poor Jennings. Nothing I can come up with makes any sense. Then again, none of this makes a lick of sense start to finish. I don't know if I should just be honest with him. I mean, he knows he is a donor child, but—"

Her voice broke, and she blew her nose. The uneasy silence prompted me to speak.

"Maybe she's wrong. Maybe you're wrong. I honestly can't imagine Dr. Addison doing something so…" I rose from the couch and paced the room, pausing at the Christmas tree to right an ornament before making my way to the sliding door. Outside, water dripped from the icicles that clung to the eaves as the sun broke through the heavy clouds. Pieces of the story she'd told me that morning fought against my hopes that it was all a mistake. If Dr. Addison were innocent, why had he killed himself and his family?

"Horrific is one word for it! I feel so dirty. Like I've been violated." She was crying again.

"I can't imagine. Have you told Edward?"

"No, he isn't doing so well. I don't want to upset him, especially until I am certain. Anyway, I thought you might want to bring Lauren over so Carol can collect a sample from her as well."

What was she implying? Her suggestion was ludicrous.

"Hello? Are you there?" she asked.

"Yes, yes, I'm here. That won't be necessary. I've never doubted Lauren's paternity. You know we didn't need a donor. There'd be no reason for him to have used his own..." I couldn't finish the sentence. My mind flashed to the day I sat alone in Dr. Addison's exam room. I'd never told Roger. Had never told anyone.

Nancy was quick to jump in, making assumptions about things she knew nothing of. "Really? You think you're special because your husband had viable sperm? You think Dr. Addison's deranged moral compass guided him to do the right thing in your circumstance? Don't be so naïve! Besides, I already know of one other patient who also thought she was getting her husband's semen."

She paused, waiting for my reply. I hoped she hadn't heard my gasp. Roger could never know that I'd returned to Dr. Addison. It was a secret I'd buried so deep inside me. I never expected it to be called into the light of day again.

"Yeah, Sally Caldwell. She and her husband had trouble getting pregnant again after their first child. They went to Dr. Addison for help. It was a year or so before Jennings was born. Sally felt like something was off from the minute her son popped out. She could never put her finger on it; figured she was making things up. Until now. Now she knows. She is patient number one, the first person Carol reached out to. She was one of the patients who Carol suspected of having an affair with Dr. Addison. Carol always felt a weird vibe between Sally and the evil doctor. She sensed something all right, just not what she expected. So, yeah, I think it is necessary. In fact, it's urgent considering the relationship between my son and your daughter."

I heard her words, but like everything she'd revealed to me so far, they didn't register immediately. The onslaught of unbelievable allegations served to drown the volatility of what she said. I tried to keep up as she continued.

"I'm not sure if they've taken their relationship to a physical level yet. I mean, I don't know how far they've gone, but think about it. If Dr. Addison used his sperm to impregnate you, our children would be half-siblings!"

I couldn't believe what Nancy was insinuating. Not that I didn't think it possible Dr. Addison was Jennings' father. It just didn't seem possible he'd done something so depraved as to use his own sperm. Almost as preposterous was her assertion that my daughter was somehow involved with Jennings. It was ludicrous.

"Relationship between your son and my daughter?" I muttered. Her speculations began to congeal. The woman was mad to even imply that my daughter was having sex with her son, never mind her ridiculous inference that they were related. "I have no idea what you mean!"

"They could be half-siblings. They need to know before they take this little romance any further. God forbid, they have already… Ugh, I can't even think about it."

A gasp rose in my chest, but shock snatched the sound before I could utter it. I lost control of my body. My knees buckled, and I reached for the arm of the sofa to slow my descent. The free fall landed me on the couch. Nancy's words were barbed. As if every syllable she uttered was meant to lay its hooks into me and back me into a corner for easy picking. I wouldn't allow it. There was too much to process. My breathing was deep and ragged, and a roaring wind whirled in my head.

"Little romance?" The words stumbled out of my mouth.

Nancy dropped her voice. "It'd be like incest."

The word fell on me. Silence hung on the line as I absorbed what she was saying.

"Stop it! Stop it right now!" I yelled into the phone. "What are you even talking about? Romance? Incest? Lauren isn't having sex with your son! She isn't having sex with anyone! She says they're like brother and sis—" The word dropped from my lips unfinished.

"You're kidding, right? Wait, you're serious? You didn't know they were together? Why would she hide something like that from you? They've been an item for who knows how long. Why do you think she's always over here? I mean, we have an open-door policy. I don't think she's even been up to his bedroom. I can't keep an eye on them every second, but I've caught them on the couch a few times. Fully clothed, of course. They are teenagers. It's only a matter of time. You're kidding yourself if you think they're just friends. They are head over heels for each other."

"She's never..." I stopped myself, unwilling to give Nancy any more fuel to light my world on fire. "She's a late bloomer, like me," I uttered.

How long had Lauren been lying? Why would she keep this from me? She wouldn't. Nancy was the liar. It was the only plausible explanation.

"Look, I'm sorry your daughter hasn't been up-front with you about her relationship with my son. Hell, there's so much I'm sorry about in this situation. Maybe you just need some time to think things through. I know I'm still trying to process it. But you can't hide from it forever. If our children are related, even if it is in some sordid way neither of us can be blamed for, we need to provide them with answers. We owe it to them."

"You're wrong about this. I don't know why you want me to believe my daughter is having a fling with your son. If it's some tactic of yours to drag me into your little melodrama regarding the questionable paternity of your child, well, that's lower than I'd expect, even from someone like you." I didn't recognize my own voice; it was corrosive. "Let's be honest here. There could be a few candidates who might be able to call Jennings their son, aren't there?"

"Excuse me?"

"Maybe the guy you were with the day we met. What was his name, Chaz, or something? The guitar player at the restaurant. How many others have there been since then? Did you keep track? I wouldn't think you'd want to go down this paternity-test road. Are you really prepared to keep going until you find the right patsy?" I hoped my words stung.

"How dare you? You know nothing about me."

"Oh yes, I do. I know that no man is off-limits to you, not even my husband! You'll be lucky if you get a match with Dr. Addison. At least then you would actually know who your son's father is! As for me and my family, leave us out of it!"

I punched the phone to disconnect and didn't move until the turning light outside moved shadows from one side of the room to the other. Tormenting thoughts spun through my head, keeping me pinned to the place I sat. Outside, the steady drip of the melting ice only served to stoke the madness swirling inside me.

I couldn't tell Roger I'd returned to Dr. Addison without him. We had never told Lauren about our difficulties conceiving. None of it seemed to matter at the time. In light of Nancy's revelation, none of it mattered still, if it weren't for her obvious intent to make things public. She couldn't force my hand. I wouldn't allow it. Maybe that was the reason she created this story about Jennings and Lauren being in love. She was hell-bent on dragging skeletons out of my closet, but why and how would she do it? She didn't know the whole story, didn't even know half of what she thought she did.

Still, the stakes were too high for me. If Roger knew about my betrayal, he might leave me. I'd lose my home, my security, the life I'd built. What if Lauren sided with him and I lost her too? There was too much at stake, and I wasn't willing to let Nancy Ellington uproot my entire world.

Despite all the ramifications of Nancy's bombshell, I struggled most with the idea Lauren could be lying to me. Nancy had to be wrong. Maybe Jennings was just a lovesick boy. Who would blame him? Lauren was beautiful, not to mention smart, funny, kind, talented. But she'd never lie to me about something like having a boyfriend. I believed her wholly. Sure, they were close, but she herself had said they were more like siblings than anything else. While that analogy was chilling, given Nancy's allegations, I'd take my child's word over Nancy's any day.

I knew my daughter better than Nancy knew her son. After all, he'd been raised by a nanny. He was a fixture, a gift to her ancient husband. A token, actually—the man didn't even care he wasn't the true father. Nancy lived in a realm outside of reality. She had no bond with her child; not like I did. While I felt sorry for Jennings, I had no sympathy for his parents, and I was not going to let Nancy's delusions throw my life into the chaos she thrived on.

The phone rang, yanking me out of thought. I was too afraid to answer it, fearing it would be Nancy hounding me further. The answering machine in the kitchen kicked on. I listened to my cheery voice asking the caller to leave a message.

"Alice? Alice, are you there? Guess not. Just wanted to let you know I made it back to town. I'll be home within an hour as long as traffic isn't too bad. Okay, see you soon."

I sleep-walked to the kitchen and went through the motions of making the dinner I'd planned. When I'd put the dish in the oven, I went to the garage to check on the cats. The deep freeze had passed, the sun was chasing the biting cold away, and they were eager for their freedom, so I released them. I hid the litter box behind the bushes on the side of the house in case I needed it again before spring arrived. When I returned to the kitchen, I heard Lauren come in.

"Mom, I'm home. Hitting the shower. Hope dinner is soon; I'm starving."

That night we ate as a family. Roger and Lauren kept up the conversation. I found myself staring at her. She was so comfortable. I could detect no hint she was hiding something from us and began to relax. She spoke of Jennings and how their rehearsals were going. There were no sparks in her eyes when she mentioned his name. No tells to betray her. Nancy was wrong about them.

Later as I lay in bed, my mind went to work convincing me further that I had nothing to fear. If I didn't give Nancy a chance to storm my world, this would all blow over. I would simply have to avoid her. Surely she wouldn't go behind my back and say anything to Lauren.

A bout of the flu spared me that concern for a time—Jennings woke the following morning with a fever and insisted Lauren stay away. His illness allowed me to relax over the holidays. I relished the time with her. We baked cookies and wrapped gifts and watched Christmas movies.

"What do you think of my hair?" she asked a few days before Christmas, after returning home from the mall with Sadie. She'd told me she was going to buy a last-minute gift for Roger.

"Your hair," I whimpered. I didn't recognize her. Her blonde ponytail was gone. Her hair fell just under her chin, and the color was an abomination. A harsh, unnatural, glassy red. I stammered for a response and bit back tears.

"Well, I see you aren't a fan. It's okay, I love it. I cannot wait to show Jennings." She stood in the foyer, toying with her hair, picking at strands, tucking some behind her ear. "I'm super bummed he's sick. I hope he's better by New Year's."

"Do you two have plans?" I muttered, relieved she'd offered me a reprieve from having to comment on her hair. *Her hair.* I approached her, reaching out my hand but unable to carry out the act of touching her. She turned to look at me. Shock rattled my senses again. "You're not going out, are you? It's one of the most dangerous nights of the year to be on the road," I said, trying to sound casual.

"Mom, you're such a worrywart. No, we aren't going out. We were going to have a Harry Potter movie marathon. His parents put in a sick home theater."

"Of course they did," I replied, louder than I intended.

"Mom, take a chill pill!" she said with a laugh as she passed me and plopped down on the sofa in the family room. "They're not that bad, you know. I mean, I know Mrs. E can be a lot, and it's kind of weird his dad is so old, but they really are fun. Well, she and Jennings are anyway. They make me feel like I'm part of their family. It's nice."

I coughed to hide a choking hitch in my throat as her words hit my heart.

"She's just rubbed me the wrong way from the day we met," I replied, then changed the direction of the conversation, afraid I'd said something I might regret. I wondered how Lauren might feel about Nancy if she knew how close Nancy and Roger had been, perhaps still were. Maybe she wouldn't idolize the woman so much if she knew what a predator she was. But now wasn't the time to play that card. "Want to help me make some Christmas cookies? The dough should be ready."

"Sure," she said, bounding up.

She looked so different. Unrecognizable almost. Not like my Lauren.

"We have sprinkles, don't we? Hey, when we're done, maybe I can drop some at the Ellingtons'."

I brought Jennings up many times during the week and watched her intently. While she spoke of him, it was never in a way to cause concern. They were nothing more than good friends. Doubt flickered in my chest, but I doused its spark.

THIRTEEN

MOTILITY

By New Year's Eve, Jennings was well enough for him and Lauren to celebrate together. I joined her in the foyer as she prepared to leave for his house. She was dressed casually, in sweatpants and a hoodie, further cementing in my mind the two weren't a couple. If she were trying to impress him, she'd have chosen something more fetching, wouldn't she? I'd been unable to ask her about her relationship with Jennings; unsure of what I was afraid of most—her actually being in love with Jennings or that she would lie to me about it.

"Where's Dad? Do you two have any plans for the night?" She spoke into the mirror, pinching her cheeks and applying lip balm.

"Well, he does." I paused, noting sparkles in what I thought had been lip balm. The harsh light of the entryway highlighted the gleam of her mouth. I'd never seen her wear something so shimmery. "He's working. I doubt I'll see him at all." I fussed with her hair. I still hadn't gotten used to her new look, and was mourning the loss of her golden ponytails, but I bit my tongue and feigned approval. At least it wasn't something permanent.

She batted my hands away and hugged me, planting a kiss on

my cheek as headlights swept across the front of the house and a horn beeped outside.

"Well, that sucks. He should put in more of an effort. I feel kind of bad leaving you here all alone on New Year's."

"Don't worry about me. I'm used to it. I've got a good book and Dick Clark. Who needs anything more?"

"Whatever, Mom. That. sounds so lame," she said, reaching for the doorknob.

"I'll wait up. See you at midnight."

"Oh." She paused, looking over her shoulder. "Didn't Dad tell you? He said I could stay out until one. Give us time to watch the ball drop."

"Oh, really? He didn't mention it to m——"

"Don't wait up!" she chirped, cutting me off.

I watched from the front porch as she bounded down the drive to Jennings' car. My fingers rose to the cool spot on my cheek where she'd brushed me with a kiss, and they got stuck in the tacky blob her lips left behind.

In the car, she rolled the window down and shouted, "Love you!" as they drove away. Bud crept out from the bushes and wove himself between my ankles. I bent down to scratch his ears and heard the phone ringing inside. Abandoning the cat, I sprinted to the kitchen, grabbing the phone without thinking.

"Happy New Year, Alice."

It was Nancy. I considered hanging up, but knew she'd just call back.

"What do you want, Nancy?" I asked coldly.

"Well, someone isn't in the holiday spirit."

I didn't respond but moved to the head of the hallway so I could see Roger should he actually step outside his office.

"I just wanted to update you. We had to postpone the paternity test due to Jennings' illness, but Carol came by yesterday and collected the sample. It takes at least two weeks for results. I don't know how I'm going to keep it together so long. The wait is already killing me."

She paused, waiting for a response, but I didn't cave.

"Have you thought any more about testing Lauren? I suppose you could wait for my results, but that seems ridiculous. Carol said six other former patients of Dr. Addison's have learned he fathered their children. Six! It's like the man wanted to populate the entire town single-handedly."

Again, she paused. I remained silent.

"You should also know that of those six, two believed their husband's semen was used. It's appalling!"

"Are you done?" I asked.

"Alice, why are you so deep in denial?

I waited for her to continue.

"Have you ever noticed they kind of look alike?" she asked.

"Who?"

"Lauren and Jennings. Similar eyes, same hair color. Well, her natural hair color anyway. Her new hairdo is adorable!"

"You're reaching. Lauren has my father's hair color and my eyes."

"Maybe, but if you look at it from this new, albeit twisted angle..." she trailed off.

"I'm not testing my daughter. I hope you get the results you are expecting, but—"

"Oh, they're here." Her next words were muffled, as if she covered the receiver. "Hey kids, Happy New Year! There's popcorn and soda in the theater room, but the pizza should be here soon, so don't fill up on junk before other junk arrives!"

I considered hanging up. There was nowhere else for this conversation to go.

"Have you ever heard of consanguinity?" she asked. I noticed now her words were slurring. Of course, she was drinking.

"Consangu-what? I really don't have time for this," I lied.

"Consanguinity. By definition, it means a relationship between two people descended from the same ancestor. But there is some psychology that suggests an attraction can be stronger between two people who share genealogy, even if, or maybe especially if, they are unaware of their genetic connection. Like you can be more attracted to someone who shares your genes. Maybe that's why our kids are so close."

"That is sick! I'm not going to listen to any more of this!"

"Hear me out, please. How many of them are living right here in this town? Walking the same halls as our kids? Say Jennings and Lauren aren't related, and all this is just a colossal mix-up. If you're right, Lauren is Roger's biological daughter, even if Jennings comes from Dr. Addison—wonderful. Things work out for them."

Her tone had climbed to an optimistic note but dropped suddenly to a whisper as she added, "But what if … what if they are related? You are just as much a victim of the despicable Dr. Addison as I am, and our children's hearts are broken. They'll get over it, right? I mean, they're young. The chances of their relationship progressing to marriage are slim at best."

"Marriage! You're going way too far with this! Are you drunk?"

"Maybe," she replied. "But what happens?"

At first I wasn't sure if she was replying to my question, but she continued as if she hadn't heard me. The mention of the word marriage still saturated my mind. She seemed so certain of a rela-tionship between the two. It simply couldn't be. Not because I believed for one second my daughter and Nancy's son shared a father; that was absurd. My fingers lifted to my cheek again. I rubbed at the gooey blob of lip gloss, needing it off my face.

"They move on," Nancy continued. "Find someone new. But think about it. The next person they fall for could be a product of Dr. Addison's clinic too. We don't know how many of them there are. This is for the rest of their lives, Alice! They won't be able to simply fall in love. They'll always have to wonder. Is this person my half-sibling? Zero spontaneity until they settle down with someone who has been vetted."

I'd moved into the living room and sat on the couch. Her words pelted me like stones. I was outside myself. I tried to conjure an image of Dr. Addison in my mind, but couldn't. When I closed my eyes, I saw Jennings' face. Jennings in a white coat. How had I never noticed it? Jennings did bear a resemblance to the doctor, at least how I remembered him.

A new layer of horror filled me. If Jennings was the offspring of a man capable of the atrocities committed by Dr. Addison and Nancy was his mother, then he was damaged. He was the child of two horrible people. A man who would defile women and a woman who cared more about herself than she did about her children. I didn't want my daughter close to any of the Ellingtons. It was all too much.

"Yes, they'd have to vet their romantic partners for the rest of their lives." Nancy's voice brought me back to the conversation. The monsters grappling for space in my head quieted as I focused on her. "I mean, I suppose they could leave. Travel far away, leave the country, I don't know."

"I don't see how your son's paternity has anything to do with my daughter's life!" I needed her voice to stop talking so I could think. "You really need to find someone else to have these ridiculous discussions with. I am not that person. You can sit around and obsess about this all you want, but leave me out of it!" It felt good to unload these words, but as I did so, the fear of the damage the unhinged woman could cause stopped me. "And if I catch wind of you revealing any of your delusions to my daughter, so help me, Nancy!"

"I would never do such a thing, Alice. While I don't understand why you are so reticent about at least knowing for sure, I would never divulge something to your child that belongs to you. But don't expect me to let this lie, especially if Jennings turns out to be..." She was sobbing now.

"I understand how stressful this is for you, and I am sorry, but I'm holding you to your word. You can't speak to Lauren about any of this. It sounds like you have weeks to go before you have any verification, anyway. I'm not the person who can help you through this. Our situations are completely different. Please leave me alone. Happy New Year. Good luck." I finally mustered the resolve to disconnect the call.

Before the changing year registered in my mind, while I still scrawled an eight over the seven when dating checks, life changed. Nancy's preposterous claims about Lauren and Jennings being more than friends slapped me in the face. No longer could I deny the depth of their connection as I saw it with my own eyes. While trudging through errands one blustery winter day, my illusions were shattered, forcing me to stoop to shameful lows to protect my family.

FOURTEEN

X, Y

2008

July 6, 2006

    Dear Diary,

    I shouldn't start out that way. So lame. Oh well, beginner's blunder. Note to self: no more "Dear Diary" BS from this point on, but it's my first entry, so.

    The whole reason I bought this dorky thing is to have a reminder, a lifelong record of the most wonderful thing ever. It has to be perfect. Yes, I did practice writing it all out on another piece of paper so I wouldn't scratch anything out here. And yes, that piece of paper also has the words Lauren Elizabeth Ellington written on it about eight-thousand times. And of course I edited it like thirty times. Ugh, I'm so cliché. I do have to say Mrs. Walkiewicz would definitely give me an A+ if I turned this in, minus all the kissy-heart stuff, that is. It took me all night to come up with it, but here it is. My perfect kiss.

    He kissed me. A single, soft, perfect kiss. His fingers held the back of my neck with gentle warmth, melting me from the inside. When our lips met, a tingly heat swirled through my body. Though only seconds passed, in an instant we became one and the world stopped. Just for us. It was magic. It was love. Love I've never known was possible. When I opened my eyes, he was looking at me with a knowing smile on his face. I giggled. He asked why. I rested my head on his chest in reply. A single, soft, perfect kiss. He didn't try to batter-ram his tongue between my teeth like the other bumbling boys who've kissed me. One was at Quartz Mountain Camp, the other under the bleachers at the away game in Springer. I can't remember their names, and besides, they don't matter. I could search my mind and try to dig them up, but I'd just be unearthing faces that don't mean anything, like hunting for trinkets in the sand with a metal detector. But there is no need. Those guys are forgotten. Meaningless. If I'm never kissed again in my life, at least I had this one single, soft, perfect kiss.

But I do hope he kisses me again. Like many, many times!

Okay, so maybe not A+ material after all, but a solid B. I should have added the part about the fireworks. There were fireworks, literally. It was the Fourth of July. First, he serenaded me with a song he said he learned just for me. He plays guitar … like really good … dreamy! The song was "The Killing Moon" by Echo and the Bunnymen. I'd never heard it before, but now it's my favorite song of all-time! We watched the display from the riverbank. We were two in a sea of people on picnic blankets. The patriotic explosions reflected in the slow-moving stream. The breeze off the water blew the sticky air enough to lift my hair as he leaned in. After, he walked me home with an arm around my shoulder.

I'd kissed him before. On stage. How many times? Goofy little stage kisses, the awkward ones that you try not to think about for the first six weeks of rehearsal, don't count. Ones that made Mr. Spencer blush when we blocked the scene. The worry of what everyone's parents might think was always scribbled all over his face. None of those kisses ever lit a fire inside me like this.

I can't tell my parents. Can't tell anyone, actually, in case it got back to Mom and Dad. Actually, Dad might shrug it off, but Mom is a whole different story. I swear I think she dreams I will join a convent. We aren't even Catholic. After her reaction when I first tried to talk to her about my feelings for Jennings, I was reminded that she was my mom, not my friend. She'd die if she knew. She hates the Ellingtons. Not sure why.

Oh well, gotta go.

TTFN,

Lauren Ellington (I love how that sounds. It's the perfect stage name!)

I closed the diary and lay back on my daughter's bed. I'd read the entry three times; each time hit like a new blow to my heart. I hated myself for resorting to such shameful tactics, but I didn't know what else to do.

Memories of the morning came flooding back. The day started out as any other—the post-holiday slump, boxes of Christmas decorations stacked in the garage. I'd considered hauling them up to the attic before running errands, but weather conditions were deteriorating, and I wanted to be back home before the frigid rain turned to snow, so I abandoned the boxes and headed out to tackle my chores. If only I'd taken the time to store the boxes, our entire existence would be different.

But the weather forced me out, and I hadn't even checked the first thing off my to-do list when the life I knew, had so thoughtfully crafted and nurtured, became something unrecognizable. What I witnessed rocked me completely, leaving a stain on my psyche, one that wouldn't come out and had damaged the fabric of my beliefs, leaving me feeling soiled, discarded. It forced me to invade Lauren's privacy. Now, as I sat on my daughter's bed, her diary burning my hands, her words taunted me and my thoughts returned to that horrible moment earlier that day.

The bells jingled above my head as I entered the butcher's shop. Mr. Smit lifted a beefy hand to welcome me. Dried blood under his nails looked like empty smiles. He returned to the rack of lamb on the counter, and his scalpel-sharp blade glided through tendon and gristle with a crisp *whish.*

"Ah, Mrs. White, welcome. Happy New Year! I've got some lovely porterhouse cuts today. Mr. White's favorites!" His thick accent was warmer than his shop.

"Well, I can't say no to that, Mr. Smit."

"Klaus."

"Klaus, yes. Add three to the usual order, please," I replied.

"Coming right up."

I moved to the front of the store. My weekly trip to the butcher was one of my least favorite chores. I'd rather buy the prepackaged cuts at the grocery store. The coppery stench of freshly cut meat sickened me, and the feel of it under paper turned my stomach. Grocery store meat was sealed tightly under plastic wrap. While unsightly, it was less of a blow to the other senses. But Roger found meat from anyplace other than the butcher unacceptable.

My gaze shifted across Cherry Street to my next stop; croissants and bagels from the bakery and coffee shop were on my list. I saw a young couple sitting at the window counter. I might not have noticed them if it weren't for the girl's hair. It was the same shocking shade as Lauren's recent dye job. Their heads were pressed together, denim-clad legs entwined beneath the narrow bar. The girl threw her head back in a silent laugh, and I realized it *was* Lauren. The other half of the couple was Jennings. Their fingers looped together like twisted vines.

I didn't hear the tinkling bells as I sleep-walked out of the bloody shop. I floated to the bus bench outside and sat, never taking my eyes off them. Why weren't they at school?

The passing traffic was no distraction as it blurred by unnoticed. Jennings and Lauren were oblivious to the world around them. Completely entranced with each other. An angry driver laid on their horn as a group of kids crossed against the light. I jumped but did not avert my eyes, even as the couple's heads snapped in my direction at the noise.

Someone tapped my shoulder.

"Why are you sitting outside in the cold, Mrs. White?" Klaus asked.

I looked at him but had no reply.

"Oh well, at least the rain has slowed, but the clouds are gathering; snow is on its way. Here you go. I hope Mr. White enjoys the steaks. Don't let him overcook them! It'd be a sin. I'll charge your account. Have a nice day!"

I took the package, oblivious to the feel of it in my hand. Nancy's words swirled through my mind. She was telling the truth. My daughter was in love with her son.

I could think of no other boy I believed would be worse for my daughter. Jennings wasn't the problem, actually. He seemed to be well-adjusted despite being raised by Nancy and a man old enough to be his grandfather. The real issue was Nancy. A life with Nancy as my daughter's mother-in-law. The idea of sharing grandchildren with the woman was inconceivable. It couldn't be. I wouldn't spend a lifetime wondering if she and my husband would reignite their interest in each other and resume their tryst. Assuming it had ever ended.

Just the day before, Nancy had called me. She choked out the news between sobs. The fertility test proved Jennings was the offspring of Dr. Addison. After breaking the news to me, she pressed relentlessly, insisting I prove Lauren's paternity. But I still had my doubts. For all I knew, Nancy could have slept with Dr. Addison, and this was all a ruse to cover an affair her precious Edward didn't approve of. Whatever her motives, her determination to drag me into her drama mystified me. Her rotting family tree was none of my concern. Saving my daughter from its blighted branches was all that mattered.

Maybe the dalliance between Lauren and Jennings was a passing thing. A fling, soon to be forgotten when another boy caught her eye. There was only one way for me to find out. Especially if I wanted the truth, and not some glazed-over version Lauren might try to sell me. Maybe my daughter was right about pursuing a career in acting. Turned out she was better at it than I'd ever given her credit for.

Foregoing the stop at the bakery and the other to-do items I'd intended to tackle, I rushed home, paying no heed to the boxes in the garage. I tossed the meat into the fridge and ran to her room to search for the diary, remembering the day she bought it. She'd been so insistent she needed it immediately and pleaded with me to drive her to The Snow Goose. She chose a pink embossed leather journal with a tiny key attached by a cord. The heart-shaped lock must have given her a false sense of privacy.

I located the journal in her bedside table. The key still clung to the binding by a frayed pink string. She hadn't secreted it away in her jewelry box or under her mattress. Invisible eyes peered at me from every corner of the room, unblinking. Shame pressed against me. I shook the notions from my mind. She'd left me no choice, forced my hand.

The first page confirmed my suspicions. She'd written those

words years ago, and their relationship was still growing to this day. It wasn't a passing phase. And it had been going on for over two years.

How had I been so blind? I thought I knew everything about my daughter. And yet, I never glimpsed the shift. Had never sensed a change in her. She'd fallen in love, lived a life she kept hidden from me, and I never noticed. What did that say about me as a mother? What did it say about my daughter? Our relationship? I'd expected her to share it all with me the way we had when she was young. When she'd fill the hours with stories of playground antics and her favorite scenes from musicals. The realization that things had not been what I believed them to be for years fell on me with a devastating heft.

I sat back up, intent on completing my mission of learning all I could about how deep my daughter's relationship with Nancy's son was. Sweat snaked down my spine, and I shrugged my coat off. I cracked the journal open again and flipped the pages, landing at random on a day less than two weeks before.

December 23, 2007

I did it. Cut my hair. Colored it too, Cherry Bomb.

Kinda emo. Allison Kirk can never call Jennings and me the Bobbsey twins again. Such a lame diss. She got it from her mom. Bobbsey twins, like, what are you, eighty? I swear she's been saying it since we were in the 7th grade, and I'm totally over it.

I love my new do; it's rad. Jennings is warming up to it, but Mom, well, she may never.

She looked at me when I got home and said, "Your hair." Which is Alice White for "it's awful." Perhaps I'll cry it out on my satin pillowcase tonight. She's never mentioned it again, but I see the distaste in her eyes. A look of shock hits her face every time I walk into the house. I try not to laugh. Hope she didn't get a million scrunchies for my stocking like she usually does. My scrunchie days are over.

I wish I could have discussed it with her before I whacked it all off and got it colored, but she is impossible to talk to and she wouldn't have let me. She always has these ideals of what I should be, how I should act, what I should look like, who I should befriend. It's totally weird. I don't get it. It's like she lives in some little world of her own where there's only room for her beliefs. And she has this knack for denial that is whack. I can't tell her anything and I can't trust her with my secrets. It's like she doesn't have the capacity to keep things to herself. Such a drag.

I told her my new do was for a role. Total lie. I'll be wearing a wig on stage. Anything for my art! Ha-ha! And no, the irony doesn't escape me. I complain about my mother being a liar, while I keep everything from her. Lies of omission are still lies in my book, but she forces my hand. She makes it impossible for me to be honest with her.

Finally figured out how to get my curfew extended for NYE. Just gonna tell her Dad said I could stay out late. She'll totally buy it. She and Dad never compare notes. Sometimes they make it too easy. Mrs. E said we could toast with real champagne! Chills!

G2G

L.E.E.

I felt like I was reading the words of a complete stranger. These couldn't possibly be the musings of my daughter—a child I believed I knew like the back of my hand. I fanned the pages and went backward in the book, selecting another day at random.

October 23, 2007

Jennings and I are running away together. Well, planning to. And it actually won't be a legit runaway. I'm trying to psych myself up to let Mom and Dad know I'm moving to NYC under the guise of taking a gap year. And really, that's my intention. I'm telling them it's a gap year to soften the blow of my never going to college. I seriously can't see myself joining a sorority, living the Greek life. Lame! I want to experience life, not follow in the footsteps of my boring parents. Go to college, get married, have a kid. Yawn! No thanks! Pass.

J's rents are totally down with him going, and he said we could get a place together. It will be some crappy studio walk-up, but who cares? How could I pass up the chance to live in the Big Apple? Walk down Broadway. See Times Square outside my window. It's going to be so boss.

Even if I can't convince Mom and Dad, I'm going. Nothing can stop me. So, I guess it would be running away if they force my hand. What if, like for real, what if we land roles? Even if they're just ensemble or understudy parts, way, way off Broadway? It'd be bomb.

Bonus points for living with Jennings. He's so awesome. I can't imagine ever *loving someone else. He's all I need. I can't wait to graduate. We're so out of here.*

It'd be best to have their approval. Mostly for the sake of money, but I'm totally down with getting a job. Every great actor waits tables at some point in their life, right? But Dad's credit card would make things so much easier. So it's my mission. It will be tough. Some might say impossible. Mom is such a tight-ass. She never lightens up. I'm sure she's convinced I'll end up like Uncle Daniel. And yeah, I get it. NYC is probably the biggest monster of her worst nightmare. But if she loves me, she'll support my dream. Fingers crossed! LOL.

TTFN

My stomach crept into my throat. Beads of sweat sprang forth and slithered down my face. How dare she give voice to such insanity? Who was she? I pressed on, despite wanting to slam the book shut and maybe toss it in the fireplace, erasing these nonsensical musings of a delusional child. I fanned the pages, searching for the latest entry, needing to know exactly where things stood.

January 3, 2008

New Year's Eve was dope! I drank champagne for the first (definitely not last) time. Jennings gave me the best NYE kiss ever! I let him go farther than I ever have, but not all the way. We came close, but we've decided to save it for prom night. Might sound lame, my bad. I mean we'll be all dressed up, have an excuse to get a room, blah, blah. Jennings suggested Valentine's Day but reluctantly agreed to let me have my way… Countdown to giving it up is on. Prom night, take my—

The doorbell rang, and I clambered like a thief who'd been caught with her hand in the till. I slammed the book shut and did my best to tuck it back in where I'd found it. I closed the drawer and jumped up, pausing to give the room a once-over, darting back for my coat and to smooth the comforter and fluff the pillow.

By the time I made it to the foyer, the person at the door was gone. Probably someone trying to sell me a security system or new windows. I paced the living room. The words of a stranger I thought was my daughter rushed through my head. It was almost time for Lauren to get out of school, if she'd even attended that day. She'd never ditched before as fast as far as I knew. Jennings was a bad influence. She likely wouldn't come straight home despite the deteriorating conditions outside, but I could never be certain. As much as I wanted to rush back to her bedroom and read every word she'd written, I would have to wait.

I wondered if I would recognize her when she did barge through the door. My image of her twisted into something mysterious, foreign. I grieved the loss of the daughter I believed I had.

FIFTEEN

SURROGACY

An ambulance skirted the roundabout at Coventry Springs as I arrived for my Wednesday shift. Its lights were off. I waved at the driver, who I recognized. Ambulances at Coventry Springs were as commonplace as airplanes at an airport.

Heavy clouds churned across the sky, cloaking the sun, graying everything, especially my mood. I trudged through the lingering slush. Lauren's diary entries gripped my thoughts in a chokehold. The raw sense of betrayal hadn't let up in the weeks since I'd learned of her relationship with Jennings. In that time, I felt as if I was living in a nightmare. Disbelief suffocated my shame. How could I have been so blind? When had I strayed so far from my child? How could I keep my daughter from running off to New York, where anything could happen to her?

My life had become a raging sea of red. Grave choices bobbed to the surface arbitrarily, and their weight dragged me down, threatening to drown me. Time was an additional foe as prom and graduation loomed, but I felt powerless to take action, to address Lauren's deceit and try to put an end to the relationship. Now I knew how my mother felt, I guess. But I couldn't destroy Lauren the way Mother had ruined my chances at true love. I couldn't just forbid her to see Jennings outright. I wouldn't have Roger's support, I was certain. Lauren would side with him, and where would that leave me?

The automatic doors to the lobby swished open, blasting my body with a gust of hot air that did nothing to warm me. Inside the nursing home, I was greeted by an onslaught of paper hearts and cupids; red and pink splashed throughout the main hall, hanging in the windows and from the ceiling. Roberta waved at me from a corner where she and a nurse aide strung a garland of fake roses around a bulletin board proclaiming, *Love Is in the Air!* The dot of the exclamation point was in the shape of a heart.

I smiled and waved but groaned under my breath as I removed my coat and hung it on the hooks by the front door. For weeks, I'd searched for opportunities to get back to Lauren's diary, but fate and paranoia were a toxic mix that prevented it. I jumped every time the phone rang, fearing a call from Nancy. I watched Lauren closely, looking for signs she knew Dr. Addison was Jennings' father, but sensed nothing. Then again, she'd hidden much from me over the past few years. The idea I'd be able to see past her facade mocked me from the pages of her journal. I knew as much about her life as Roger knew about me returning alone to Dr. Addison, against his will.

My eyes were drawn down the hall, where a cluster of residents and employees milled outside a patient's door. It wasn't unusual for guests and staff to make a show of welcoming newcomers, but this particular room had been renovated and was now designated as a medical suite, something new to the facility. The incoming director insisted specialized care was the wave of the future and would usher in a new era for Coventry Springs. Strategically positioned close to the nurses' station, it was outfitted with equipment to care for someone with medical needs too cost-prohibitive to keep them in a hospital. Curiosity drew me to the group.

The residents who hovered near the door began to disperse as I approached. They shuffled past on their way to the common room, with smiles and nods. Nurse Jackson stood just outside the door. I peeked inside, expecting to see an elderly individual, perhaps in the final stages of lung disease, hooked up to oxygen, or someone bedridden but alert. I was surprised to see a child.

The bed swallowed up her tiny figure. An IV was plugged into her bony arm and her skin glowed ghostly white. Twisted scars, still healing, laced across her face and exposed flesh. Their thick, ruddy tracks seemed monster-like against her porcelain complexion. Monitors behind her cast colored shadows on her yellow hair. She was beautiful, ethereal in a way. Like a sleeping princess in a fairy tale. If you took away the scars that marred her, she could have been Lauren a few years ago.

A nurse snaked a tube out of the patient's narrow nostril. How did such a length of plastic fit inside such a small body? A doctor I didn't recognize lifted a blanket at the girl's midsection and guided the attendant in connecting a new tube to a port near the child's navel.

The shock of what I saw forced me to withdraw. I felt ashamed, as if I were rubbernecking at an accident scene, nosing myself into an intimate moment.

"Sad, isn't it?" Nurse Jackson whispered, standing next to me at the threshold. "Never thought I'd see the day when I'd care for a child in this home. *Tsk.*" She moved the gold cross she wore around her neck with her fingers, clasping it tightly and bringing it to her lips where she kissed the pendant and released it.

"Who? Why?" I stammered.

"Accident victim. Her body survived the crash, but her brain didn't." Nurse Jackson walked away, shaking her head.

I chased after her. "What do you mean?"

She paused and glanced around to see if anyone was nearby.

"You didn't hear this from me—I really shouldn't be saying a thing. This new director is really cracking down on confidentiality, and Lord knows, things are hush-hush about this one, but you're practically one of us, so no harm, no foul. She's in a permanent vegetative state. Won't ever wake up. The saddest thing I've seen in these halls, and I've seen my share of sadness. Mm-mm."

She continued down the corridor and disappeared into the

nurse's lounge. I wanted to go back to the room and check on the child. Where were her parents? Why was she alone?

"There you are, Alice," another volunteer called out, waving at me from the community room. "The library delivered some new books. Could you help me sort them onto the cart? I'll deliver them to the patient rooms as soon as I can."

"Of course," I said, entering the room and joining her at a table.

"There's some good ones here," she continued. "I know several people who've been waiting to get their hands on some of these." She pulled books from a box, put them on the table, and pushed them at me. "The new one by Grisham—Mr. Snell has been waiting on it. Oh, *The Stolen Child*. I've never heard of this one, but it looks good."

I tried to focus on sorting my stack, but my thoughts drifted back down the hall. The mystery of the child patient calmed the angry waters that stirred in me and rescued me from the riot in my head, at least for a little while.

———

I lingered at the facility longer that day, waiting for an opportunity to learn more about the mysterious new patient at Coventry Springs. There was always someone who needed help, so finding something to occupy my time was easy. A group of middle school students arrived with Valentine's cards for the residents. I settled on decorating mailboxes for each resident, collecting empty cereal boxes and aluminum foil from the kitchen staff and construction paper and glue from the arts and crafts closet. I set up in an under-utilized storage room near the medical room, propping the door open under the guise of needing better airflow in the stuffy space.

From the impromptu crafting station, I watched as doctors and caregivers came and went. No family or friends visited. Who could leave such a young child in need of care? Nurse Compton had been assigned as the girl's primary point of contact. While I had a good relationship with the woman, she was a stickler for the rules. I couldn't rely on random conversations or feign innocent curiosity to garner more details.

When it was time for Nurse Compton's break, I exited the storage room and went to the water cooler in the hallway.

"I've just updated her chart and administered her meds," Nurse Compton said to the aide as I listened in. "There shouldn't be any issues, and I'll only be gone for an hour. Just stay close. Monitor her vitals. She seems stable. There haven't been any changes in hours, but it's her first day, she's very fragile. Keep a close eye on her, please."

Nurse Compton nodded at me as she passed on her way to the cafeteria. I raised my cup to her with a smile and took a sip, then lingered, enjoying my water break watching the aide. She sat behind the station desk, flipped through some papers, and picked up the phone. Soon she was giggling and speaking in hushed tones.

An alarm pierced the hall, a familiar but grating blare. The overhead speaker crackled to life with a voice calling for an aide in a distant section of the home. The woman behind the desk slammed the phone down in a jump and rose. She craned her neck, looking down the corridor. Indecision worked its way over her body. Again the voice echoed through the center, this time with a tinge of poorly disguised alarm. At the end of the hallway, a faint red light flashed outside a resident's room. It was likely a fall—commonplace but always cause for immediate action. The woman abandoned her station and jogged down the hall.

The beacon fell silent and the hall remained empty. I glanced at my watch: two o'clock, a time when many residents napped. Most were so wiped out by this time that even an alarm and the ensuing hubbub wouldn't be enough to pull them from their rooms. This was my chance.

I set my cup on the nurse's desk and stole another glance around me. I ducked inside the medical room, a cover story taking shape in my mind should I be found. A rhythmic series of beeps kept time with her heartbeat and muffled the drone of countless monitors. A metal chart hung at the foot of the girl's bed. It kept her secrets. Secrets I now had access to.

The room was dim, dismal almost, with the blinds drawn tight. The freshly tiled walls absorbed any warmth that might have penetrated the sterile space. A soft light above the bed cast upon the girl's face, highlighting the twisted scars. Despite their aberrant form, they did nothing to distract from the beauty of her features. Yes, she reminded me of Lauren when she was young. I could envision the milky blue of her eyes under her taped lids. Her golden hair lay in a halo around her face, draping onto her shoulders. I picked up a soft strand and drew my fingers through it. She would look pretty in braids.

Her finger twitched, causing me to recoil, certain she would spring to life and call me out. But no, it was involuntary. A spasm. It served to shake me from the spell she'd cast and pressed me to look at the chart.

With shaky hands and eyes on the door, I removed the metal file from its hook and opened it. My gaze fell to the name at the top of the page—*Addison, Shelby R.* Her date of birth indicated she was only ten years old. I slammed the file shut, returned it to its place, and ran from the room.

My craft project forgotten, I hurried to the entrance of the nursing home and retrieved my coat, fleeing to my car and fumbling the keys out of my pocket as I did. Safely inside the vehicle, I went to work to lower my pulse that pounded in my ears, trying my best to even my ragged breath.

The girl was Dr. Addison's daughter, Jennings Ellington's half-sister. If the rumors were true, she was also the half-sister to countless other unsuspecting children. She was the sole survivor of the tragic crash that claimed the lives of her entire family. She had no one. The thought was overwhelming, and a flood of sobs wracked my body. A tidal wave of tragedy crashed into me.

Coventry Springs was no place for someone so young. But where else was she to go? An orphan with a broken body and a shattered mind. I wept for Shelby. For all the things she would never experience. For the cruel fate that had left her discarded in a place where the only certainty was death. How long would she languish, frozen among the aged and fading? It wasn't fair. And on top of all the grievous injustices weighing on such frail shoulders, she had to endure it all without a mother's love.

Once I'd calmed myself enough to drive, I struggled with the notion that I should return to the poor girl. Perhaps I could embrace her. Hold her. Braid her hair. Do anything to show her she was not alone. I forced the intrusive thoughts out and left her behind. She would spend her first night in the living tomb alone. I had my own family to tend to.

I arrived home to a quiet house. Roger was on another business trip; his flight wouldn't be in until late. Lauren was at rehearsal, but with no real idea of when she might return, I fought the urge to pry into her diary again. While I now knew she and Jennings were closer than I ever thought possible, I still needed to learn more. We were rushing toward prom season, and she had already begun searching through magazines for the perfect dress. At least I knew Nancy was wrong when she suggested Lauren and Jennings had already known each other intimately. I should have guessed Nancy would jump straight to sex without any evidence.

Moving through the house, I flipped on the lights. In the kitchen, the answering machine light flashed. I pushed the button, and Lauren's voice split the silence.

"Mom, something horrible has happened!"

My heart stopped, and I froze on my way to the refrigerator, waiting for her to continue.

"It's Mr. Ellington. He's at the hospital. I'm here with Jennings. We were at rehearsal, and—" She was quiet for a time. "They aren't sure—" A hitch in her throat cut her off. "Oh, Mom, they don't think he will make it. I'm not sure when I'll be home. I need to be here for Jennings. I'll keep you posted. Love you!"

The machine clicked. I considered calling her on her cell phone, but refrained. She'd phoned about an hour before I arrived home. Given her state of upset and my apprehension of when she might return, I resolved not to cave to my longing to lose myself in her words. An internal war waged within me. I held a card that could lay waste to their romance and believed the day was fast approaching where I'd be left with no choice but to play it.

Roger's possible reaction held me back. What would I do if he left me? The world I'd created for myself and for my daughter would be obliterated. My mind grappled with scenarios of how he might handle the news. I was sure he would see my betrayal as too great to overcome. We'd grown so distant. There was no affection left in our marriage. How could things have spun so out of control? If it weren't for Dr. Addison's despicable actions and my daughter's betrayal, my secret would have stayed safe forever.

SIXTEEN

INDUCED

Roger and I huddled under a black umbrella at the graveside. The sky grim and gray, heavy clouds pelted the mourners who gathered to lay Edward Ellington to rest with icy rain. He'd suffered a coronary but clung to life for several days before succumbing to the damaging blow to his heart.

Lauren sat next to Jennings and the Ellington family under the shelter of a black canopy in front of the gilded coffin. Nancy clung to her son, her eyes veiled in black tulle. Her gloved hand clutched a kerchief to her nose. Jennings sat between the two women, stoic, a solid structure for his mother to lean on.

After the burial, the Ellingtons hosted a reception at their home. I implored Roger to bow out after the service, but he insisted on attending.

"We should be there," he'd countered. "For Lauren. She and Jennings seem to be good friends. She's pretty busted up by all this."

Somber music floated through the foyer when we escaped the downpour and entered the Ellington home. A string quartet sat drawing their bows in the expansive entry. We deposited our coats and umbrella at the coat check. Fragrance from dozens of sprays and bouquets permeated the house. Lauren stood with Jennings in the main room. She didn't notice our arrival among the sea of people clad in black.

I excused myself to the restroom, passing by the line outside the powder room to ascend the grand staircase. I made for the bathroom I'd last been in so many years ago, when I was so full of hope and excitement. The door to the room that once served as Jennings' nursery stood ajar. I could not resist having a look inside. It was a completely different space, but no doubt still Jennings' bedroom. The creamy Persian rug was gone. The mural had been painted over in a tame shade of green; the walls were now adorned with posters from Broadway shows, movies, and music groups. A photo of him and Lauren sat framed on his nightstand. I scanned the hallway before exiting to ensure no one spotted me in a place where I shouldn't be.

The bathroom was completely remodeled as well, looking nothing like the room it was when I'd last visited. A jolt of envy prodded at me in the stylish space. I'd been trying to convince Roger to update the interior of our home. He was adamant a remodel wasn't warranted and only made repairs when needed. The aesthetics didn't matter to him. He spent little time outside his home office.

I left the bathroom and stood on the stair landing, scanning the room for my daughter. I hoped to join Lauren to offer condolences and make a quick escape. She hadn't moved from the spot I'd seen her in earlier. Now Roger and Nancy stood with her. Nancy held Roger in a long embrace. He rubbed her back. I stood mesmerized, wondering how much longer they'd remain in each other's arms. If anyone else caught sight of them, surely they'd be as taken aback as I. The interaction was far too lengthy and intimate for the two of them to be passing acquaintances, much less for a grieving widow during her husband's funeral.

When they finally let go of each other, Roger's arm remained on her lower back, and Nancy rested her head against his shoulder. Lauren and Jennings stood in conversation with them, none of the party showing disdain for the adults' behavior. I fought the urge to clamber to his side and stepped back into the shadows to observe.

Nancy's shoulders hitched, and her knees buckled. She clung to Roger as he helped her to a chair. He knelt next to her with a veil of concern across his face—a look he'd never shown to me. Lauren and Jennings moved away to a buffet table. They were a blur in the crowd as my eyes stayed locked on Roger and Nancy. The other guests disappeared. The room belonged to my husband and a woman I despised.

His hand rested on her knee. She clutched it and leaned in close. They had to be whispering, their lips nearly touching; they could feel each other's breath. Roger's mouth dropped open. He stood, shaking his head. Nancy slumped forward and buried her head in her hands; her shoulders bucked. Roger's eyes darted about the room, landing on Lauren. Nancy rose and hugged him again. They didn't release each other until Jennings approached with a highball in hand. He passed it to his mother, and she drank readily, draining the glass and passing it to Roger. He dutifully took it and made his way to the bar, returning to Nancy with a drink for her and one for himself.

I'd seen enough. Now I descended the stairs, returning to the spot where I'd left Roger before using the restroom. I stayed there, making small talk with those who passed by. There I remained for another half hour until the waiting gnawed at my nerves. It seemed as if Roger forgot he'd brought a plus-one to this event, and I gave up on him seeking me out. I started to push back through the crowd to find him when I spotted him moving toward me. I could tell by the sway in his stride he'd no doubt downed another drink or two.

"There you are," he said as he approached.

"Right where you left me," I replied coldly.

"I hope you're ready to get out of here. I've had about all I can stand," he whispered in my ear. The stench of Scotch invaded my nostrils.

"I should drive," I said.

"Why? I'm fine."

We retrieved our coats and exited. The rain had stopped, but low clouds still cloaked the sun. Roger broke the silence as he drove down the long driveway and turned onto the street.

"Have you spoken to Nancy lately?" He said her name with a comfortable familiarity that crawled on my skin.

"Only when absolutely necessary," I replied, tightening my jaw.

"Has she told you about that doctor? What was his name?" He paused, his finger tapping the steering wheel. "Addison? The charlatan you insisted could get you pregnant…"

A bead of cold sweat trailed down my spine. I sat frozen in panic as the car's heater threatened to ignite my skin. I leaned forward and punched the button to extinguish the blowtorch.

"The nerve! Using his own"—his voice lowered to a whisper as he searched for the word—"stuff to knock up how many women? How is that not against the law?"

He paused at a red light, and I scrambled to find a response. Nothing came, and he continued as the light turned green.

"She says he fathered Jennings. Can you believe it? I mean, she always knew he wasn't biologically Edward's son, but man. Were you aware? I'm guessing not. I can't imagine you'd be able to keep such a juicy piece of gossip to yourself." He threw a glance in my direction. My eyes wouldn't meet his.

He gave up on waiting for a response from me.

"She hasn't even told the poor kid yet. He's still oblivious. Said she was trying to come up with a way to break it to him when his dad, well, his—I don't even know what you'd call him—Edward. When Edward had the heart attack. Can you believe it?"

The weight of his words worked through his body, and his foot pressed harder on the gas pedal as he spoke. He was driving too fast. I should have driven, should insist he slow down. I considered asking him to pull over, but I knew it would only anger him more.

"We sure dodged a bullet. You're welcome. Can you imagine if I'd let you continue treatment with him? What if he'd done the same thing to you? Disgusting!"

My mind raced. I knew I had to come up with something to appease him. He'd obviously run out of words and was waiting for my reaction.

"She mentioned something," I said, trying to force an air of indifference into my tone. "You two didn't talk about our time with Dr. Addison, did you?"

"You mean you knew?" He slammed on the brakes and pounded on the horn at someone who pulled out in front of him. The car's tires struggled for grip on the wet road.

"I knew I should have driven," I said, hoping the errant driver would prove distraction enough to pause the conversation. He ignored my comment but didn't answer my question.

"You knew about this rogue sperm doctor? Knew he'd fathered Jennings?"

"Well, yes. It's not like you and I have regular conversations. When was I going to bother you with something that held no consequence to us?"

"I don't know about no consequence. She also said her son and our daughter were quite the twosome these days. Were you keeping that little tidbit from me as well?"

"No!" I replied, grateful he'd offered me something to hang the conversation on. I geared up to feign shock about Lauren and Jennings' tryst, already clasping my hand to my chest, but he didn't give me a chance to further convince him of how I felt.

"I mean, good for Lauren. She could do way worse. From the looks of their mansion, he may be coming into a hefty inheritance."

"Roger! That's inappropriate!"

"Whatever." He stopped short, almost skidding through a stop sign. He kicked the wipers to the highest speed as rain broke from the clouds again and craned his neck in both directions. The tires spun in the current of the flooded street. "Wish I had that kind of money."

He was quiet for a moment, and I considered taking a jab, calling him out, questioning his tryst with Nancy when a thought flashed in my mind. Nancy was back on the market now, not that she'd ever considered herself off the market. But now she could flaunt her single status and was no doubt already on the hunt. I wanted to pummel him with accusations, threaten him, secure my place in the marriage, warn him away from Nancy. But I couldn't alienate him at this point. I needed to keep a level head. I had to bite my tongue and tread carefully.

"I think we should invite them over," he continued, "for dinner or something. I'm sure Nancy could use the distraction, and it sounds like we need to get to know this boy better."

"I don't think that's necessary." My voice was shrill as I rushed my words, attempting to stay on course without losing sight of my objective. Distracted and panicked, I lobbed a ridiculous statement. "Even if they are dating, it's a high school fling. It's not like he's going to propose." I wished I could draw them back in as the words spewed out of my mouth. I felt foolish, like I'd allowed Nancy into my head and I was arguing with her instead of my husband.

"I don't know," he said. "Sounds like they've been an item for some time now."

Not him too? Of course, Nancy took the chance to put her spin on everything, poisoning my husband's opinions with her own. I needed air and wished I could roll the window down, but the rain continued.

"I'm kind of surprised Lauren kept it from us all this time." He sounded as if he were speaking to himself and not to me.

Traffic slowed to a crawl. The rain fell harder, making it nearly impossible for the wipers to keep up. We sat motionless for some time, and quiet filled the car. My mind grasped at thoughts that slipped by too quickly for me to grab. Roger spoke again.

"You know Nancy wants Lauren to go to New York with Jennings after graduation. Sounds like it might be a win-win for Lauren and for us. She said Lauren could live with Jennings rent-free. I feel like a heel depriving her of such a great opportunity. Maybe we should rethink things."

I sat in stunned silence, grappling for a response. My need to uncover what the two might have shared about my time with Dr. Addison was now forgotten. It was just like Roger to cave to whatever Lauren wanted, despite any consideration of what was in her best interest. Running off to New York with the Ellington boy was preposterous. Anything could happen to her out there in a city notorious for crime. Not to mention Lauren remaining in the grips of

Nancy's claws, beholden to her for what, free rent? The implications of Roger's position expanded inside me. His mouth opened as if to speak, but I cut him off.

"Out of the question!" The words rushed out of me on a wave of emotion. Releasing them did not ease the terror building within me. "Why are you so hellbent on assisting our daughter in ruining her life? She's staying here. She's going to college. This New York pipe dream must be forbidden. By both of us. For once, we need to present a united front."

We'd inched along in the traffic enough to spot the problem. Ahead of us, a car sat with its blinkers on. The driver of the car sheltered from the deluge under the hood. We skirted around the stalled vehicle, and soon traffic flowed smoothly again. I shifted my eyes to outside the car, trying to force out the splash of red that blinded me. The landscape flashed by quicker as Roger increased the pressure of his foot on the car's gas pedal.

"And slow down! I knew I should have driven. You've had too much to drink."

"Well, get used to it. Too much to drink is my state of existence these days. I haven't landed a new client in months, and I'm barely hanging on to the ones I have." His words had sharp edges. "You think it's easy to keep all this afloat? I'm not getting any younger, and the industry is evolving so fast. I'm really struggling, Alice. I thought by my age I could just coast into retirement on the clientele I'd built. But nothing is good enough for you, so I can't slow down."

I focused on taking deep breaths. It was just like him to dodge the matter at hand and shift the focus onto himself.

Roger sighed as he stopped at a red light.

"Why do you think we know what's best for our daughter?" he asked as the light changed. His tone softened as he said, "Why would you want to pigeonhole her into this lifestyle? Marriage, mortgage, career pressure. Maybe she's destined for something more. Something better."

"Something more?" I scoffed. "Better?" His words lit a fire inside me, threatening to throw me off course. I'd dedicated my life to building this family and thought I'd done a pretty good job.

Lauren was happy, and once we eliminated this Jennings nonsense, she'd be back on course. Roger had a respectable career, a loyal wife, a nice house, and a happy child, and if he could see past his own ego, he'd realize I was the one who held it all together. Or maybe he knew but didn't believe my efforts were good enough.

I wanted to ignore his baseless comment and draw him back to Dr. Addison. Had Nancy hinted at anything that might expose me? I tried to douse my anger and think of ways to redirect him back to the matter that could give him enough ammunition to walk away from the life he wished was better, but he answered my rhetorical questions.

"Yes, Alice. Something more. Like following a dream, blazing a new trail instead of limping along in the ruts of a life we created for no other reason than it was what was expected of us. Don't you ever get tired of what we chose? Ever think about how things could have been if we'd made different decisions?"

"No, I have not!" I yelled in a shrill and unsteady voice. "I've been too busy working hard for this life, for this family. We've spent over twenty years building—"

He countered in a monotone hush, cutting me off.

"Oh, I don't need to be reminded. Twenty years of scrambling to keep up with a lifestyle I'm not sure I ever really wanted."

"You don't want this life? Me? Our daughter?" I tugged at the seat belt as it clamped tighter against me. "We aren't good enough for you? You're so selfish, Roger!"

"I'm selfish?" His voice hardened again. "Everything I do is for you and Lauren. Every sleepless night, every endless day, busting my ass to put a roof over your head and give you the child you wanted. I'm the selfish one, right! It's no wonder Lauren wants to run as far as she can from this stifling existence. At least one of us still has options, and I don't think we should take them away from her."

"Well, I'm so sorry Lauren and I are such disappointments to you. Am I just not pretty enough? Flashy enough? Don't have enough family money? Nancy Ellington has all those things going for her."

I focused on his face, watching for the expression I believed he'd reveal, knowing what I did of his fondness for Nancy—his desire to toss me aside for her. There was no reaction, so I pushed further. "Of course she does. But you know what she doesn't have? One shred of self-decency, one ounce of mothering skills, or any clue what loyalty is. I could go on, but I'm sure you're aware of all Nancy has to offer and what she's lacking."

"What's that supposed to mean?"

He looked baffled. He was better than me at hiding his feelings. Now I knew where Lauren got her acting skills.

"Don't pretend you don't know what I'm talking about. I've done all I can to be the wife you wanted and the mother Lauren needed. So yeah, to find out twenty-some years in it's all just some colossal disappointment to you, well, it stings."

"Maybe I'm just disappointed in myself," he retorted. "And maybe depriving our daughter of her dream will just be one more disappointment I am forced to live with. Hell, maybe I should go with her. Try my hand at advertising in the big city."

Was he threatening to abandon all we'd built? He'd never so much as hinted at wanting another life. Finding out I'd betrayed him all those years ago could be all he needed to decide to walk away.

"Really? And where does that leave me?" I asked.

"I don't know. Maybe you could get a job like you're always prattling on about. Maybe you can find yourself a handyman to bed who can update your precious house. The world could be yours, Alice. You never know."

My hand tensed on the door handle. I fought the urge to throw the door open, to leap out of the moving car—anything to end this conversation. How dare he? I fought for air, my throat tightening as if struggling to keep more noxious words from escaping my lips. Roger broke first.

"Look, I don't know how the paternity of Jennings Ellington spiraled into this argument, but the fact remains Lauren is eighteen, and as soon as she graduates from high school we won't have a say in what she does with her life. We can take a stand against her dreams and deny her the opportunity, but if we do that, we could risk losing her. Maybe we let her sow her own oats. Maybe she'll respect us for it. Besides, she really is talented."

"Don't you dare encourage her!" I growled. "And don't you dare give her your permission before you think through the ramifications. I'm warning you, Roger. I want what's best for Lauren, and it certainly doesn't involve New York City or Jennings Ellington." The steely tone of my voice surprised me as much as it surprised Roger. He glared at me with his mouth agape. My words had silenced him.

I was relieved to see the turn to our street ahead. I still struggled to breathe. Getting out of the car and away from this conversation was the only way I'd be allowed to inhale. I cursed Nancy for telling Roger about Dr. Addison. I'd yet to come up with a way to untangle my child from the wreckage of Nancy's pathetic excuse of a family while keeping myself safe. I needed time to think. I remained silent until Roger parked the car.

"I didn't realize the life we built was so abhorrent to you. You can't imagine all I've done for this limping rut of an existence!" I snatched my purse from the floor, exited the car, and slammed the door behind me, never looking back as I bolted for the house. Bud trotted out from a row of shrubs while I dug the key out of my bag. I thrashed at the cat with my foot and hissed at him, warning him off. He leapt over a puddle and scurried back to his hiding spot.

SEVENTEEN

RIPE

Two days after Edward's funeral, I stood in the kitchen waiting for the bread to pop out of the toaster when the doorbell rang. Through the peephole, I saw the back of a woman's head. I didn't recognize the pixie cut, platinum-blonde hair and considered tiptoeing back into the kitchen. I was already running late for my shift at Coventry Springs. Before I could retreat, the woman turned, and I was shocked to see Nancy. How had she managed to change her look completely since I'd seen her just days ago at the service? She knocked on the door. I flinched with each blow.

"Alice, I know you're in there. Your car is in the driveway. Save me from this wretched beast now, please!"

Through the fisheye lens of the peephole, I saw Bud wind his way onto the porch and slink toward Nancy. She nudged at him with her pointed shoe as he approached. I took a deep breath and opened the door.

"Nancy, now is not a good——" I began. She pushed past me, shoving an empty casserole dish into my hand as she did. I almost dropped the platter but recovered and grasped it before it slipped from my hands.

"Thank you for the…" she started as she took her sunglasses off.

"Oh, what was it? Chicken and rice, lasagna? Whatever it was, I am sure it was delicious. Not that I've been able to stomach a bite since Edward…" She extracted a handkerchief from her jacket cuff and dabbed at her nose. The whites of her eyes were laced with swollen red tendrils.

"Oh no, Nancy. This dish isn't mine. I didn't bring any food. I apologize; I should have brought something, but I wasn't sure and time got away from me. I'm very sorry, it was…"

"Never you mind. I had to throw so much food out. I felt simply horrible about it, but the outpouring was overwhelming." She removed her jacket and hung it on the coat rack, but then stilled, tears pooling in her eyes. She looked at me with the most human expression I'd seen on her face in all the years I'd known her. Sympathy nudged at me, but I shook my head, breaking myself away from her gaze and reminding myself to keep my distance.

Before I could rebound and focus on getting her to leave, she snatched the dish from my hands, set it on my entry table, and made her way to the kitchen.

"Might I bother you for a cup of coffee? I've been meaning to have a heart-to-heart with you for weeks, but other matters prevailed." She took a seat at the kitchen table, and I felt powerless to evict her. Instead, I made my way to the coffeemaker and began preparing a fresh pot. I busied myself retrieving mugs and spoons, feeling the heat of her gaze on me as I did.

"I really don't have time," I said, removing my toast from the toaster and tossing it in the trash. I wiped down a spotless countertop to avoid sitting with her.

"You need to make time for this. Besides, if you're running off to the old folks' home, they can wait. What are they going to do, fire you for volunteering your time?"

The coffee maker sputtered and spit out the last droplets of the umber liquid. I'd only made two cups in hopes she would depart quickly. I filled each cup and brought them to the table, reluctantly sitting across from her.

"Thank you," she replied, reaching into her bag and withdrawing a silver flask. She twisted the cap off and poured a generous splash into her cup. "I don't know how to function at this point without my trusty friend." She raised the vessel and wagged it in her hand as she tossed a chuckle out the side of her mouth and used the teaspoon to churn her drink. After making a show of blowing on the hot beverage, she closed her eyes and downed half the drink.

"As if losing my husband wasn't enough, I'm still reeling from learning my son is indeed Dr. Addison's son." She shuddered, her earrings dancing madly with the motion, unhindered by the longer, auburn locks that framed her face days earlier. "Those words leave a bad taste in my mouth. Dr. Addison's son. It isn't right. I swear that repugnant phrase is what put my poor Edward in his grave." Again, she plucked the kerchief from her cuff, this time dabbing at her eyes and wiping her nose. "I can't help but wonder if he'd still be with us if I'd just kept the news to myself."

For several moments, the only noise in the room was the ticking of the clock hanging above her head. When I believed I couldn't take the coiling tension another second, she spoke. "If I'd kept my mouth shut, he could have left us without that knowledge. Learning what Dr. Addison did to me, to our family … it destroyed Edward. I'm trying to find some peace in knowing he doesn't have to bear this complete indignity we've suffered as a family. He is free of the aftermath."

Disquiet forced me from my seat. I rose and paced the kitchen, pretending to search for sugar. She stuffed the handkerchief back into her sleeve and finished her drink. I leaned against the counter, abandoning my search for sugar, and picked at a hangnail while envy prodded at me. Nancy playing the victim, when in reality she had a whole new lease on life. She'd always known Jennings' father wasn't Edward. Why did she continue to make it such an issue? She had everything, and now she had even more, without the fear it could all be ripped away from her on her husband's whims. She'd been wanton with her fertility her whole life, but now it mattered who fathered her child?

I wondered if she ever cared this much about the paternity of her daughter. Of course she didn't. This debacle with Dr. Addison provided her with a new tool. Now she had the added fuel of being a wronged widow—a wealthy, wronged widow at that, and one who was lucky enough to know who her son's father was. The son of a doctor, of all things. The nerve! I inhaled deeply and slowly as I waited for her to go on, knowing she wasn't finished.

"I've spoken to my lawyer. I've spoken to my therapist. Hell, I've spoken to anyone who would listen, but I haven't spoken to my son. Every time I think I can break the news to him, I freeze up. I don't know why. He's grown up knowing Edward wasn't his biological father. So, it shouldn't be difficult to tell him. But I feel so violated. My lawyer can't drum up one violation, at least according to the law. It's ridiculous, isn't it? A man can essentially force himself upon you, put something inside you that you didn't agree to accept, and there is no legal recourse? It isn't right. I liken it to rape, and don't think it isn't. We were assaulted, Alice. Some of us are considering a class action suit, but how do you file a lawsuit against a dead man? Especially when he left one innocent survivor behind after his final insidious act. Any money he had should be used to care for his last victim."

I was drawn back to the conversation. "His last victim?"

"His daughter. She survived. Rumor is she resides in a nursing home now. She's a child! The absolute horror!" She drummed her long red nails against her teacup and cleared her throat. Without asking, I went to the coffee pot, scooped more grounds into the filter, and pushed the brew button.

"How did you hear about his daughter?" I hoped I'd tempered my tone enough. If Nancy had information regarding Shelby Addison, I wanted to know. In the weeks since the girl's arrival, I'd become a fixture in her room at Coventry Springs. The nurses called me in to braid her hair after they washed it. I read to her and watched MTV with her, hoping to stir life into her endless sleep. They'd dubbed me her surrogate mother.

Despite the turmoil my life had become outside of Coventry Springs, being with Shelby centered me. It was like reliving early motherhood, but without the sleepless nights and gnawing self-doubt. Of all the patients I'd served at the nursing home, my time with the only survivor of Dr. Addison's horrific act was the most rewarding. The nurses insisted that her color had changed and her vitals improved. Some attributed it to being in a more comfortable environment than a hospital, but I believed it might be due to the attention I gave her. I wasn't about to share my knowledge of Shelby's condition with Nancy.

"Oh, here and there. So-and-so heard something; this person knows someone who cared for her at the hospital, the usual. She is in a coma or something, never to recover, from what I hear. It's tragic. But enough about her; she's just one of the many half-siblings Jennings now has, even though he doesn't know it. But since my dear son is indeed the offspring of that monster, it is even more crucial you test Lauren. They could be related too, and while I didn't think it was possible, they've actually gotten closer since Edward's passing."

I pulled the pot from the maker and filled her cup. Nancy promptly topped it off with a splash from her flask; the spoon tinkled against the porcelain as she stirred. I returned to my seat across from her and sipped my coffee.

"Nancy, enough. I don't know how many times I have to tell you I am one-hundred percent certain Dr. Addison is not Lauren's father." I wondered if she remembered running into me that fateful day at the fertility clinic. She hadn't mentioned the specific incident, but she knew my secret. What she didn't know was that it was indeed a secret. One held so tightly inside me it became my reality.

Roger believed Lauren had been conceived by sheer happenstance, that he'd been right and we didn't have fertility issues. It had all been a scam. But my desperation had allowed me to be preyed upon by a charlatan, a man who could do such vile things. If Roger knew what I'd done, I could lose everything. My entire life could disintegrate around me.

Nancy's theories and allegations were a significant threat. I could tell her the truth, but I didn't owe it to her. It was none of her business that I'd been forbidden to seek further treatments. She would mock me for my weakness. She wasn't dumb either. She'd seen me in the office that fateful day. She could do the math. My pregnancy aligned closely with the visit. If she kept on, she could expose my secrets. How could I have ever known those misconceptions would be so relevant all these years later? My future rested on a very thin line, one that she could overstep at any moment.

As I waited for her to reply, images spun in my head. My home with a for-sale sign in the front yard. The rooms emptied of furniture. I rose, growing uncomfortable in the heat of Nancy's closeness. I walked to the kitchen's entrance. My fingers traced the carved notches on the trim that tracked Lauren's growth from a toddler to a teen as the visions swarmed me. The memories of Lauren's childhood echoing through an empty hall. Me hunting for a job. I'd never even balanced a checkbook. Me searching for an apartment. It was an uncertain future I had no means with which to navigate. I'd have to leave my home, my cats.

I'd never been on my own, and I wouldn't let Nancy destroy all I'd lived for. Roger couldn't know. I had to prevent her from upending my life.

Too consumed by racing thoughts, I hadn't noticed Nancy studying me. How long had she been fixated on me? I did my best to wipe the panic from my expression, forcing the abysmal images from my mind, and joined her at the table. She reached for my hand, and I withdrew it, placing it in my lap.

"But what if you're wrong, Alice? All the evidence we have proves anything is possible. Dr. Addison was an evil man. A megalomaniac. We can't risk delaying things any longer. Because if she is…"

She paused, her lips quivering. Her gaze shifted to a bird perched on the window ledge outside. She inhaled deeply and took a long draw on her coffee. "If she is Jennings' half-sister, we must tell them so their relationship doesn't grow deeper. As it stands, the news will devastate them. But if they get closer, the consequences could be dreadful. What if…"

She paused again, draining her coffee cup. Out came the flask. She dumped its contents into the empty cup and took a swig. "God forbid Lauren got pregnant. I don't even want to think about it!" Again the handkerchief appeared, but before she could use it her head fell forward and she collapsed onto the table, sobs wracking her body.

As I watched her cry, it hit me. I had the perfect solution to the biggest problem I faced: making sure my daughter didn't run off with the likes of Jennings Ellington. If he and Lauren were to keep seeing each other and someday marry, we'd be stuck with Nancy forever.

Lauren could not go to New York. She could not stay in a relationship with Jennings. Nancy had been trying to cram the answer down my throat for months. I did have a way to end the relationship. The biggest obstacle I faced was my husband. But my priority was my daughter. It always had been. What if Jennings and Lauren were related? I rose again and paced the kitchen as burgeoning thoughts invaded my head.

"How can you be so certain that you weren't a victim too?" Nancy pressed. "You got pregnant months after he did it to me. You were in his care. I saw you there right before you announced your pregnancy. Why do you think you're so special? That you were spared from his twisted scheme?"

She did remember our encounter. Ideas were falling into place, and now I had one more piece of the puzzle. Roger couldn't find out, but that problem could be addressed. I now knew what I had to do, and I needed to change course with Nancy. The first step was to give her an inch.

"I don't know," I whispered, willing tears to build and my chin to quiver. "I'm not sure what to think. Maybe the idea is just so … so … too horrible to allow in." I silently applauded my performance. I could do this.

"I swear I find myself staring at them when they are together," Nancy said, seemingly untouched by my unfolding. "The more I do, the more I am convinced the similarities are impossible to overlook."

She searched through her handbag again. I was certain I would have to remind her there was no smoking in my house, but instead she shoved a photo in my face. I'd never seen it before. Lauren in a top hat emblazoned with *Happy New Year*. Jennings with a noisemaker clenched between his teeth. Their eyes were alight, their smiles pulsed. Their happiness with each other emanated from the photo, leaving zero doubt of their feelings. My heart plummeted.

"What's this?" I feigned indifference.

"Look at them, Alice," she said, holding the picture closer to my face. "Look at their eyes, their smiles. They look so much alike."

I wanted to snatch the photo away from her and toss the bits in the garbage to obliterate its existence. The joy radiating from my daughter was something I rarely saw. Something I only gleaned when she was onstage. I gazed intently at the image, then looked away. I chose my next words carefully.

"I've always been certain Roger was Lauren's father. But now…" I fluttered my fingers at her, asking for the picture without saying so. She pinched the photo between her long red nails, holding it just outside my reach. I leaned in, squinting, making myself believe I saw what she saw when I looked at the young sweethearts. "I guess I can't deny the similarities."

"Right?!" she exclaimed, flipping the picture and drawing it near her face. "They could be twins, couldn't they?"

My stomach rolled, and coffee, still warm, rose in my throat. I choked it down and pressed on.

"Maybe not twins, but yes, there is a slight resemblance."

Nancy straightened her spine as if proud of some accomplishment and pressed on. "I can get you a testing kit. It's painless. She just has to swab her cheek."

I stood up and forced myself to convey all the proper emotions: confusion, doubt, reluctance. I moved to the window and stood as long as I believed was necessary to pull her in, realizing any display of reticence was needless. With shaking hands, I turned back to her, sighed deeply, and nodded my head while diverting my eyes.

She sprang from the table. Now her eyes danced, no hint of the watery, bloodshot mess from when she arrived. She reached out to me, grabbing me and drawing me in. Gone was the flowery fragrance she used to emit. Now she smelled like my mother—booze and age.

"I knew you'd come around," she whispered.

I did my best to accept her embrace, but was convinced she'd squeeze the life out of me. Gently, I withdrew and brushed away a nonexistent tear.

"You have to make a promise to me, Nancy." I regarded her solemnly.

"A promise?"

"You have to let me handle this my way. In my own time."

She took her purse from the table.

"Time is of the essence," she said. "They are only falling deeper in love."

I winced and hoped she didn't notice.

"I understand I can't ruminate any longer. I need to submit her DNA for testing, which I will do quickly. But you have to stay out of it. Don't say anything to Lauren. This has to be handled with care."

"Understood," she said, making her way to the front door. I picked up the casserole dish off the table and held it out to her. She put her jacket on and reached for the dish. I clenched it tightly in my hands, forcing her to make eye contact with me.

"I mean it, Nancy. Not a word to Lauren or Roger until I say so."

She tugged at the dish. I did not relinquish it.

"My lips are sealed. I'll contact Carol to get you a test. But please promise you'll let me know when the results are in. I swear I haven't been sleeping. I can't eat. I can't even properly grieve my husband. I need this resolved. At least this part. My most fervent hope is that I am wrong. That Roger is proven to be Lauren's father. Jennings will need her to help him come to terms with his own paternity."

I let go of the dish and opened the front door, resisting the urge to shove her out of my house. She exited but turned back to me before I could close the door.

"We'll get through this, Alice. And so will our children. At least you still have your husband. I've never needed my husband more." Her eyes quivered. Tears pooled, threatening to spill over.

I closed the door on her without another word.

EIGHTEEN

HATCHING

The following Thursday, I sat in the lobby at the table closest to the entrance of Coventry Springs, losing a chess match to a new resident. Chess was never my game, but was an obvious favorite of Mr. Pendleton. He pondered each move at length. My mind was elsewhere, and my eyes were on the door. Nancy had arranged for Dr. Addison's former nurse to deliver a DNA test kit. She questioned why I insisted on the package being delivered to the nursing home instead of my house, but quieted down when I reminded her I was handling the matter on my own terms.

I recognized the nurse immediately, despite the passage of nearly two decades. She smiled at an elderly woman who crept by using a walker. The smile hadn't changed. Impossible to read, an expression that held an abundance of unspoken nuances. Good news? Bad news? A look that somehow conveyed both.

My knee knocked the table as I sprung up, toppling the chessmen. Mr. Pendleton grumbled and set about righting the game pieces, oblivious to my departure.

"Mrs. White, it's wonderful to see you," she said as she approached, hand outstretched. In her other hand, she held a brown paper bag, giving the exchange a sordid feel.

I scanned the room, not wanting to answer questions should someone see my guest. Mr. Pendleton was the only person in the lobby, and his focus was on where he had placed his knight after the last play. I snatched the bag from her hand, avoiding her invitation to shake.

"I'm sorry," she said, dropping the volume of her voice. "I should be more discreet. But there is absolutely nothing to be ashamed of. Dr. Addison's abuse was not your fault."

I was powerless to conceal my incredulous expression and struggled for a reply. She shook off my reaction and continued.

"I apologize for not getting in touch with you, but to be honest, this has all been so overwhelming. Word of mouth keeps bringing me more potential victims, but I never imagined how many women he'd done this to. Not to downplay your trauma."

"No need to apologize," I replied. My eyes darted about—to the door, then the main hallway. I'd hoped to complete this transaction with no intrusions and kicked myself for not setting up a more discreet meeting place.

"I never grasped how diabolical and far-reaching his methods were. I believe Mrs. Ellington filled you in on how this all got started. I knew something was amiss, but I didn't think anyone would believe me. I thought my notion that he was having affairs with patients was bad, preposterous even to some. I had mouths to feed, bills to pay, and only a couple of mismatched blood types as evidence that something was amiss. I couldn't risk my job, my livelihood, my reputation on suspicions. Besides, if he had been sleeping with his patients, well, he and the women I suspected he was bedding were consenting adults. It would be scandalous, but not devious. I confronted him, you know?"

Tears welled in her eyes, and she flinched like she could hear the crash and twisting metal that stole the lives of the Addison family. "I'm trying not to blame myself for the deaths, but it's hard not to. I just couldn't keep quiet any longer, and once my granddaughter was subject to her own paternity test, I realized I could figure it all out. I could prove that he'd been sleeping with patients. I never dreamed…"

She shook her head. "I'm still in shock. I wonder if we'll ever determine how many women he victimized. For all I know, there could be women pregnant with his offspring right this moment. He fired me, of course, so I can't gather any more evidence. Law enforcement can't help. The lawyers for his practice are doing their best to cover it all up, even after his death. Forgive me for rattling on and on. I just wanted to say how sorry I am. I'll never get over the guilt."

"No need for explanations or apologies," I said. "None of us could have imagined the horrors." I stressed finality in my tone, hoping she'd take the hint and leave. She did not.

"The instructions are inside the bag. It is very simple, almost foolproof. If you have any questions, my phone number is in there as well. I added a name to the return envelope. I have a contact at the lab who knows to test these samples against Dr. Addison's DNA. Should he not be your daughter's sperm donor, the results will be available for further testing as you see fit."

"That won't be necessary," I said. The crumpling noise from the paper bag echoed through the nearly empty room as I opened it and peered inside.

"Or if you would prefer, I can administer the test myself. Is your daughter here?"

"No!" I snapped. My voice pealed louder than the crinkling sack. I quieted myself to a whisper. "I'm sure I can handle it fine. Thank you for the delivery." My hand was on the woman's shoulder, steering her to the exit.

"You're more than welcome," she said, conceding to my nudges. "I hope you get the results you're wishing for."

Once the doors opened, I turned my back on her. She continued her departing sentiments as the doors slid closed. I scurried back to the table, apologizing to Mr. Pendleton and cramming the bag into my purse, which I'd tucked under my chair. He'd used my distraction and the misplaced pieces to his advantage.

"Check," he exclaimed. "Your king is surrounded." He leaned back in his chair and admired the board.

"Nice win, Mr. Pendleton," I said, feigning disappointment. "I need to introduce you to Gracie Wilcox. She's just down the hall from you and is a much better player than I am. A challenging opponent would do you good."

"Well, you aren't horrible, but a new adversary is always a good thing," he replied, gathering the pieces and setting up for a new game. "Keeps the mind sharp."

"I'll go find her. If she's available, I'll send her your way. I'm needed in arts and crafts now," I said, grabbing my purse. I rose and pushed my chair in.

"Oh, I think my mind has had enough sharpening today, but thanks for the offer."

I fled before he finished speaking and made my way to the ladies' room. Inside the stall, I pulled the bag from my purse and examined the contents. There was an instruction sheet, a pair of latex gloves, and an envelope with a mailing label. A bright orange biohazard sticker blared across the return envelope. Sealed inside heavy plastic were a tube and long cotton swab. I scanned the instructions four times, ensuring I understood the steps without having to refer back to them.

It was almost time for a shift change at the station outside Shelby's room. I tucked the swab into my pocket and the rest of the bag's contents back into my purse. Once outside the stall, I washed my hands, smiling in the mirror at a candy striper who had entered the restroom. I concealed my purse beneath the sink, making sure anyone entering the bathroom wouldn't see it.

In the hall, the nurse was not at her station so I moved swiftly to Shelby's room, peering through the frosted glass window that flanked the entrance to her room. She was alone. I entered and closed the door behind me. In order for my plan to be foolproof, I had to make sure the DNA I submitted for comparison held the genetic makeup of Dr. Addison. I couldn't take any chances, and I wasn't ready to test Lauren yet. While I hated the existence her father had cursed poor Shelby Addison to, I couldn't have asked for a better opportunity to exact my plot. The child's horrible fate played right into my hands.

I stood over Shelby's bed. Her hand twitched as I stroked her hair. The ribbon I'd placed in her hair was askew. I took a moment to fix it and removed the swab from my pocket. I moved to the other side of her bed for a better view of the door in case anyone approached. Leaning in, I gently pulled her lips apart. She didn't respond to my touch. I nudged the swab past her teeth, noting several teeth were missing; no doubt they had been left in an icy field months earlier. Recalling the instructions, I moved the tip of the swab around inside her mouth, pressing firmly into the inside of her cheek before rolling it to the other side. Outside, the hallway remained silent and still. Confident I'd performed the task properly, I inserted the swab into the tube and placed it back in my pocket. I exited the room to a still-empty hall.

In the supply closet, I located a box of swabs. I shrugged, uncertain what the facility used them for, and crammed a few of them into my pocket. On another shelf, I found some old vials that looked similar to the test tube I'd tucked the sample into. I snatched two of them and hid them in my pocket as well. While not exact matches, Lauren would not know the difference when it was her turn. I hated subjecting her to my version of a DNA test, but it would be critical to the outcome I envisioned.

Leaning around the open door, I peeked into the hallway and was relieved to find it unoccupied. I strode back to the bathroom, retrieved my purse, and departed Coventry Springs without saying goodbye to anyone.

On my drive home, I tried to calm my nerves. The first step of my plan had gone off without a hitch. The next moves were far riskier. I dropped the sample at the post office, not wanting to risk it being discovered at home. I scrawled Lauren's name on the sample and slipped the package in the mailbox. The results wouldn't arrive for a couple of weeks, buying me a little time.

At least I knew the results would show what I needed them to reveal, despite how things may have played out in Dr. Addison's lab of horrors. While many women were betrayed by the monster doctor, others had escaped his vile scheme. Who knew what the madman's methods entailed? What triggered his choice of a woman to impregnate? For now, what mattered most was that I get confirmation the sample I submitted was from the offspring of Dr. Addison. Shelby's wasted life proved invaluable to me.

After the post office, I made my way to the community college a few blocks away. The visit to the school was another step in the great changes I planned for my life. Dozens of people milled about on the lawn, where tables and displays for various courses dotted the quad. It was an enrollment event, one I'd learned about at Coventry Springs. A new course was being offered that taught people about new coding being implemented for medical billing—something I could complete within nine months; the skill was needed at the nursing home as billing practices were evolving rapidly. I'd already discussed a job opportunity with the director of the facility when I approached him about becoming an employee rather than just a volunteer.

"What piqued your interest in medical coding?" asked the counselor as she accepted my post-dated check for the course.

"I've volunteered for many years at Coventry Springs Care Facility. I would love to have a job there, but I don't have any work history and abandoned my education when I got married. The director told me about their need for CPT coders." I forced a casual air into my tone, despite this being one of the more momentous occasions in my life. "My daughter is heading off to college soon, so I thought I'd take up a new adventure and join the workforce," I said with a shrug, my heart fluttering with excitement. I hadn't told Roger or Lauren of my plans to return to school.

I stopped at the grocery store on my way home. I felt like celebrating. I had accomplished so much in one day. A recipe I'd cut from a magazine was tucked in my purse, something new I'd wanted to try. Without referring to the clipping, I gathered the ingredients. It was all part of the unfolding of the new me.

———

Later that evening, I knocked on Roger's office door.

"Come in," he replied after releasing a loud sigh.

Inside his office, I stood and watched him as regret overwhelmed me. Why hadn't I just been honest with him from the get-go? I wouldn't now be faced with the unthinkable if I had. How would he react if I told him I had returned to Dr. Addison, against his wishes and without his knowledge? Perhaps if I had just come clean all those years ago, the thrill of becoming a father would have over-shadowed my deception. But to tell him now? No, he wouldn't forgive me. My betrayal would push him away and devastate Lauren, sending her right into his arms. After all, he was willing to allow his only child to give up any hope of a normal future and run off to New York, with a boy no less.

It was an impossible situation. There was no world where Roger learned the truth and accepted it, especially now that Dr. Addison's evil deeds had been exposed. Roger would leave me. My daughter would side with him. I'd thought of little else since my last discussion with Nancy, playing out different scenarios. They all ended the same: me alone. I couldn't accept it, especially not on Roger's terms. There was only one way out of this predicament. If I was going to be alone, I would do it my way.

His gaze was intent on his computer screen, and he ignored my presence until he reached for a storyboard to the side of his desk.

"Yes?" he asked, not hiding his displeasure with the interruption. "What do you need, Alice? I've got a lot of work to do."

"Right, sorry to intrude. I made a plate for you. I thought you might be hungry."

"Thanks," he said without looking at me. "You can leave it on my desk. I'll get to it when I can."

"It will be better hot," I replied. "It's meatloaf, but I made it with ground turkey."

"Turkey loaf?" He eyed the plate. "Sounds enticing. My mouth is watering."

"I've just been thinking of making some healthy changes. We're not getting any younger, you know. And there's your blood pressure to consider."

He reached across his desk and palmed the mirror dusted with white powder, tucking it into a desk drawer. "Mm-hmm," he murmured.

"I've got your pill organizer too." I placed the plate on his desk, steam still rising from the mound of mashed potatoes, and retrieved the multicolored plastic container from under my arm, shaking it. "There are a couple of new ones in here. I read an article about fish oil. It has a lot of health benefits. It's good for the heart, cardiovascular—" I made a move to sit in the chair across from his desk, but bounced back up when he spoke.

"Right, right. Thanks for thinking of my ticker, but I really need to get back to this."

"Of course, sorry to interrupt. It's just with the death of Mr. Ellington, you know, it got me thinking. It's never too soon to take better care of ourselves."

"Well, I dare say the late Mr. Ellington had at least twenty years on us, but yeah, an ounce of prevention and all." He peered at me over his glasses, an expectant look on his face. I realized his only expectation was that I leave.

"Okay, then, have a good night. I'll see you in the morning." I moved to the door. I opened it, and as I exited, I paused and leaned back in. "Oh, I also got rid of the half-and-half. It's laden with cholesterol. I got a non-dairy version instead."

"Sure, sure. Can't wait to try it."

"It's powdered. It's sitting by the coffeepot."

"Powdered? Sounds decadent."

"Don't knock it till you try it," I said, coercing a strained chuckle. "Some say you can't tell the difference. Well, maybe you'll drop a pants size, but aside from that, you probably won't miss it."

"Good night, Alice," he replied, dismissing me.

NINETEEN

WASHING

An ill wind whispered me awake the next morning. It lifted the gossamer curtains in a dance that swayed in rhythm with a nearby wind chime. I opened my eyes to shadows of the elm outside my window dancing across my face. A chill caressed my shoulders as I rose and the blankets fell. The window was still open. Roger would have closed it if he had come to bed last night. He'd slept in his office again. I reached for the window sash and pulled it down, driving out the cold of the early spring morning.

A bird shot from the tree and smashed into the window. I flinched and gasped as the tiny creature's battered body slid to the ledge, where it lay twitching. I snapped the curtains closed. A scream shattered the morning, hitting me with another shockwave. It was not the death cries of a flailing bird, but the shriek of a woman. A resounding wail, so loud the closed window provided no buffer.

I yanked the drapes open and surveyed the area. Bud sat lapping something up on the front walk. He greedily devoured the mess, ignoring the bird that lay dying only feet away. Another scream reached my ears. The ghastly peal did not dissuade Bud from the feast he'd discovered.

"Someone call nine-one-one!" a woman yelled. I heard her voice before I saw her. She repeated her pleas as she ran up my front walk. I didn't recognize the woman who was dressed for a morning jog. Bud hissed at her but wasn't willing to abandon the milky puddle.

I snatched my robe and threw it on as I ran down the hall. Lauren exited her room, rubbing her eyes.

"What's happening?" she grumbled.

Lauren fell behind me as I rushed past. Unaware of how close she was, I threw the door open, and it hit her in the head, knocking her back but graciously blocking her view. Before my mind could comprehend what I saw out front, I knew it was nothing she should witness. It was a scene familiar to me, but instead of my father laid out on his bedroom floor in his pajamas, it was my husband splayed on the front walk in a business suit. His tie was knotted around his neck, and a coordinating pocket square tucked smartly in the chest pocket waved in the breeze. His travel mug, though still loosely held in his hand, lay on the ground, and milky liquid seeped into the brick pavers around him. Roger always took more creamer than coffee in his morning cup. A frothy stream of spittle leaked from his mouth, converging with the creamy pale puddle. I clapped at Bud, shooing him away, and he retreated into the bushes.

"Go back to your bedroom and stay there!" I yelled to Lauren, hoping with everything in me that the last time she would see her father was last night and this image of him would never pollute her mind. She rubbed her forehead as she dissolved into tears. But she did as I asked, and her door slammed shut moments after she fled.

The woman skidded to her knees and began loosening Roger's tie. His briefcase had come open; a swirl of loose papers skittered across the lawn. She balled her hands together and pounded Roger's chest. His coffee cup rolled from his fingertips.

"Did you call nine-one-one?" the woman yelled at me, still pumping her fists on Roger's chest. "I don't have my phone with me."

I ran back inside the house and grabbed the phone, punching

the keys. My memory dulled the moment the dispatcher asked, "What's your emergency?"

The next several hours were a blur. If my life depended on it, I'd be hard-pressed to retell the events with any sense of clarity or detail. There was an ambulance, a trip to the hospital, Lauren's confused cries. Jennings drove us home. I arrived back at our house with my purse and a white plastic bag plastered with the words *Patient Belongings*. Inside were Roger's shoes and wallet, his belt, and his wedding ring. The suit he'd been wearing when he left for work had been cut from his body.

I remembered sitting alone in a small room down a quiet hallway at the hospital, clutching the bag to my chest until a doctor arrived and told me every effort to save Roger's life had been unsuccessful. He surmised Roger suffered a stroke and offered little else to help me process what he was saying. His words sounded muffled as I struggled to hear them above the ringing in my ears. The conversation seemed far away. It was impossible it had occurred only hours before.

I asked about an autopsy. The doctor replied with words like *Type-A personality, age, smoking*. I considered bringing up his cocaine usage as a possible contributing factor, but decided it wasn't necessary. I didn't want Lauren to ever have to know certain things about her father. When I pressed for a direct answer, the doctor assured me an autopsy wouldn't be called for, given the circumstances. I knew I had that card to play should there be any questions.

"Here, Mrs. White, let me take that," Jennings said, tugging gently on the white bag as we stood in the foyer of our home. I released it, and he put it on the entry table. His arm never left Lauren's shoulder. She clung to him as if he were a life preserver she seized as she battled an invisible sea, a torrent of unseen waves battering her, attempting to pry him free from her grasp.

The space felt different. As if the house knew an enormous shift had occurred. I sat on the couch, still unsure of what my next move would be. Unsure of what had happened since I'd awakened to an open window earlier that very day. Years seemed to have passed during those hours. We woke as one thing and ended the day as something completely foreign.

I looked up to see Jennings and Lauren sitting across from me. Her head rested on his shoulder. Her hair obscured her face. She was crying, but her sobs were almost imperceptible. I had yet to shed a tear. As I watched Jennings comfort Lauren, I wondered if I'd ever cry for my husband. The thought stirred nothing in me. No emotion sprang forth except relief.

"You both must be hungry. I could go pick up some food," Jennings offered.

If Lauren replied, I did not hear her. But the mention of food awakened a ravenous hunger in me. I'd not eaten anything all day, and now the sun hung low in the sky.

"I can make something for us to eat," I replied, not comprehending what that entailed, but rising from sheer convention. My mind scanned items on hand, already developing a dinner plan as I moved toward the kitchen.

"Oh, no, Mrs. White! You've had such a long day. I'd be happy to go pick something up." Jennings tried to stand, but Lauren held him down. He pressed his head to hers and whispered something I could not hear. Whatever it was, she allowed him to rise. He placed a soft kiss on an odd bruise on her forehead and rushed to my side. Offering his hand, he guided me back to the couch.

"I'll be back before you know it. Maybe you want to go wash up while I'm gone, Laur?"

She was still wearing the flannel pajama bottoms and T-shirt she'd worn to bed the night before. Shadows hung below her eyes. A blemish stood out on her chin. She didn't rise, but leaned into the warmth Jennings had left behind, curling herself into a ball.

"I'll be back soon," he said, closing the door behind him.

Bud and Kane paced on the back porch, their dark forms shadow-like in the fading sun. They hadn't eaten all day either. I went to the sliding door and opened it wide. The cats were hesitant to cross the threshold into an unknown world. I left the door open and went to the kitchen pantry where I got a can of tuna and ran it through the electric opener.

Back in the living room, Lauren had fallen asleep on the couch while Bud and Kane still circled just beyond the open door. I tapped the can, and the cats froze. Crouching down in front of them but still inside the house, I waved the can in their direction, enticing them with scent. They paid no further heed to the potential for danger and rushed inside, circling my feet, threatening to trip me as I guided them to the kitchen. There, I placed the can on the floor. Kane attacked the food, but Bud lay down on the banquette seat and fell asleep. I walked back to the patio door, closed it, and left Lauren asleep in the living room as I went about setting up a litter box for our new house cats.

I finished the chore and showed the new box to Bud and Kane. Bud convulsed as if coughing up a hairball. He choked up a mess that I refused to look at while I wiped it away with a paper towel. I'd just put the disinfecting spray back in the cabinet when I heard a knock on the door. Lauren sat up, rubbing her eyes. I rushed to the door. It was Jennings. Following him up the walk was his mother.

"Oh, you poor dear," Nancy exclaimed, rushing toward me, arms outstretched. I considered closing the door, but Jennings was already skirting past me, his arms laden with fast-food bags and a drink carrier.

Nancy grabbed me in an embrace. Her perfume turned my stomach, but as soon as she released me, the aroma of the food drew me in.

"I'm so sorry I wasn't here sooner. I took a drive up to our lake house. We don't get good reception up there. I came as soon as Jennings reached me," she said as she removed her jacket.

"It's really not necessary," I began, but stopped when the smell of the food pulled me away from Nancy. Jennings was removing items from the bags and placing them on the coffee table. I sat across from him in Roger's recliner, mouth watering, waiting for him to hand a burger over.

Nancy entered the room and hurried to Lauren's side. Lauren stood and collapsed into Nancy's arms. She stroked Lauren's hair.

"There now, you poor sweet girl," Nancy murmured.

I took a bite of my burger, and before I finished chewing, I said, "You should eat now, Lauren, while the food is still hot."

"I couldn't," she replied as Nancy released her from the embrace.

"Your mother is right. You need to keep your strength up," Nancy said. She unwrapped a burger and passed it to Lauren. Lauren took the food and nibbled on the bun.

Nancy busied herself doling out napkins and ketchup packets to Lauren and Jennings, and we ate in silence. As soon as we finished, Nancy swooped in to clean up the mess. Exhaustion overwhelmed me. I wanted to tuck Lauren into bed and get out of the clothes that were steeped in hospital germs. A hot shower, a clean nightgown, and curling up under the blankets were all I could think of. It was difficult to maintain a sense of courtesy in the face of such an alluring prospect.

"I can't help but think of the … irony? Coincidence? I don't know which words suit this horrible situation best. Both of us losing our husbands so close together. It isn't fair." Nancy spoke over her shoulder as she moved to the kitchen to discard the fast-food trash.

Jennings spoke up. "She's right. Both of us losing our fathers back-to-back."

"Opening night is in two weeks," Lauren said. "Will we be able to pull it off? I don't think I can." She crumpled into him again as sobs overtook her.

"Neither of you should worry yourselves with such a thing right now," Nancy said as she came back into the living room. "Alice, which funeral home did you send him to? I hope you used Fitzgerald's for the service. They did a wonderful job with my Edward. Very compassionate and detail-oriented. I wouldn't trust anyone else with my loved one's remains."

Loved one's remains. I pondered the words. They sounded so genteel, yet inappropriate, especially from someone who had carnal knowledge of the person she spoke of. She was looking at me expectantly, forcing me to speak.

"I hadn't really… I mean, I'm not sure," I stammered. "I was considering cremation." I regretted the words as soon as they left my lips and I saw how they impacted Lauren.

Lauren looked up, a look of horror taking over her face. It was just like Nancy to make things worse than they already were, asking me questions I didn't know how to answer, prying into our time of grief.

"Well, I don't know about that," Nancy said, with an expression on her face saying she not only disapproved, but I was barbaric for considering cremation. "But I also don't expect you to have thought it through so soon. It's a shock to the system. There will be plenty of time tomorrow to start planning a service. I'll be at your beck and call; it's all so horribly fresh to me still." She pulled a tissue from the box sitting on the side table, blew her nose, and dabbed her eyes.

I yawned loudly. Too loudly.

"Where are my manners? Can I get you anything else? A cup of tea, perhaps?" Nancy didn't wait for my reply. She was already in the kitchen. I heard the clatter of the kettle and slamming cabinets.

"You must be tired too, Lauren," I suggested, hoping Jennings could take a hint better than his mother.

"So tired," she replied, her voice dreamlike, distant.

"I'll help you," Jennings offered, standing and holding his hand out to Lauren. She took his hand and curled into him as they moved toward her room. I should have protested, but I didn't want her to be alone. I should have been the one she leaned on. Why could none of them read my cues?

In the kitchen, the kettle whistled. I sat by myself, listening to Nancy take over my kitchen, wishing I could just be alone. Within minutes, Nancy swept into the room and set a cup and saucer in front of me, steam still rising from the tea. She moved to the entry, retrieved her purse, and approached with her flask in hand. I didn't stop her from adding a splash to my cup. She took a draw straight from the flask before recapping it and handing me the mug.

"This will help," she said.

I blew on the hot liquid. The whiskey burned my nostrils. I tested the drink. The heat was comforting, and I felt my muscles relax as the elixir ran down my throat.

"Please tell me," Nancy said, moving close to me, her voice barely a whisper. "This didn't happen after you told him the news, did it?"

I stared at her blankly.

"You know, Dr. Addison, the potential that Lauren isn't his. When will you have the test results?"

"No, of course not," I hissed.

"Of course not what?" she asked.

"I didn't tell Roger, and I have said nothing to Lauren yet."

"What?"

"Keep it down! This is not the time."

"But I gave you the test last week. You haven't even swabbed her? Told her why?"

"No, I haven't. It's a lot to process, and now this. It's going to have to wait. She can't lose her father one day and then cop to a paternity test the next. Have some compassion."

"Compassion? This has nothing to do with compassion! Hell, they could be doing…" She dropped her voice again. "Doing 'it' as we speak!"

"Don't be vile!" I snapped. "Is that all you ever think about?" My heart thrummed loudly in my ears, resounding and amplifying the pressure I felt. Part of me wanted to run down the hall and throw Lauren's bedroom door open. I'd be damned if my daughter used my shock as a means to get away with the unthinkable. A bigger part of me wanted to hurl Nancy's coat and purse onto the front lawn and kick her out of my home. I imagined slamming the door on her and her son. Instead, I finished the remaining tea, the whiskey now burning my throat more than the heat of the drink.

Jennings rescued me from his mother.

"She fell asleep before I could even get her shoes off," he said, joining us in the living room. "I'm pretty beat too. I'm sure you are as well, Mrs. White. We should give them some space, Mom."

"Yes, of course, you need your sleep, Alice," Nancy cooed. She leaned in to hug me and added another splash of whiskey to my teacup. "This should help," she whispered.

"We'll let ourselves out, Mrs. White. I'm so sorry," Jennings said from the entryway after helping his mother into her jacket. He reached back inside and turned the lock on the front door before closing it behind him.

I downed the whiskey in one gulp and left the cup on the coffee table. As I rose, I called for Bud and Kane, and the two followed me down the hall. They were curled up together, sleeping soundly on the unmade bed when I stepped out of the shower. Despite bone-aching exhaustion, I couldn't bring myself to retire. Instead, I went to Lauren's room and quietly cracked open the door. I stood at the threshold and listened to her sleep, losing all track of time. Her slumber was peaceful; she barely moved. Listening to her steady breath gave me solace. All would be well. We would weather this storm together and come out stronger in the end.

Feeling calmer than I had in weeks, I closed her door and climbed into bed. Sleep took over faster than I expected.

Kane woke me some hours later while the sky was still dark. The cat pawed at my face and kneaded my hair, yowling loudly. I rolled over, and my foot caught on something. As I sat up, I saw it was Bud. I prodded him gently with my toes, but the cat didn't stir. His body was lifeless. I reached out to him, hoping to coax him from his sleep. He was cold, stiff.

"No, no, no," I cried, startling Kane. She jumped down from the bed and fled the room. I sat on the bed with my dead cat, one who had only known the warmth of a home on his last night, a night when he should have slept in safety and peace, out of the grasp of predators. I stroked his matted fur while I sobbed.

"I'm so sorry," I whispered as I wrapped Bud in a sheet. Anger at myself boiled within me; regret tempered the rage. I buried Bud in the backyard before calling the funeral home to make arrangements for Roger's service. While I didn't relish either task and wanted to curl up with Kane and mourn the loss of her kin and my companion, there was too much work left to do. At least now I had something to cry about. It had been so hard for me to feign tears.

TWENTY

MORPHOLOGY

I convinced Nancy to keep her mouth shut until we'd buried Roger. The days passed quietly. Lauren kept to herself much of the time, but she stayed at home, which brought me comfort. Jennings was a fixture in our house. He stayed glued to Lauren's side but made himself available to me as well, accepting flower and food deliveries, running errands, and screening phone calls. His demeanor impressed me. For someone so young, he possessed innate abilities to manage crises, instill calm, and find ways to help. Most likely, those life skills could be attributed to a nanny who barely made enough money tending to him to provide for her own family.

The service was on Friday, and by the following Monday, Lauren was ready to go back to school. I'd hoped she would take more time off, but she believed a return to routine would help and was adamant the performance would take place as scheduled.

"Mom, I'm fine. I can't just mope around the house indefinite-ly," she argued. "Graduation is closing in on me, prom is almost here, and, most importantly, the show is days away."

"People will understand, Lauren," I said. Having her at home with me had been an unexpected perk, and I soaked her presence in. The lazy days when no one expected anything from either of us were a godsend.

I'd started a conversation with the school about allowing her to graduate early and end the school year now, so she wouldn't struggle. She was an exemplary student and had a solid GPA. I was certain they'd make an exception so close to graduation. I was expecting a return phone call from the school principal. If I could convince her to stay home today, maybe she'd never have to go back. Her acceptance at TU was already secured. One round of finals and a few more weeks of school wouldn't be necessary.

"I'm sure they'll understand, Mom," she replied. "But I'm doing this for myself. I don't want to shirk my responsibilities. Throwing an endless pity party for myself isn't fair to the cast."

As I walked her to the door, Jennings arrived, concern and apprehension etched on his face.

"Are you sure you're ready for this, Laur?" He took her backpack from her. "Everyone will understand if it's too soon. Mr. Spencer said we could postpone the show."

"I'm tired of lying around the house. I need to get back on the stage," she replied, turning to hug me. "Maybe you should go to Coventry Springs today, Mom. Get your mind off things as well."

"That's a great idea, sweetie," I said, holding her embrace longer than necessary. "If it gets to be too much for you, I'm happy to call the attendance office."

"Won't be necessary," she said, releasing herself from my arms. "Let's do this," she said to Jennings.

I watched them drive away. When they'd left my sight, I closed the door and went to Roger's office. My classes started the following week, which meant I needed to transform the room into my own space by then. His secretary had already come by and taken items pertinent to his clientele and the agency. As I began purging what remained, the phone rang. I ran to the kitchen to answer it.

"Did she do it? Go to school?" Nancy asked. She didn't wait for me to say hello.

"Yes, yes, she did."

"She's a strong young woman. You've done well. However, I

must tell you, it's harder without a father figure around. Jennings tries to hide his pain, to be strong for me and for Lauren, but he's different. I hate that they are both suffering. How are you holding up?"

I wasn't sure how to respond. I believed I was handling things well. Roger's life insurance would carry us well past the time by which I hoped to be earning my own income. Lauren's college expenses were covered, and the mortgage was paid in full. I'd already scheduled a contractor to start refreshing the house a bit. I was still devastated at the loss of Bud, but I wouldn't speak of that with Nancy.

"Oh, I'm holding up, I suppose," was all I could offer.

"Listen, with all the turmoil of the past few weeks, I still haven't told Jennings about his paternity, and now I'm thinking perhaps we could tell them together. Sit them down this evening and break the news to them. Maybe it will be easier to take if they aren't alone."

"That's absurd!"

"Absurd? Why? They are very close. This impacts all of us."

"I think we should wait until after the show run. Neither of them needs another blow of this magnitude before they go onstage. It would just be cruel." And prom wasn't for two weeks after the close of the show. I had time.

"I hadn't thought of the show. I guess you're right; another week won't hurt," Nancy said, drawing the words out as if trying to convince herself. "But after that, I can't put it off any longer. It's getting harder to see them together with all this fear over my head. Each day we wait, they grow closer. Each day we wait will amplify the pain. They've both been through so much. I'm so worried about them."

"I understand your concerns," I said, softening my tone to keep her on the same page with me. "Lauren is holding up very well under the circumstances." I wanted to tell her not to worry about my child, but I played along. "I'll consider your suggestion, but I'm not so sure telling them together is the right way to go. The day after closing night, I'll tell Lauren and swab her. You are free to proceed with Jennings as you like, but you have to let me handle things with my daughter in my own way."

"Yes, yes, I know. In your own time. You've made it very clear," she said. Her tone was one of a harried mother speaking to a toddler. Before my anger had a chance to simmer, she made an abrupt shift. "Have you heard the latest?"

"Probably not," I said, forcing an air of indifference into my tone.

"You remember Monica Gilbert, right? Her twins and Jennings grew up together. I used to joke that Jennings was their triplet. They were so close, like brothers." She paused for dramatic effect, but I could see where the story was going. I remained silent.

"Turns out," she said, stretching the words. "They are brothers! Monica just got her test results. The poor woman is beside herself. They were like you and Roger. Her husband was chock-full of healthy swimmers, and still the barbarian had his way with her. I haven't seen the Gilbert twins in days. Apparently, the shock has been overwhelming for them all."

"That's horrible," I replied, now attempting to force concern into my voice.

"It is! Those poor boys. The three of them have been like family their whole lives, and now to find out they are. Truly unbelievable. But this highlights the importance of not putting this off. Maybe they can all support each other, even Lauren and Jennings. Hell, maybe especially those two."

"Enough, Nancy. We don't know anything yet. Just because poor Monica was abused by Dr. Addison doesn't mean I was."

"Well, we can't sit around and hope for the best any longer."

"One more week, Nancy. Give the kids a chance to catch their breath."

She was quiet for a moment but agreed to wait. I ended the call with her and returned to my new office, where I gathered several full bags of trash. I boxed Roger's plaques and awards. The ones I'd dutifully hung on the walls throughout his career. It had been an act I'd hoped would show my pride in his work in our early years. He never seemed to notice, turning the loving act into a chore I forced upon myself. Rather than remove the nails from the walls, I retrieved Maisy's solander box and decorated the space with her needlepoint art. Afterward, I took down the heavy curtains and opened the blinds; light flooded the room. While it'd take some airing out to free the space of lingering cigar smoke, it didn't look anything like the office where Roger chose to spend his time hiding from us.

There was only one more task to take care of. One thing that would purge Roger from the room once and for all. I'd found his stash before his secretary arrived and tucked it into my keepsake box. Surprisingly, I'd found no proof of his infidelities; no receipts or notes divulging any untoward relationships. Like Lauren, he was good at hiding things. With Roger in the ground, no questions being raised about his cause of death, it was time to get rid of my safety net. I pulled the baggie from the box and dumped it into the toilet, flushing multiple times to make sure the powdery substance was completely washed away. I wadded the baggie inside a ball of toilet paper and went to the kitchen, tucking it deeply within the garbage can. With those chores complete, I returned to my office.

I sat at the computer and booted it up, determined to learn a bit more about how to use the machine before classes started. Kane nosed the door open and crept in. I got up and moved to the best spot in the room, enticing her to roost in the window seat. The doorbell rang. The cat trailed behind as I went to the entryway.

"I'll need you to sign for this one, Mrs. White," the mail carrier said, pushing a clipboard in my direction. A green index card was clamped to it, and a pen attached by twine. I scrawled my signature with shaky hands, noting the letter was from the DNA lab. I handed the clipboard back and closed the door as the postal worker thanked me and wished me a good day.

Turning the envelope over in my hands, I was reluctant to open it. My reaction was foolish. I had no reason to doubt the results were what I needed. There couldn't possibly be any question about Shelby's paternity. I'd never considered any alternative but proof that Dr. Addison was Shelby's father, but as I moved down the hall, the small package grew heavy in my hands. What if Dr. Addison's wife took her own secrets to the grave? My carefully devised plan would unravel should the test results show Dr. Addison was not the father. All my efforts would be for naught.

I sat at the desk and pulled the letter opener from the drawer. My hands shook as I slid the blade through the thick paper. I extracted the letter from the envelope and clamped my eyes shut while I unfolded it. I pressed it onto the desk and smoothed the creases. I sat for a moment, eyes closed, hands caressing the cool paper as if I could impart the desired results onto the page by pure will.

With a gulping breath, I opened my eyes, tossed the cover page aside, and scanned the document. Four columns comprised the majority of the page. The first contained a list of letters and numbers that were seemingly random and made no sense to me. The second column was blank; its header said 'Mother, Not Tested.' The word 'Child' topped the third column and was followed by more meaningless numbers. 'Alleged Father' hovered over the fourth column, with similarly patterned numbers listed.

At the bottom of the page, all the ambiguous statistics and odd labels were deciphered with the phrase, "The alleged father cannot be excluded as the biological father of the tested child. Based on the analysis of STR loci listed above, the probability of paternity is 99.999999%."

My shoulders relaxed, and I exhaled so heavily my breath shook the paper. Mrs. Addison had been true to her husband, at least when it came to the conception of Shelby. I now had what I needed to dissolve the relationship between my daughter and Jennings, and more importantly, to eradicate Nancy from my life forever.

Of everything I'd done to execute my plan, the worst was yet to come. I hated the thought of breaking Lauren's heart. She was still reeling from the loss of the man she'd always known as her father. Now I was forced to shatter her again by breaking her away from the young man she believed was her future. I'd played out the scene in my head countless times. There was no denying Lauren would have her doubts. I took the proof I needed to discount those uncertainties and returned to my keepsake trunk, placing it inside.

Closing the trunk, I pushed it deep under the bed before returning to the office to familiarize myself with the computer.

A short time later, the front door slammed with a heft that shook the windows. I glanced up from the computer screen when Lauren's voice boomed through the house.

"Mom!"

There was fire in the word.

I rose on shaky legs, fearing school had proved to be too much for her. Lauren blew past the office. She'd not see the work I'd been doing to dismantle her father's den. There was no reason for her to search for me there. I opened the office door in time to see the blur of her body flash by. She didn't see me as she'd already passed. With heavy feet, she tore further down the hall and threw my bedroom door open without knocking. Shock pushed me into the hallway, and I ran to her as she entered my room.

"Mom?" she yelled. "Where are—" She turned, and we collided.

"Lauren!"

She backed away. Her face was on fire, her eyes filled with sparks.

"How dare you?" she said, her voice simmering.

"What are you talking about?"

"I got called into Principal Stone's office today," she began, dropping her shoulders and closing her eyes. She flicked her hands in an effort to shake off the storm. "You asked him to release me without finishing my year? What is wrong with you?"

"Honey, I—"

"You had no right!" she screamed, unable to temper her anger. "Why would you do something so whack? Like I'm some fragile little flower who can't deal with life's blows."

"No, Lauren," I pleaded, blindsided by her fury. "I didn't mean—"

"Didn't mean what? To think you could control my life? God, Mom! I can't believe you'd do something so weird and completely off base!"

"Sweetie," I whimpered, approaching her with tears pooling in my eyes. I knew she might be angered by the request I'd made to the school's leader, but I never expected her to be this upset. I'd only done it out of care.

"No," she said, the temperature of her voice lowering. "You can't just make decisions about my life, my future, without talking to me. Leaving school early was never even on my radar. I'm busted up about losing Dad, trust me. But I don't think he'd want me to throw the last days of my education out the window. He'd want me to experience all the things I've looked forward to for so long. So I told Mr. Stone I wouldn't be leaving school. You need to accept it. And don't ever lie to me again."

"I didn't lie," I said.

"Really, Mom." Her words were so cold I expected them to dissipate in a puff of vapor. "Semantics? Omission is a lie. Lying is a lie. Whatever you want to call it, I won't stand for it! No more lies! And stop trying to control my life! I'm eighteen now. If you keep treating me like this, you'll leave me no choice but to walk away. It has to stop!"

She pushed past me and left me standing alone in my bedroom. A chill remained.

———

The crowd, which had been enthralled from the moment the curtain rose, erupted into a standing ovation. The spotlight landed on Lauren and Jennings as the two held hands and bowed. He drew her in for an embrace before the light shifted to land on the performance's two special guests. Nancy and I sat in the front row, side by side in the spotlight's glare. It had been the director's idea.

I ducked my head and shielded my eyes from the beam while Nancy stood and turned to the audience. The playbill held a tribute to the stars' recently deceased fathers, alerting attendees to the tragedies. Some well-meaning cast members dedicated the show to Nancy and me, the widows.

The director presented us each with bouquets as the crowd extended its standing ovation for us. I hated every moment of the attention, but Nancy shone, clutching her kerchief as she waved to the crowd. She bowed and whispered words of gratitude with a hand held to her heart. She closed her moment by embracing me. I suffered through, wanting to shrug the woman off. This night was about Lauren and Jennings. The two displayed tremendous resilience in the face of misfortune. All Nancy and I had done was bury our husbands.

Lauren had broken her silent-treatment punishment the day before to inform me of the upcoming fuss, forcing me to scramble for a new dress. She'd said she forgave me but hit me with the accusations of lying to her again. I still didn't believe I had lied. Not about that anyway. I firmly believed that ending the school year for her was in her best interest, but also knew she'd forbid me to do so if I'd discussed it with her first. She didn't understand sometimes lies are for the best. I was just grateful to be back in her good graces, so I bit my tongue.

Lauren moved to the front of the stage and clapped, tears streaming down her face. She mouthed the words, "I love you." I wasn't sure, but it appeared the words were directed at Nancy and not me. I shook off the envy and focused on making the night memorable for Lauren.

The four of us went to dinner after the performance. Despite the sense of loss hanging over the evening, Lauren and Jennings kept the conversation light.

"I almost flipped when Becky forgot her lines," Lauren said.

"Right!" Jennings exclaimed. "She's never missed a cue. I thought she was going to call, 'Line!' right there on stage."

"I'd have died!"

"The two of you were mesmerizing!" Nancy gushed. "I can see your names in Broadway lights already!"

"Stop it, Mrs. E! You're making me blush," Lauren replied. She brought the napkin up to wipe her mouth but buried her face in it.

"Nonsense! The talent you two have is rare. You share a gift. It's almost as if…"

I wasn't sure what Nancy intended to say, but I made a move to kick her under the table. Her shin was spared by the arrival of the dessert cart.

"Ooh, those all look amazing! One of each!" Nancy told the waitress. "We can share them!"

While I didn't relish the idea of sharing anything more with Nancy, I was grateful for the well-timed interruption.

Jennings dropped us off later that night, walking us to the door. Reluctantly, I excused myself and left them on the front porch. I saw little harm in letting the two have one last romantic moment.

I checked the cat bowls and retired to my room. After changing into my pajamas, I pulled the box out from under my bed and removed the items I'd collected to administer Lauren's DNA test, laying them out neatly on my dresser. As I climbed into bed, I heard Lauren shut and lock the front door. Kane curled up on Roger's pillow, and I drifted off to sleep.

QUALITATIVE

The following morning I let Lauren sleep in. It had long been her habit to do so the day after closing night. I busied myself in the kitchen making her favorite breakfast. Kane stayed close by, ready to clean up anything I might spill. She'd taken to the life of an indoor cat quickly. When I heard Lauren stir, I poured the batter into the waffle iron and whisked the eggs.

She entered the kitchen, yawning and stretching, still in her pajamas.

"It smells so good in here. I'm starving." She bent down to pet Kane as she wound between her legs. "Cheesy eggs and waffles?"

"Of course, cheesy eggs and waffles, plus bacon. Have a seat."

"Coffee first," she said, pouring a cup and taking it to the nook table.

I put a plate in front of her. She held her fork over the plate, waiting for me to shred cheese over the eggs and top them with green onions. Kane jumped up in the seat next to her, the cat's nose twitching close to the plate of bacon. I shooed her down and sat with Lauren, watching her eat, rehearsing the words I planned to use to break the news to her.

She devoured a waffle, two strips of bacon, and a mound of eggs, washing it down with coffee.

"That was bomb," she said, pushing her plate away.

"I'm glad you liked it. I figured you'd be ravenous. There was so much dancing in this show."

"Yeah, there was. I'll have to watch what I eat now that I don't have rehearsals to burn calories. Prom and all."

"Don't be silly. You're waif-thin. You don't have to worry about calories."

"If you say so," she replied, rising to take her dishes to the sink.

"Don't worry about those. I'll get them later. I have something I need to talk to you about."

She sank back down in the banquette seat and took another sip of coffee.

"Is it about Dad? We really haven't talked much about him." She swiped at a tear that slid from her eye.

"Oh no, we don't have to talk about him. I mean we can, but first I have to tell you something."

"It still doesn't seem real, you know? Like I expect to run into him in the hallway when I leave my room. I actually miss hearing him typing as I fall asleep. It used to bug me, but now—" Her words drifted off and her gaze fell on the garden outside.

I wasn't sure how to reply and didn't want to veer off course, so I changed the subject.

"Have you spoken to Jennings this morning?" I asked casually as I took her plate to the sink and started rinsing it. Nancy probably waited outside the boy's bedroom door to break the news to him now that there were no more roadblocks keeping her from doing so.

"No, he won't call until he knows I'm awake. For a guy, he totally gets the need for beauty sleep." Her words were wrapped in admiration, her feelings for the boy laid bare in the quality of her voice.

I turned to see the smile on her face and paused. Grief ripped through me, knocking the air out of my lungs and forcing me to brace myself against the sink. Doubt flickered in the recesses of my mind, but I suffocated its spark and pushed forward, abandoning the dishes and joining her at the table. I took her hands in mine, inhaled deeply, closed my eyes, and began.

"There are things your father and I never told you about, Lauren. About your conception."

"Ew, seriously? I just ate." I sensed she felt the weight of my words somewhere inside her and wanted to lighten the mood.

I chuckled softly and tucked a piece of hair behind her ear.

"You see, I struggled to get pregnant. Struggled for years before I learned I was pregnant with you."

"Oh wow. That's pretty heavy stuff." She pulled her hand away from mine and slumped back on the bench, her eyes darting around the room as if she were looking for the right reply. "How come you never told me before now?"

"I'm not sure. It just didn't seem important. I mean, we were over the moon when we finally got pregnant, and we never looked back."

"So you're saying you got pregnant? You're not springing some 'you're adopted' plot twist on me here, right? Lizzie's parents did that to her, you know? Just told her one day right before her sixteenth birthday. She was shocked. Never dreamed she wasn't related to her parents. Seems like she should have known. Her parents are both redheads, and she has jet black hair, but whatever."

"No, you aren't adopted. I did get pregnant, but I required…" I faltered, unsure of what to say next. Now that I'd finally broached the subject, the countless hours of rehearsing what I might say eluded me, gone in a puff of anxiety. I'd managed to get through the first sentence, which I'd carefully crafted to make sure I wouldn't be painted as the sole deceiver. But I still feared she would shut me down with accusations of lying, forcing me to focus on extracting sympathy from her to replace the condemnation.

"Spit it out, Mom. Now I know I'm yours, and as long as you spare me any closed-door secrets about you and Dad's love life, I think I'm good. Did you do any fertility treatments? It's nothing to keep hidden. Did you know Mrs. E used a sperm donor? Jennings has always known he wasn't biologically his dad's kid. It's not that big a deal. Honestly, I think I'm more upset about you keeping it from me than anything else."

I ignored the Jennings' comment and tried to redirect.

"Yes, your father and I relied on fertility treatment. We saw the same doctor Nancy used, but we didn't use a donor."

"Whew! That didn't really hit me as a possibility until I mentioned Jennings being a donor baby. So we've established fertility treatment, no big whoop. No donor, kind of a big whoop, but not in my case. So what's the big deal? I'm a test-tube baby? Kind of cool, actually. Except for the shrouded in secrecy part."

"Well, that's just it. Recently, some things have come to light. Their implications are, well, shocking, unbelievable, heinous—you pick a word." I hoped I was edging my words with enough pity she wouldn't focus on the omission.

Lauren straightened from her slouched position. Down the hall her phone rang. She ignored it.

"Heinous? Sounds ominous. You're kind of scaring me." She took my hand now and began toying with my wedding ring.

"It turns out Dr. Addison employed some less-than-ethical methods in his efforts to help his patients become pregnant."

"Unethical methods? What are you saying?" Her grip on my hand tightened. Deep inside the house, her phone chimed again. Again, she ignored it.

"It seems Dr. Addison took liberties with his donor samples."

"Liberties? You're not making sense. Just spit it out. Are you crying?"

I hadn't noticed my own tears. I swiped at them, brushing them away while not understanding where they'd come from. The conversation put me back on that paper-covered table, my feet in stirrups, the aura of the light blinding me as my pelvis pulsed with stinging pain.

"He was deceptive in his practices. He used his own..." I hesitated again, not wanting to delve into the repugnant details, but there was no way around it. I couldn't force my eyes to meet hers and slid my hand from her grasp, rising to pace the kitchen. The kit I'd improvised from the supply closet at Coventry Springs leered at me from the spot on the kitchen counter where I'd placed it this morning.

"Used his own what?" she asked, attempting to piece together the meaning of the words I couldn't bring myself to say. "Oh, wait. No way!" Now Lauren was on her feet, moving toward me. She took my hand again. "Please don't say he used his own semen."

Hearing the word from my daughter's lips was like a slap to the face. We'd never discussed sex. Roger insisted she'd learn everything she needed to know in school. I'd willingly accepted his opinion, as it spared me the uncomfortable conversation.

"Mom, is that what you're saying? He used his own sperm to impregnate his patients? What a sicko!"

We stood in silence for some time. I could see her mind turning over the revelation, trying to make sense of what it meant to her. To me.

"Wait," she said, her eyes widening. "Are you saying Jennings is…?"

She paced now, gnawing on her lip.

"Yes, it turns out Jennings is the offspring of Dr. Addison. He didn't use the donor sample Nancy thought she was getting."

"Oh my God! Poor Mrs. E! Poor Jennings! Why didn't he tell me? I need to call him." She moved to leave the kitchen, but I stopped her by grabbing her arm.

"He didn't tell you because he doesn't know."

Her phone rang in her room. Her eyes darted toward the sound. She tried to extract herself from my grip. I held firm.

"That's probably him." The phone went silent. "Wait. He doesn't know? Why are you telling me if he doesn't know?"

"Nancy has been trying to find the right time. She only learned about it herself right before her husband fell ill. Then, when he passed, she couldn't bring herself to break the news to poor Jennings."

"Oh, wow," she said, sinking onto the breakfast bench again. She tucked her legs underneath her. "That's what the test was about. She totally faked him out."

"What do you mean?"

"She gave him a test like weeks ago. With everything that happened, I forgot all about it. I bet Jennings did too. Man, this is so uncool." She ran her fingers through her hair, and I saw the thoughts churning in her mind.

"What are you talking about? What test?" She had details I now realized could be beneficial to me. I focused my energy on the question to block out the distress of knowing my daughter had never said anything to me about it.

"Well, we didn't know what it meant at the time. Mrs. E said it was some family tree thing she was doing. She made him swab his cheek, but then she totally brushed it off. Acted like it was no big deal."

I retrieved my own testing materials from the counter. Lauren tracked my movements from her seat at the table. Her eyes fell on the items in my hand as I approached.

"What's that?" she said, rising for a closer look.

"Is this the type of test he took?" I asked, feigning naiveté.

She inspected the items as I placed them on the table and sat.

"I don't know. I guess," she stammered. "But why do you have a test kit? You said you didn't use a donor sample."

"I didn't. But there are some women who believed their husband's samples were used to impregnate them, and it turned out Dr. Addison deceived them too. The man was mad. He used his own seed even when there was no need for a donor."

"What?" She slammed her hands on the table, rattling the items on the dishtowel. "That's sick! How? Why?" She paced again, running her hands through her short hair.

"No one can answer the why. I don't think anyone even understands the how. We'll never get the answers we want. Dr. Addison killed himself."

She turned back to me, her eyes wide, grasping for the meaning of it all.

"Killed himself? So you think—" She collapsed into the seat next to me. "No, it can't be. You've always said how much I looked like Dad when he was little. There's no way."

"You're right, honey. You do bear a remarkable resemblance to your father. This is just"—I hovered my fingers over the items on the towel before rolling my hand into a fist—"just a precautionary measure. For our peace of mind."

"Wait!" Color drained from her face as realization coiled into her. "If Mrs. E already knows this sick doctor fathered Jennings, and you suspect you were a victim too, that means Jennings and I could be… Oh, my God, Mom. This can't be happening!"

"I know." I reached to stroke her hair, but she rose again, not allowing my fingers to touch her.

"No, you don't know! You're saying I could be Jennings'—" She faced me, her expression lost and dumbstruck, her mind still grappling with the implications. "I'm going to be sick!" She bolted down the hall. I heard her retching from where I stood in the kitchen. The toilet flushed, the faucet turned on, then off, and then I heard sobs. Jolted from my spot, I ran to her and found her on the bathroom floor. I knelt beside her, and she swatted at me.

"Leave me alone! Go away! How could you do this to me?" She sat up and pushed me away, but her eyes caught mine and she crumbled into me. Her wails echoed down the empty hallway. The warmth of her body felt so good. I breathed her in, and in my mind she was a little girl again. All she needed was her mother's love. My love could heal her hurt. I held her tighter.

"I'm so sorry, sweetie," I cried, rubbing her back. "I never meant for any of this to happen."

We sat there for some time until her sobs subsided. She sniffed, and I reached for the toilet paper, ripping off a wad and using it to dry her eyes and wipe her nose. It felt good to take care of her. To know I brought her comfort.

"It can't be. I mean, it's ridiculous. It just can't be."

I rose and helped her up. She stared at herself in the mirror. I wondered what she was thinking. Was she identifying every trait that might prove she was mine and Roger's, or was she looking for something in her appearance linking her to Jennings or to a stranger she'd never have the chance to meet?

I looked in the mirror too and studied my reflection, seeing my mother, but looking for my father. For the first time since that awful night when the father I believed was mine died and my mother divulged her horrid secret, I didn't recognize myself. What traits did my daughter carry that she'd been given by someone I never had the chance to meet? Did she look like her grandfather? A man I never knew. The world threatened to cave in on me. I shoved those thoughts aside and trampled on them.

Lauren leaned forward, taking the tissue from me and wiping her eyes. She tucked her hair behind her ears and straightened her T-shirt before turning to me. "Let's take the test. I want to put an end to this."

I followed her back to the kitchen.

"What do I do?" she asked, lifting the swab from the table. "Just rub it on the inside of my cheek like they do on TV?"

"Here," I said, "let me help."

———

"I paid extra to rush the order," I lied to Nancy later that day when she called to ask how things had gone.

"I didn't even know that was an option," she replied. "Has she come out of her room yet? She's not answering Jennings' calls. Is she all right?"

"Well, obviously, it came as a shock. I'm giving her space. I hate that we have to live with the uncertainty hanging over our heads for another week, but I had to wait for the right time."

"The timing of everything couldn't be worse. First, I learn what that despicable man was capable of, then I lose my husband, and then you lose Roger. It is all too much for kids their age to struggle with. My heart breaks for them. Jennings is handling it better than I expected, but he doesn't for one second believe Lauren, you…"

"Nancy," I whispered when I heard Lauren's door creak open. "I have to go." I disconnected the call without waiting for her response. Lauren entered the living room and sat next to me on the couch. She had changed, done her hair, and was wearing makeup.

"How are you doing, sweetie?" I asked, taking her hand.

"I don't know. Pretty sure this is going to be the longest week of my life. Waiting to find out who my father is… It's beyond lame."

"Yeah," I replied. "What are you all dressed up for? You aren't going out, are you?"

"I am," she said, standing and making her way to the entry hall. "I need to see Jennings. I don't know how we don't make it weird, but whatever happens, he's my best friend."

She turned to look at me as I approached and followed her to the door. Tears shimmered in her eyes before spilling over. She made no move to wipe them away. For a second, I thought she might tell me more. Let me know Jennings was more than just her best friend, but she didn't.

"Mind giving me a lift to the Ellingtons'?"

I wanted to deny her the ride. Beg her to stay home with me. What did she plan to accomplish at Jennings' house? I cursed myself for not testing her sooner. I had the results I needed tucked under the bed. Waiting for the other results was pointless, and while I knew I wouldn't actually be waiting for additional results, the delay and the ruse were necessary for my plan.

"Sure," I conceded. "I need to run the test to the post office, anyway. The sooner we mail it off, the sooner we'll have answers. Let me get my things."

I went to my bedroom and put my shoes on, grabbing a mailer from my desk on the way back down the hall. In the entry, I made a show of placing the stamp on the package, keeping the blank mailing label out of her view. She was too busy petting Kane to notice that the envelope remained void of details. I tucked it into my purse and grabbed my keys. She was already out the front door, moving to my car.

TWENTY-TWO

QUANTITATIVE

The week dragged as if it were a heavy weight I was forced to bear, chained to me, holding me down. I hardly saw Lauren at all. It was spring break, and we'd canceled our plans to visit the Grand Canyon after Roger's passing. She was at Jennings from the moment she woke until her curfew. Nancy called every day asking if I'd received the results.

"I'm going to call the lab today," I told her Friday when she called. Lauren had just bolted out the front door to Jennings' awaiting car. She said they were going to the mall. "School starts back up next week. I don't want to wait any longer."

As I spoke, I went to the front door, stepped onto the porch, and pushed the doorbell. "I'll call you back. Someone is at the door. I think it might be the mail carrier." I disconnected the call and went to the kitchen for a glass of water and pondered how long I should wait to call her back. I did some chores and went to the laundry room to clean the litter box.

I was sweeping the back porch when the doorbell rang. I ran to the front of the house and peered through the peephole. Nancy stood outside, tapping her heeled foot and inspecting her manicure.

Panic washed over me like a wave. The test results were still tucked under my bed. I rubbed my eyes and mussed my hair and looked in the mirror. Convinced I didn't appear distraught enough, I bit the inside of my cheek hard. A coppery brine flooded my mouth, and my eyes watered. I reached for the door and opened it slowly, stepping back into the shadows of the entryway instead of onto the sunlit porch.

"I couldn't wait another second. The suspense is killing me." She pushed past me. "Was it the test results? Do you have them?"

I turned without responding and moved to the living room, falling onto the couch in as dramatic a fashion as I could muster. I should have anticipated Nancy would come over. She wasn't one to wait for a return call. I focused my energy on shifting my anger to sadness and folded my head into my hands.

"Oh, no. Please say it isn't so. Let me see it." She rushed to my side and wrapped her arm around me. I knew she wanted to hit me with an 'I told you so,' but she just held me. She was quiet, showing a patience I didn't know existed within her. I sat with her until I couldn't stomach it any longer.

"I'll be right back," I said, rising and swiping at absent tears. I left her in the living room and went to my bedroom, where I retrieved the box and pulled the results of Shelby's DNA test out. I examined it again closely, now worried maybe I'd missed some identifier that could lay waste to my scheme, something I hadn't noticed before that might jump out at Nancy. I was being ridiculous. I hadn't submitted Shelby's name on the document. To the world, these results were for Lauren. Only the cover letter was dated, and I'd tossed it when I received the results. I slid the box back under the bed and exited the room.

Nancy was in the kitchen helping herself to my coffeepot.

"I thought you might need a cup," she said as she poured fresh grounds into the filter. "I know I need something to spike."

"Thank you," I replied. I moved to the nook and sat, fixing my face with the most despondent expression I could rally.

Nancy started the coffee maker and joined me at the table, removing her flask from her purse. She tilted it at me. It wasn't yet noon, but I figured a swig might help me play this out. I took it from her and sipped, trying not to screw up my face too much as the liquid lit fire to my throat.

"Is that it?" she asked, motioning to the paper in my grasp. "Can I see?"

I pushed the document toward her, but kept my fingers pressed hard against it, forcing her to tug a bit to remove it. She scanned the page silently, seeming to know exactly where to direct her focus. The last damning section—the spot with the pertinent information.

"Oh, Alice," she said, without moving her eyes from the paper. "I'm so sorry. I had really hoped you'd escaped his madness. How many more of us are there?" She pushed the paper back to me and rose, moving to the cabinet where I kept my mugs. There, she removed two cups, poured coffee into them and brought them to the table.

She offered me her flask before she added any to her drink. I took it and poured a splash, careful not to pour too much. The last thing I needed was to lose control of my emotions. Anger simmered just below the facade I presented. I needed to keep it contained.

I stirred my finger in the cup and took a drink. She watched me, sizing me up, trying to read me. I thought about her reaction to the news and did my best to emulate shock. I couldn't think of anything to say, but knew she'd fill the silence before it became too heavy.

"Does Lauren know?" she asked.

I shook my head. "I don't know how I'm going to tell her." I took another drink.

"Wait… They're together right now, aren't they?" she said, adding some of the flask's liquid to her coffee. "Of course, they are. They are always together. She's been so adamant the results would be different. In every conversation we've had, she's worked to convince me there is no way you were a victim as well."

I swallowed hard. Lauren had barely said a word to me about the whole ordeal, but Nancy seemed to know exactly where my daughter's head was. Resentment battered me, but I fought it off, reminding myself I'd soon be free of these conversations. My daughter's relationship with Nancy's son would be a thing of the past, which meant her bond with Nancy would be broken as well. My lips twitched, forcing me to morph my smile into a grimace.

"She'll be devastated," I said.

"They will both be destroyed," Nancy agreed. "Maybe we should tell them together. I could call Jennings and ask him to bring her home."

"No, that'd be too obvious. Give them the afternoon before their worlds implode."

We sat in silence for some time. Kane entered the kitchen, and instead of recoiling from her, Nancy waved her hand, shooing the cat away. I was grateful for the distraction. It was clear she wasn't going to leave unless I kicked her out. Unable to handle the stifling silence, I thought of something to say.

"How many others are there now?" I asked, my voice barely a whisper.

"You don't want to know. It seems like someone new joins the ranks every day. I really can't fathom how what he did is not illegal. My lawyers are still trying to come up with an angle, something we can use to get justice. The contracts we signed were so lax. It's as if no one could ever have conceived of a situation like this. Pretty shortsighted, if you ask me."

"I wouldn't say shortsighted. You'd have to have a mind as warped as Dr. Addison's to conjure up something so evil." I searched my memory for the conversations I'd had with Nancy when she exposed Dr. Addison's techniques to me. Unable to muster the emotion she had expressed, I resorted to shocked silence. It was easier and understandable. Masking my emotions was more comfortable than expressing them.

"Have you eaten?" she asked. "I know you aren't a drinker, and I don't want you to get sick. I'd be happy to make you a sandwich or something."

I shook my head.

Lauren and Jennings entered the house, and laughter tumbled down the hall. Their exuberance tore through the gloom as they moved toward us, Jennings' arms laden with bags.

"You look ridiculous," Lauren said to him. "Why did you buy those things?"

"Don't knock 'em till you try 'em," he said, and laughed. "They're super comfortable."

"They may be comfy, but they look like clown shoes." Lauren stopped when she saw Nancy and me sitting in the breakfast nook. Her words faded with her smile.

"Oh, my dear, sweet girl," Nancy cried, rising and rushing to Lauren. She swept my daughter into her arms.

Lauren stared at me from Nancy's embrace. Confusion slowly drained from her face, replaced by a devastating realization. She writhed free of Nancy's grasp and shook the woman off her.

"No," she whispered. "No, no, no!

Each denial grew louder as she made her way to the paper that now sat between our coffee mugs on the table. She snatched the document up and drew it near her face. Her eyes darted, scanning the page before landing at the bottom. She sank into the banquette seat, her jaw slack. Her face was pale. Heavy shadows settled under her eyes. All the joy she'd brought upon her arrival shattered around her.

"Lauren?" Jennings asked. "Mom? Mrs. White? What's going on?" He wiggled the shopping bags from his arms and dropped them on the floor.

The table trembled with Lauren's sobs. She clamped her hand to her face and shook her head as if her denial could change the words on the document.

"Is that…?" Jennings pointed to the paper.

Why was Nancy not speaking? Since she was here and we were doing this as a group now, I expected her to dive in, relish the moment, and provide commentary. For the first time since I'd known her, she was stone silent. I kept my voice clenched inside, and my fists balled as I searched for something to say. The right words always escaped me, and I needed Nancy to fill the quiet and at least put an end to Lauren's pitiful cries.

Lauren got up and ran down the hall. The slamming door echoed through the house.

"Can I see the results, Mrs. White?" Jennings asked. He'd aged since he'd entered my kitchen. He was now a sage, hardy and resolute. Not the gleeful boy who'd entered moments earlier. I wished he belonged to anyone but Nancy.

I retrieved the document from the table and gave it to him. His cheeks flamed, and his hands trembled. I could see his mind working, hardening him to the reality.

"How can this be?" he asked, never taking his eyes from the test results.

"Oh, darling," Nancy finally said. She rushed to his side. "I'm so, so very sorry." Tears coursed down her face, leaving veins of exposed white skin.

"This can't be," he said. His gaze shifted from his mother to the hallway. He moved to the entrance of the kitchen but stopped before leaving. "I don't know if I should go to her."

"I could go talk to her," Nancy suggested.

"No," I said, too loudly, my tone acidic, forcing me to backtrack. "I mean, maybe she needs some time to herself. This is a lot for all of us to digest." Suffering was safer in solitude.

"Alice is right, Jennings. Maybe we should go home. We all need some time to absorb this news." She was already gathering her purse. "Come, dear." She took Jennings' arm. He pulled free of her grip and turned to me.

"Can you tell her something for me?" He held my arms, and his eyes pierced my dread, quieting it, calming my pulse. How could Nancy's son be so poised?

"Of course." My muscles softened in his grip. "Anything you need me to say to her, I'm happy to deliver the message."

"Tell her that no matter what, I love her and she'll always be my best friend." Tears pooled in his eyes.

His words knocked the air out of me. There was no way I would deliver that message to my daughter. He'd dared to speak the truth about their relationship when my own child wouldn't. I learned about her first love from an outsider. Perhaps it was better this way, easier to deny coming from Jennings and not Lauren. It didn't matter anymore, I reminded myself.

"Of course I will," I replied. I did my best to hug him. The liquor-tinged coffee rose in my throat, and it took everything in me not to push him away.

They left me standing in the kitchen. I heard the door shut and both their cars start in the drive. I knew I should go to Lauren, check on her, hold her, but something stopped me. Maybe it would be best to wait for her to come to me. Perhaps I should give her some space.

I paced the kitchen and downed the remaining coffee. This was all going better than I ever expected it to. There was no way Lauren and Jennings could remain friends under the circumstances. They might try for a while, but the reality of it all would become unrelenting. To transition from friendship to romantic partner to siblings would overwhelm them. Despite their closeness, I didn't fear that any aspect of their relationship was salvageable. The divide would become too great.

Believing the hardest parts were behind me, I decided to start dinner, settling on shepherd's pie, Lauren's favorite. Maybe a nice meal with her mother would help. I went about the tasks with a lightness I hadn't experienced in some time. The whole house sighed with relief as if the windows had been thrown open, chaos sucked out in the pull. With the dish in the oven, I went to her door and knocked.

"Lauren, honey, how are you?" I asked through the door.

She did not reply.

"Can I come in?"

"No! I just want to be alone right now."

"I understand. I can't begin to tell you how very sorry I am, sweetie. I never meant for any of this—"

"Alone, Mom!" she shrieked. "Go away!"

Her words hit me like a punch. I backed away from the door without replying. I ate dinner by myself, sharing a few bits of lamb with Kane.

TWENTY-THREE

DILATION

The following morning, I stopped outside Lauren's bedroom door on the way to the kitchen. I hadn't heard anything from her all night; she hadn't left her room even to brush her teeth as far as I could tell. I pressed my ear to the door, panicked that perhaps she'd done something unspeakable. Maybe she escaped out her bedroom window, or worse. Dread forced me to knock despite the early hour. There was no reply.

"Lauren?" I rapped on the door more sharply.

The door opened as my fist connected with it. Lauren still wore the clothes she'd been wearing the day before. Her eyes were drawn, her hair a webbed halo. She was adrift in loss.

"Mommy," she cried, falling into my arms, almost taking me to the floor. I braced myself against the doorframe to hold her up as she sobbed. Her grief poured into me. I absorbed it like a sponge. It was my job. What kind of mother would I be if I didn't feel her pain? But I'd saved her from so much more heartache. I don't know how long we stood in the hall, clinging to each other as she drained her tears. My heart lilted.

"I don't know what to do now," she said into my neck. "How do

I go on? He was everything to me, Mom. We were going to New York together. We were meant to be together forever, and now…"

I stroked her hair. The dampness from her tears seeped through my sweater as her words pummeled me, and my rapture was snatched away. I let what she said roll around in my mind, hoping I could find a way to ease her pain, to lift the gloom, and mend her broken heart. Her suffering was a dark cloud hanging over me, but this dark cloud's gilded lining came to me quickly. My daughter had confessed. Finally, she had put her trust in me and shared her biggest secret. With me. Rather than shrink away from the news, I embraced it. We were already closer.

As my heart soared again, I clamored for something to cinch the seam. A deeply planted seed sprouted in my mind. Could I share my pain at learning my own paternity could be questioned? It had never been confirmed, and I'd chosen to deny it as the venomous musings of a drunken, vacant woman, but it could give us a connection. It could be another thread that could open doors and deepen our bond.

But I yanked the sprout up, roots and all. I couldn't. Giving voice to that part of me would force it into the world. What if my real father was a wretch? A criminal? And what if it made her think less of me? Cast further doubt on her identity? It was too risky.

Should I tell her of my own lost love? Let her know of the one my mother deemed unworthy, the one who got away? Tell her how I felt I'd never love again? Confess that I never had? Maybe an anecdote about heartache would help her, comfort her, give her hope. But what if I didn't get it right? She could be offended by the comparison. Everyone believed their love was the greatest of all. Everyone but mothers. We knew the purest love was between a mother and her child. I couldn't chance it.

Nothing else came to me, so I continued to hold her until she pulled away.

"I need something to drink," she said. "Do we have any coffee?"

Finally, something I could do to help.

"Of course, come to the kitchen with me. I'll start a pot."

"Gonna use the bathroom first," she replied, sniffing and wiping her nose with the sleeve of her sweatshirt. "I'll be there in a minute."

She made her way to the restroom. I'd never seen her so aimless. So distraught. It was up to me to bring her back. I moved to the kitchen and went about making a pot of coffee. Before Lauren joined me, the phone rang.

"Hello," I said, noting that it was Nancy. I'd have been more surprised if it had been anyone but her.

"How is she doing?" she whispered.

"Not good."

"My heart is breaking for them. Jennings is a mess too. He hasn't left his room since we got home. How do we help them, Alice? I've never felt so powerless."

"I wish I knew the answer." It was the most honest response I'd given to any question hurled at me in days.

"Wait, I think I hear him." She was quiet for a moment. "Yes, he's coming downstairs. I'll call you back." The line went dead. A few minutes later, as the pot sputtered to a stop, Lauren entered the kitchen. She slumped into the banquette, and Kane hopped into her lap. She nuzzled her face against hers, sensing her distress. Maybe the cat could lift her spirits better than I had.

I poured a cup and took it to her.

"Thanks." She reached for the mug, then tucked her knees up to her chin and cupped the mug in her hands. The cat settled next to her. I sat across from her and tried to shift the expression on my face. I knew I appeared needy, eager for her to speak, wanting desperately to know what she was thinking.

"Can I make you something to eat? Waffles, maybe?"

"No, thank you. I'm not hungry. But the coffee is helping."

"Well, that's something."

"I don't know what to do now. Like, how is this even real? I just want to wake up from this nightmare. I want Dad back. I want my old life back." Tears poured down her face. "It was a good life."

Pride bubbled in my chest. I'd given her a good life, she said so herself. I stomped the feeling out before it reached my expression.

Now wasn't the time. I reached for her hand and said, "I know, sweetie. I wish I could make that happen."

"How do I go to school on Monday? How do I go to prom? He was my date. He was my future. I can't go to the prom with my, my…" She collapsed into sobs again. I sat with her and let her cry. "My half-brother. I've kissed my half-brother, Mom. And I should be totally skeeved out by it, but I'm not because he doesn't feel like my brother. He's my best friend. More than my best friend. He's my soulmate."

Her eyes were distant, searching, unblinking. "I can't believe this is happening. Please tell me the test results were wrong. Please, Mommy, tell me this is a nightmare I'll wake up from soon. Please!"

Soulmate? My mind got lost again down the wrong path. Now that she'd revealed her closeness to Jennings, I wished she'd stop reminding me of it. I scooted around the table to be closer to her, nudging Kane off the seat, wrapping my arms around her, tracking down the right response.

"You don't have to make any decisions right this minute, honey. It's going to take time."

"I know you aren't going to understand this," she said, shaking free from my embrace and rising. "But I've got to go see Jennings. I need to talk to him."

She was already in the hallway by the time I realized what she'd said. I got up and chased after her.

"Lauren, sweetie, I'm not sure that's a good idea."

She stopped outside her bedroom door and turned to me.

"I'm not so sure it's a good idea either, but it's the only thing I can think of right now. Besides, if he can't help, I bet Mrs. E can. She always knows what to do." She went into her bedroom and closed the door.

Now I was the one who felt lost. Running to Jennings was the last thing I expected her to do, but what could I do to stop her? And what could Nancy do for her that I couldn't? I was still standing in the hallway when she came back out of her room. I was frozen, my hands knotted. Panic shivered through me. Why would she go to

Nancy when I was right here with her, tending to her needs? She'd changed into her bathrobe.

"I'm going to take a shower first," she said, brushing past me and going to the bathroom. The motion stirred me but offered me no recourse.

I went back to the kitchen and started cleaning. There was no mess, but I couldn't think of anything else to do. I was floating in a space of doubt and disbelief. I tried to talk myself down.

"It's fine. It will all work out."

"She needs to process it all. It's not like she's going to continue a relationship with her brother."

"You've done all you can now, so you have to be patient. Don't do anything to push her away."

"You're a great mother. You've saved your daughter from a wasted life."

I'd convinced myself that all would be fine by the time Lauren joined me in the kitchen. Despite her breaking heart, she glowed. I silently berated myself for not having done something more productive while she showered. Maybe I could have convinced her to stay home with me if I'd made a batch of her favorite cookies or found a movie to watch. Instead, she stood with her backpack in hand.

"Mind giving me a lift to the Ellingtons?" she asked.

Some moms would refuse to do so. Would try to talk sense into their lovesick daughter. Share sage advice to dissuade her from making things worse and offer insight that would ease the ache in her soul. But this might be just what was needed to close the door. What was she going to do at this point? Go to prom with him? Give herself to Jennings now? Of course not. It was best to go along with her, allow her to do what she wanted. It might help things dissolve more rapidly.

"Um, sure," I said, moving to the entryway for my purse and keys.

We drove in silence. As I rounded the circle drive to the Ellingtons' front walk, Lauren turned to me.

"Do you want to come in? Mrs. E has had more time to absorb what that horrible man did to the two of you, to us. Maybe it'd be good for you to be together now, share things. I hate how you're always alone."

The thought of entering Nancy's showcase home and listening to her blather on about how wronged she was made my stomach turn.

"I don't think so. I need time to myself. To process it all."

"I get it," she said, leaning over and kissing me on the cheek. "Thanks for the ride! I'm sure Jennings can bring me back home later."

She got out of the car and bounded up the front steps lightly, as if she hadn't a care in the world. Maybe she was more like me than I realized. It gave me hope that this would all blow over. One day she'd thank me. I watched from the car until the door opened. I couldn't see who answered. Lauren disappeared inside. I drove home.

———

I spent the day in my new office doing tutorials on the computer and researching all I could find about CPT coding. Kane lay curled in my lap while I worked. Completely lost in my studies, I didn't notice the sun had set. The cat stood and stretched, breaking my concentration. The desk lamp provided more light than the window now. Kane needed dinner. Lauren wasn't home yet.

As I went through the motions of feeding the cat, my mind swam with what-ifs. Why wasn't she home? Was she still with Jennings and Nancy? What kind of commentary was Nancy subjecting her to? How much worse was she making things with her spin? After dumping kibble in the bowl, I paced the house, pausing at the front window with each lap, watching for Lauren's arrival.

When the clock struck ten, I couldn't stand it any longer and reached for the phone. Before I could dial, I heard a car pull into the driveway. Within a minute, the front door opened. I made my way to the foyer to greet her when I heard her bedroom door slam.

I walked down the hall and pressed my ear against her door. She was crying. Softly. I knocked.

"Sweetie," I called. "Welcome home. Did you eat?"

"Go away!"

"Excuse—"

The door flew open.

"I don't want to talk to you!" she shrieked. Her face was red, her eyes feral.

"Lauren, I—"

She tried to shut the door on me, but I pushed back. She turned away from me, and her hair swirled as she threw herself onto the bed. With her face buried in the quilt, she screamed, legs flailing, like a toddler throwing a tantrum. I stood in the doorway, unsure of what to do but knowing I was right. Nancy had said something to taint her mind.

With her rage spent for the time being, she flipped over and came at me. Lifting off the bed, she crossed the distance between us in a flash.

"You did this to me! You… you ruined my life!" She shook her finger at me.

I stumbled under the weight of her words and fury. My knees buckled, threatening to give way. No words came to me. No insightful response sprang to my rescue. I said the first thing that entered my mind.

"Sweetie, you don't mean that. I know you're angry and confused, and it will take time. Time heals everything." Meaning to impart wisdom, I quickly realized I'd made things worse.

"No, it doesn't, Mom!" she exclaimed. "That's one of the most whack thing you've ever said! There is no healing! My dad is gone! Turns out he isn't even my dad." Her voice trembled, and her words lost footing. She gathered herself, her face changing from flushed to hot. Anger built in her like a pressure cooker. "It's all your fault!"

"My—" The words dried up on my tongue.

"Yes, your fault! I didn't ask to be born! Daddy didn't force you into Dr. Addison's office! You did this! Why, Mom? Your life was just too useless without a child? I wish I had never been born!"

The world fell dark. My pulse raced, and again I was rendered motionless.

"I didn't ask to be born, you know!" Her wrath did not subside. "You did this to me! You had to fulfill your good little wife life and force me into this world."

"Lauren…" It was all I had. A meaningless one-word response. Powerless.

"Maybe the universe was trying to tell you something by making you infertile!" She looked away from me. Like the very sight of me was too much for her to bear.

"What?" The word was knocked out of my mouth as if forced by a strike.

"You weren't meant to be a mother, duh! Your own body was telling you it wasn't in the cards, but you couldn't accept that! What else would the prim and proper Alice White be if she wasn't a mother? You knew you'd be nothing, so you forced it to happen. You forced me into existence! And now look how that turned out. Mom! I've lost the love of my life! Everything is ruined! My life is over!" She hurled herself onto the bed again and wailed.

I wanted to go to her, take her in my arms and hold her. It had always worked when she was younger. My embrace was once healing, transformative. I made a move toward her, and she rolled over. Her eyes bore into me with a hatred I'd only ever felt from my mother and Roger. I froze, unable to approach her, fearing the raging storm inside her.

"I hate you," she said in a low voice I didn't recognize. Her lips tightened into a white line, jaw set.

"Lauren." My heart exited my body just as surely as if she'd reached inside me and ripped it out. Tears threatened to spill from my eyes. The floor beneath me rolled, the walls writhed, all air in the space aspirated.

"Get out!" she whispered. "I need you to go away." Exhaustion and resentment had stolen her fervor.

"But, sweetie," I muttered. How could I be rendered mute at such a pivotal moment? Where was my voice? Had I ever had one?

Lauren bound from the bed and pushed past me, spinning me toward the door.

"Fine!" she said, her voice gaining strength again. "If you won't leave, I will."

She went to her closet, retrieved a duffel bag, and snatched some items off hangers. Exiting the closet, she stuffed the clothes in the bag and moved to her dresser. There, she crammed undergarments and pajamas into the satchel. I watched as if I were outside the space, a ghost looking on as life spun around my invisible figure. She left the room, and I heard her in the bathroom shuffling through drawers.

I collapsed onto her bed, unsure of what to do. The bunny, the one I'd bought before my precious daughter was even conceived, called to me from Lauren's bookshelf. I plucked it off the shelf and held it as if it were a sleeping infant, cradling it in my arms as Lauren's childhood flashed in front of my eyes. How could I make her see that all would be fine, that time did heal, especially under the safety and love of a mother's watch? Holding the stuffed animal to my nose, I breathed in the nostalgic fragrance of Lauren's childhood before returning it to its perch on the shelf. I made it to the threshold of her bedroom just as she blew past on her way up the hall. Spurred into action, I chased after her.

"Where are you going?" I pleaded.

She dropped her bag by the front door and moved to the window to stare silently out the glass.

I put my hand on her shoulder, and she shrugged it off with a jerk, then continued to ignore me.

"Please, Lauren. I don't know what to say. I'm sorry. I know it isn't enough, but what else can I do? I'm not sorry I had you. You are my everything."

Lights flashed across the window. Keeping her back to me, she picked up her bag and opened the door. Before closing it, she turned to me. She looked like she'd aged five years in the span of a day. Shadows draped her eyes. Her skin was blotchy, the still-fading bruise a pasty green line down her forehead.

"Well, to me, you're nothing. I'm alone now," she said, regarding me with hollow eyes. Her glare was bone-cold, seeping deeper into me with every icy second. "Jennings is gone. Dad is gone, and you...

Well, can you imagine how lonely it is to hate your own mother?" She slammed the door with the word *mother* still hanging from her lips. The windows in the foyer shuddered in their frames. As she fled, all the energy chased her like a shadow. Her absence left a dark void. The absence of everything.

"Yes, I can!" I screamed at the door. I'd found my voice a second too late.

I turned a slow circle in the room. Nothing looked familiar. My entire existence disappeared on the heels of my daughter. I peered out the window to see her get into Jennings' car.

I wandered through the dark house. The silence was so loud, the world a blinding gray. The air was thick with regret, making it difficult for me to inhale. My exhale felt full of pain and remorse. I didn't know what to do with myself. I finally landed on the sofa. I wasn't sure how long I'd been sitting there when my phone chimed. It was a text message from Nancy.

Nancy: *She is at my house. She's asleep in a guest room, finally. She can stay as long as she likes. I just wanted to let you know she was safe.*

TWENTY-FOUR

SURFACTANT

She was gone for three days. The only thing that drew me out of bed was Kane. I called in sick to Coventry Springs, didn't eat, didn't shower. I made sure the cat's needs were met and waited. Waited for my daughter to come home.

Nancy messaged me regularly, keeping me informed. She'd taken Lauren clothes shopping. Took her to and from school, made sure she ate, did her homework. Jennings was staying with Nancy's daughter across town. Part of me was relieved for the updates, comforted to hear Lauren was physically safe and being kept at a distance from Jennings. The other part of me despised Nancy more than ever. How dare she take my daughter? Put Lauren's needs before those of her own son? Was she trying to steal my child away from me? What a horrible excuse for a mother she was.

While I wanted to phone Nancy and implore her to send Lauren home, I didn't. I couldn't think of the words to say or how to say them. I was paralyzed, unequipped for such a task. So I writhed in the emptiness and dreamed of her return.

Shortly before sundown on the third day, I heard voices outside my front door. Lauren.

I rose from the bed, my bones aching, joints stiff and reluctant.

From my bedroom window, I watched my daughter speak to Nancy. Their words were too hushed to decipher. Lauren was home. The two embraced, clinging together as time slipped by. I closed my eyes and put myself in Lauren's arms. My daughter had never hugged me with such emotion. When they released each other, Nancy wiped tears from Lauren's eyes and kissed her on the forehead. My chest knotted with spite.

Lauren hadn't yet entered the house as Nancy drove away. Unable to withstand another moment without her, I ran to the front door and threw it open. She sat on the stoop with her back to the door. She didn't move.

"Lauren?" I whispered.

Nothing.

I inched onto the porch and sat down next to her. Close, but not touching. No reaction.

"Sweetie, I'm so happy to see you!" The words gushed out of me. "I was so worried." My hands twitched in my lap, longing to reach for her.

She wiggled closer to me and put her head on my shoulder. I was certain she could feel my heart hammering in my chest. Relief washed over me. My body shrank and my lungs expanded.

"I'm sorry, Mom. I was just so angry at the world, at you. I thought I'd explode."

I could think of no reply, but I breathed her in. The warmth of her body next to mine, the smell of her hair. Her.

"I've thought about everything a lot... Too much," she said with a pained chuckle. "It's all so much. Like my entire life has been a lie. I don't even know who I am. I'm not the person I believed I was for my whole existence. Like I'm a stranger to myself."

"Oh, sweetie," was all I could offer, still absorbing her closeness. There was amity in her words.

"I've talked so much with Mrs. E," she went on, sending waves of confusion crashing down on me. My body tensed. I wanted to scream at her to never mention Nancy's name again, in any form. I closed my eyes, breathed deeply, and dropped my chin to my chest, willing calmness. I couldn't blow it now, now that she was here with me.

"It really helped," she continued, not detecting my angst. "She suggested you and I go to counseling. I think she's right. We have a lot to work out. She and Jennings are doing it, and they think it's helping."

I wrapped an arm around her and pulled her closer. "Anything you want."

"Do you mean it?" Her eyes found mine for the first time in days.

"Yes, sweetie. I'll do anything to help you recover from this."

"It's not about my recovery. It's about acceptance." The words came from Lauren, but I detected Nancy's voice. "Accepting what has happened to us. And I need you to understand things. Things that will have to change for us to have any chance of a relationship."

Again, the world fell on top of me. Her words boomed in my ears. Was she threatening to leave me? After all I'd done for her, for us. I'd saved her from herself, from an aimless life. Nancy could foot the bill for her son. He'd have no future, at least not the one he envisioned. Jennings could meander willy-nilly, chasing stardom for as long as he wanted, waiting for his big break. But when he came to his senses, he'd have money and power to fall back on. Lauren couldn't waste those years, or she would have nothing in the end. No education, nothing to show for her life, no family. She and I had only each other.

"Mom?" she asked. "Are you listening to me? Because this is really important and I need to get it off my chest." Her voice rose as she struggled to speak. I could see her fighting for ground as tears took her down. "I need you to hear me."

I lied. "I promise I'll do anything."

She was quiet for a bit, tears trickling down her face.

"You can't run my life. You can't make decisions that affect me without my knowledge, and you can't lie to me anymore. I can't stand lies. This one has destroyed me. Do you get that?"

I nodded, wishing we could fast-forward to better days. The day when she realized I had her best interests at heart. That I'd done what any loving mother would do in my shoes. We just had to endure, and we had to do so together.

"I'm serious. I can't take any more lies. I'd rather crumble under the truth than be soothed with dishonesty. Lies only ever lead to more pain."

She was wrong, but she was young. Truth was overrated. Truth was cold and uncaring. Truth was shifting and tricky. You could make it what you wanted it to be.

"Can you promise me?" she continued. "Promise to be honest. To not protect me from things you have no right keeping from me? And don't make decisions about my future without asking me first."

"Yes, of course, sweetie," I said, my words rushing out. I gave her the answer she wanted, not the one I wanted to give.

She stood up and grabbed her bag. When she'd left for Nancy's, it was deflated. Now it bulged and the zipper strained. I stood up next to her, and she hugged me. I held on like I'd never let go.

"Jennings is leaving for New York City the day after graduation. Obviously, I won't be going with him now." She walked to the door and opened it. Kane greeted her at the entrance. I followed behind. "I'm exhausted," she said. "I'm going to bed. You should really think about taking a shower."

TWENTY-FIVE

GESTATION

2020

TWELVE YEARS LATER

"Mom, it's time." Lauren lurched into the kitchen, her hands gripping her swollen belly. A wet spot was spreading down her leg, darkening the fabric of her jeans. She waddled to the banquette but glanced at her pants and opted not to sit, leaning against the table instead.

"It's time? Like, really time?" I dropped the dish I'd been rinsing into the sink and grabbed the dishtowel on the counter, drying my hands as I hurried to her side.

"Watch the puddle," she whispered between clenched teeth. She folded her body in half, her hands clinging to the swell of her stomach. Her breath escaped in bursts and gave way to a growl that erupted from deep within her. The veins on her neck pulsed, and redness spread across her face as a contraction gripped her. Her eyes bulged, wild and scared, like a trapped animal.

I ran to the laundry room for towels. Racing back to the kitchen, I placed one on the seat. Her hand clawed the air, searching for something to grasp. I offered her mine and helped lower her to the banquette, then dropped another rag to the ground, stomping on it to absorb the pool of straw-colored liquid on the floor. Although we'd planned for this moment, had discussed it at length over the months since she'd moved back home, I felt unprepared but ready at the same time.

Today was the day we would welcome Lauren's daughter. My granddaughter. A day I feared we would never see, as Lauren spent the last decade moving from one failed relationship to another. She'd never married, a fact that would find my mother spinning in her grave, but one that found me teeming with pride. Lauren lived life on her own terms. And now, at nearly the same age I was when I'd given birth to her, she was about to become a mother.

"I'll get your suitcase," I told her. "Can I get you anything else?"

Her body quieted as the contraction released her. The flush returned to her cheeks. She pushed air out through pursed lips, like they'd shown us during the birthing classes we'd been forced to take online, practicing the breathing techniques in front of the computer screen on Zoom.

"Just the suitcase and my purse," she replied. "But I think we should hurry. The contractions started a couple of hours ago. The sun wasn't up yet. Now they are coming about five minutes apart. What if we're too late?" Color slipped from her face.

"Nope, nope!" I yelled to her as I rushed down the hallway to her bedroom. "Not too late. You're doing great."

Her suitcase sat just inside her door with her purse propped on top of it. I ran to my bedroom to get my shoes and coat. Excitement spurred me through the motions. I grabbed Lauren's bags on the way back down the hall and left them in the entryway. She was up now and moving toward me, towel in hand, when another contraction stopped her.

"Breathe," I cried, rushing to her side. I took her hand, and she squeezed as the pain jolted through her again. The contraction was so intense I almost felt it myself as she doubled over again and wailed. We stood together in the hallway and waited for the contraction to have its way with her. I felt it subside as she loosened her grip.

"Mom, I'm scared," she whimpered, tears springing forth. "It's not fair I have to do this alone!"

"You've got this, Lauren!" I cheered, nudging her to the door. "We've got this!"

New safety mandates wouldn't allow me to stay with Lauren. I was forced to remain in the car while my daughter gave birth among strangers. The world was only a few months into the pandemic, and we were still adapting to a way of life foreign to us all. Neither Lauren nor I was thrilled with the new policies, but the circumstances did little to quell my enthusiasm.

The hours passed slowly as I sat in the car, only three floors below where Lauren became a mother. It might as well have been a million miles away. There were no updates besides the few texts she'd sent after settling into her birthing room. The last message came after her epidural. My mind wound back down the path that brought us to this day.

Lauren attended TU as planned and earned her degree in teaching. After graduating, she landed a job at a nearby junior high. She was a music teacher. A slew of suitors came as the years passed. None remained. I did not know who the father of her child was. It didn't matter to me. She never spoke of him, simply indicated it was for the best that she raise the child alone. Jennings Ellington became a distant memory, one I found easy to forget.

Her decision to move back home after she got pregnant came as a welcome surprise. She'd asked for my help and wanted to save money for her child. I couldn't ask for anything better.

I thrived in my job, having advanced from a CPT coder to head of the claims department at Coventry Springs. But as the pandemic settled upon the country, I'd grown fearful. Illness, isolation, and death roamed the halls of the care center. I'd been one of the fortunate staff members allowed to transition to working from home. While the world fell apart, Lauren and I grew closer together. I remembered the day she told me she was pregnant.

"I know it isn't how things are supposed to be done," she'd started, hooking her fingers into air quotes with the final words. "But marriage doesn't seem to be in the cards for me, and I really want to be a mom. I didn't want to wait until I was in my thirties. The opportunity presented itself, so…"

She spoke as if she needed to convince me that the path she'd chosen was just. As if anything past my becoming a grandmother mattered to me. I'd insisted they could stay as long as she wanted, but her plan was to continue to live with me for the first year of her child's life and no longer, even though she had few delusions regarding the challenges she faced as a single mother.

I was honored that she'd returned to me, having worked to appease her and regain her trust over the years. Lauren might attribute our close relationship to therapy, which we did for a few months after she finished high school. She'd embraced counseling, but I was never convinced it was worthwhile. I stuck with our joint sessions for as long as I could take it. Our therapist was a man. As if any good could come from taking the advice of someone who knew nothing of the mother/daughter bond. He'd pushed for honesty and absolution. Lauren soaked up all his input, but I never trusted him with his talk of boundaries and truth. He was easy to fool, though, and never dug deeper into my life than the abuse I'd suffered at the hands of Dr. Addison.

By the time the twice-weekly appointments grew tiresome and Lauren started college, we let the sessions fall by the wayside, much to my relief. Lauren was satisfied we'd purged our demons, and I was tired of having someone poke around inside my mind.

While I didn't enjoy living alone and loathed the empty nest, I worked to improve the house and focused on my job, quieting the heavy silence of the barren home. After Kane passed, I selected two kittens from a shelter. Elle and Emmett kept mice and loneliness away. Now I had more than I ever could have hoped for. My home had at long last been refreshed; new life had been breathed into it. My career was fulfilling and fruitful, and I had Lauren to myself again. I'd readily accepted her homecoming, and now, as I sat alone in my car in the crowded parking lot, I knew things would only get better.

LAUREN: *She's here! Introducing Alana Alice White, 7 lbs 8 oz, 20* *inches long. Ten fingers, ten toes. Absolute perfection! Get your binoculars out. The nurse is bringing her to the window.*

I stared at the attached image, and tears sprung forth. A squished and wrinkled face, red and blotchy, stared back at me with soulful eyes. She was perfect. It was like looking at Lauren as a newborn all over again. I pulled the binoculars out of the console and jumped out of the car. Holding them to my eyes, I scanned the windows above until I saw the nurse waving. She held the little bundle up, and I focused the lenses on her. Alana was quiet and still in her swaddle. Before I'd soaked up all that she was, the nurse disappeared. It was the greatest moment of my life.

———

"My maternity leave is almost over. I really thought eight weeks sounded like an eternity. But it's flown by so fast. It isn't fair. She's still so tiny, so helpless." Lauren jostled the infant up and down in the familiar dance, bobbing gently to placate the fussy baby. "I can't ask you to quit your job to care for my child, Mom. We can find someone to watch her during school hours."

"Nonsense, honey."

Lauren was a natural mother, but the pandemic threw a wrench in her carefully laid plans. As she neared the end of her maternity leave, she was left without the benefit of the district's childcare program. I couldn't fathom how a music teacher could instruct eighth graders from her computer screen, but such was the new way of things.

"It will be fine," she continued. Her tone implied she was working to convince herself more than me. "Thanks to this pandemic, I don't have to leave her someplace, but with her colic I'm not sure how I'm going to juggle things even without being inside a classroom. This whole virtual thing is a joke, but it keeps me from bringing every bug home to this little one."

Lauren's words were halting. Her cadence bounced with her body, setting rhythm to her speech. "Then again, maybe a daycare is for the best. I hate the idea of leaving her in a petri dish every day, but it will build her immune system, right?"

"Out of the question," I said. "The timing couldn't be more perfect. Besides, you aren't asking, and it isn't quitting. I'm offering, and it's retirement. It's a few years early, but I can do it. My finances are secure, and working in administration at a nursing home has become pretty risky business these days, especially for someone my age."

I busied myself washing baby bottles, doing my part to help the new mother out. "Between furloughs and working from home and masks… Don't even get me started with the deaths. The suffering is overwhelming. Honestly, I think some of the residents are dying from loneliness, without even catching the dreaded virus. I can't take it anymore. The world is imploring me to retire, and I can't think of a more delightful retirement than being a caregiver for this beautiful girl."

I put the bottles on the drying rack. After I dried my hands, I moved to where Lauren swayed with her infant, reaching out to take the baby.

"It's so tempting," Lauren said, handing Alana over to me. With her arms free, she tilted her head side to side to stretch her neck and shook her hands. "But I don't want her to be a burden."

A loud burp erupted from Alana, cutting off Lauren's words. The baby settled with the release of the offending gas bubble and cooed.

"Seriously? I've been trying to get that burp up for almost an hour."

"Neither of you is a burden. There are so many pros here," I said. "And I can't think of any cons. I can lower my risk of catching this disease, help you out, save you gobs of money… I could go on and on."

Now I danced around the kitchen as Lauren made herself a cup of coffee. I'd offered to help with feedings during the overnight hours, but Lauren insisted on tending to the baby on her own as much as possible. But I was always there—well-rested, prepared. Alana got the best possible version of me. I'd bonded with my grandchild already; we had a special relationship that would only grow.

"Well, when you put it that way. Maybe it is our best option," she said, collapsing into the banquette. She lifted her arms and sniffed, grimaced, and then scratched at a mystery stain on her T-shirt.

"Why don't you go take a shower?" I suggested, noting the bags weighing heavy under her eyes and her unkempt, stringy hair.

"That'd be wonderful, but I need to pump. Gotta get my supply up." She downed the coffee. I hadn't confessed that I'd switched to decaf during her pregnancy, for Alana's sake.

"Well, my next Zoom meeting isn't for another couple of hours. I'll take care of her while you pump and shower. Maybe you can squeeze in a little nap."

"A nap? What's that?" she joked. She stood and walked to us, kissing Alana's forehead before kissing my cheek. "Thanks, Mom. I don't know how I'd get through this without you."

There was no fanfare, no going-away celebration, no retirement party to mark my departure from Coventry Springs. Gatherings were forbidden, and the nursing home was a place of mourning and fear these days. I couldn't have asked for a better job. It had allowed me to work in a place that was like a second home to me. It hadn't been the same since the pandemic, though. Empty halls, so much death.

Poor Shelby Addison contracted the disease. Instead of finding love and starting a family, she'd spent all those years in a lifeless sleep, only to die alone far too young. She'd likely contracted it from a caregiver since I was the only other person who visited her in all those years. She succumbed within days of falling ill. Her frail body had been weakened by years of forced inertia. There was no service. There were few services for the dead while the virus had its way with the world.

Having a granddaughter was like living motherhood over again, only better. Gone were the hormones that brought panic and anxiety. I wasn't trying to prove myself to anyone. No forced schedules, no comparisons to others, no competition. Just me pouring all my love into my beautiful grandchild. It was more than I ever imagined it would be, and Alana gave back to me more than I provided her.

My daughter and I made a wonderful team as we raised little Alana. Lauren didn't move out after a year. Instead, the three of us lived together. I was happy to keep them on and couldn't have imagined it any other way. The infant was the salve that healed our relationship better than all the therapy rubbish. Alana did more than mend the wounds—she erased the scars. It was an almost-perfect world. My small family lived in our happy little bubble for over two years until our lives were toppled once again by Nancy Ellington.

One morning while Alana, now exploring the world as a toddler, played with Tupperware containers on the kitchen floor, I sat at the table looking through the newspaper. Though the obituary pages were becoming fewer in number, news of the dead hadn't dropped to pre-pandemic levels yet, despite a vaccination. I scanned the announcements section when a photo leaped off the page. Nancy, now Nancy Ellington Larson, was dead.

I snatched it from the pile and drew it near my face. The obituary featured an old photo of Nancy, likely taken near the time she'd fallen out of our lives. I wondered what she looked like now... Well, what she looked like last week. There was no indication of her cause of death. I'd have put money on cirrhosis, but perhaps the virus had taken her out.

Alana toddled to me and climbed into my lap.

"I bet you're hungry," I chirped, my mood lifted by her smile. I left the paper on the table and started a batch of waffles for Alana, holding the child on my hip and narrating my actions. I let her dump the teaspoon of vanilla extract into the batter. As we drizzled the first cupful into the maker, Lauren joined us from her bedroom. She poured a cup of coffee.

"Nana is making us waffles again, I see," Lauren said, putting her coffee cup on the table and taking Alana from me. "I don't know if she needs your help." She kissed my cheek and spoke to me. "How do you hold her like that? She's getting so big. Like a ton of bricks!" She carried Alana across the room, lifting her up and blowing raspberries on her belly. Alana squealed.

"Why don't you clean this mess up for Nana before breakfast?" she said to Alana, setting the toddler back down in the sea of plastic containers. Alana began to stack the items in a tower rather than for storage, and Lauren sat at the table.

"Oh my God," Lauren gasped, snatching the newspaper from where I'd left it. The second the words escaped her lips, I cursed myself. Why had I left the obituary there? "Did you see this?"

"What's that, dear?" I asked, feigning ignorance as I placed a waffle on a plate.

"Mrs. E," she said, her voice barely a whisper. "Mrs. E is dead. Look here." She rose and crossed the room, paper in hand, tears already welling in her eyes. "Wow, this is so sad."

I took the paper from her and scanned it, unsure of what to say. I searched my mind for the right words—something supportive and not spiteful, but also something to abate the severity of the blow. Maybe I could cauterize it before it could bleed out and stain our lives. Nothing came to me. I tried to shift the tenor.

"Breakfast is ready," I said, turning to Alana, placing a plate where her booster seat sat and cutting the waffle into small pieces.

Lauren remained where she stood and scanned the obituary. I scooped Alana off the floor and put her in her booster seat.

"She'd been living outside of New York City, it says, but they are bringing her home to be buried. The service is this Friday."

"Service? Like in-person, not virtual?" Of course, Nancy wouldn't have an online service. Even in death, her ego wouldn't allow it.

"Not online, the real deal," Lauren said, joining Alana at the table. I returned to the waffle iron and dumped more batter in.

"We should go," she said.

The mixing bowl slipped from my hand, and waffle batter splattered all over the countertop. "Dammit!" I hissed.

"Mom!" Lauren said. "Little ears!" She jerked her head toward Alana with eyes wide. Alana didn't notice my slip-up as she stuffed another bite of waffle into her mouth, making a show of licking the syrup off her fingers afterward.

"Right, sorry," I said, grabbing a dish towel and corralling batter back into the bowl. "Why would you want to attend her funeral? Who knows who might be there. It could get very uncomfortable."

"True," she said, slowly chewing a bite she'd swiped from Alana's plate. "But I don't know. So much time has passed. It says here that Jennings is married…" Her words drifted off. Her eyes never left the page.

"Oh, sweetie," I said, joining her at the table.

"Whatever, it is what it is. Not like I could marry my half-brother." She straightened in her seat and put another bite in her mouth.

"Well, yeah," I said. "But still."

She wiped a tear from her eye. I wondered if it was for Nancy or for herself.

"I think we should go. Mrs. E never did anything to us but be supportive. She was like a second mom to me. Jennings and I have both moved on. It's really kind of sad that we drifted so far apart. I mean, I know why it happened. It was all too awkward, too difficult to navigate. But now, well, we're grown-ups. You and I owe it to Mrs. E and Jennings to attend."

I could read her face. The set of her jaw told me her mind was made up. I scrambled for a reason to deny her, see if I could use Alana to dissuade her.

"Think about Alana. Being in a place like that. Close quarters. She's managed to avoid the virus so far, but we'd just be asking for it if we attended a funeral."

"The numbers are way down these days," she countered. "Besides, for little kids, it's usually nothing more than a severe cold. I mean, I get it if you don't want to attend. Alana and I can go without you."

I stifled a laugh. As if I'd send the two of them into that situation alone.

"Well, we should at least wear masks," I conceded. Lauren had claimed to want the truth years ago, but I'd hidden plenty from her regarding the type of person Nancy had been. My mind raced with other arguments as to why we shouldn't go but came up empty. I prepared myself mentally for her funeral, knowing at least now Nancy was finally out of our lives for good.

TWENTY-SIX

CONCEPTION

The sun did little to warm the crisp autumn day. Leave it to Nancy to ruin my favorite season. Alana tugged on my hand as we made our way to the church.

"Shoes hurt, Nana," she complained.

"I know, sweetie," I said, attempting to placate her. "We can take them off when we find a seat."

Lauren wasn't aware of our conversation as she scanned the cavernous room. I didn't know if she was searching for someone or trying to hide from them. Alana and I should have stayed at home. This was no place for a two-year-old. The church was packed. Hardly anyone wore masks. I tugged Alana's up before adjusting mine.

"Let's sit back here," I suggested, lifting Alana into my arms and moving to a row near the rear. Lauren followed me, and we squeezed past a young couple to take our seats. Before I had time to remove Alana's shoes, the music quieted, and the procession appeared at the rear doors. We stood.

Jennings was third in line behind a man who bore a slight resemblance to him. Between this man and Jennings was a young Nancy. I'd never met her older children. Each of Nancy's children was on the arm of their spouse. Jennings' wife's cheeks glowed—her belly was full with child. I shifted my gaze from the procession to Lauren. Her eyes were locked onto Jennings, never drifting from him.

The service was eternal. A slew of Nancy's friends spouted endlessly about the woman. How fun she was. How insightful she was. How generous. Alana fell asleep. Without the distraction of the toddler, I was forced to listen to the mourners exalt the insidious woman. Obviously, none of them knew her like I did. It was almost as if Nancy had crafted each eulogy herself.

When the casket was ushered out of the nave, I grabbed Lauren's arm. "We really should get out of here." I whispered to her as we stood and waited for an opening to escape our pew.

"No, we need to give our condolences," she insisted. "I can take Alana if she's too heavy for you."

In the vestibule, we were ferried along by the current of well-wishers. Alana woke and agreed to walk, stopping and bending over every few steps to glide her finger between her heel and the offending patent leather. It seemed like time stood still in the river of soft murmurs, black attire, and polite hugs, but finally we approached the family.

Jennings' eyes lit on fire when he recognized Lauren. I wondered if I was the only one to detect the ember that still burned between them. I fought the urge to whisper a reminder in her ear: "He's your brother. He's married now."

"Lauren? Mrs. White?" He approached, arms open. He and Lauren collided, and the flint cleaved again as he hugged her. His wife looked on with a credulous smile.

"Wow," he exclaimed, extracting himself from Lauren's embrace. "It's so good to see you both. Thank you so much for coming. Mother would be touched." I detected no trace of our defective history in his demeanor. "And who is this little one?" he asked, bending to shake Alana's hand.

The child, who never met a stranger despite her life being spent without much social engagement, made her best attempt at pronouncing her own name while Lauren reached down and removed her mask.

"This is Alana," Lauren chimed, tucking the mask into her pocket. I realized then that she'd removed her own mask. Anger threatened to spill out of me. We'd agreed to wear masks. What was she doing risking Alana's health? I gnawed at my lip to contain my words as Lauren continued, "She's my daughter."

Jennings stood and took Lauren's hand. "She's absolutely beautiful. Just like her mom!"

Silence hung between them. Alana grew impatient with the reticence and pulled from my grasp, worming her way between the legs of those in line behind us. I had no choice but to give chase and wanted nothing more than to drag Lauren along with me.

I trailed the parting crowd until I caught up with Alana and gripped her hand.

"That was dangerous, young lady!" I snapped. "You have to hold hands in a crowd this big."

Her lip quivered. Her face shifted from innocence to shame in the span of seconds before her mouth dropped open. She was powerless to control her wails. Nana rarely raised her voice. I scooped her up and made my way to the doors, looking back to see Lauren and Jennings still talking. He'd ushered her away from the family line, and the two huddled in a nearby corner. I stepped out into the sunshine with Alana.

I tried my best to distract Alana outside the church. After applying Band-Aids to her heels, we searched for the biggest leaf and counted clouds as we waited for her mother. Just when I'd decided to push back through the crowd and seek Lauren out, she appeared on the steps, hand shielding her eyes from the late afternoon sun. I waved her down, and she approached, wiping tears from her eyes.

"Are you okay?" I asked as she joined us and lifted Alana into her arms.

"Let's just get the car," she whispered.

We didn't speak until Lauren pulled onto the highway.

"Well, that was weird," she said. Her chest rose higher with each breath and sank deeper with every exhale as she forced air out through pursed lips.

"I can imagine," I replied.

"You know what? I'm sorry, I need to pull over." She checked the mirror and crossed two lanes to pull onto the shoulder.

"Are you all right?" I asked, noting traffic was light along the thoroughfare. "Do you need me to drive?"

"No," she said, putting the car in park and turning on the hazard lights. "I just need a minute to catch my breath." She squeezed the steering wheel and leaned forward, gently banging her head on it. After a few minutes, she drew a deep breath and lifted her head and leaned back, her gaze on the car's ceiling. "God, he seemed so happy. I miss him so much."

I monitored the traffic, uncomfortable with our position on the busy highway since the evening rush was fast approaching. I struggled to control my instinct to pry further. What had her so upset? My mind grappled with possibilities. Had I left any holes Nancy or Jennings could have squirmed through? Something that would rattle Lauren? I'd been so careful. I could think of nothing. I wanted to scream at her and beg her to tell me what happened. I stayed quiet.

After a few deep breaths, she checked the mirror and merged back onto the highway. We drove in silence until I couldn't take the dead air.

"What happened? What did he say?"

"Well, I met his wife. She seemed nice." Her eyes scanned the road ahead as if she were reminding herself she was behind the wheel. "They are having a boy, due on Christmas Day." Her voice cracked.

"Are you sure you don't need me to drive?"

"No, I'm good," she said, swiping at a tear that dangled from her chin. "It was just weird."

She was quiet until we took our exit from the highway. At the stoplight, she looked at me.

"He invited me to join a group."

"A group? What kind of group?"

"It's made up of Dr. Addison's offspring. There are over fifty of them. Can you believe it?"

My chest seized. Air couldn't pass through my throat. I pressed the button to roll down the window.

"Fifty siblings," she said, her voice distant. "It's so unreal."

I could tell she was struggling to process the information. I wanted to give her time, let her thoughts develop, but questions jumped out of my mind in a barrage.

"What else did he say?" My voice came out in a halting screech. I hoped I didn't sound as desperate as I felt.

"He said they'd formed a community. It started at the beginning of the pandemic. He reconnected with the Gilbert twins, and they reached out to others they knew. It grew from there. He said it's been cathartic, and they've made some really close bonds."

"Well, that sounds horrible! A bunch of bastard children commiserating with each other. Over what? Their evil father? How is whining about the wrongs done to your mothers helpful to anyone?" I tasted the venom in my words and chided myself for being so indelicate. I had no idea where the vile language came from.

"Mom!" she yelled. "Those are some pretty harsh words! It's not like any of us had a choice in the matter. And it didn't just happen to the mothers. It happened to their husbands and their kids."

"You're right, honey. I guess I've just stuffed it all down so far. It came bubbling up with a vengeance." It was the closest thing I had to an apology. I still fought with what more to say. "I'm not sure that's the most constructive way to deal with any of this. I mean, everyone has moved on with their lives. You guys aren't really so different. I mean, there are plenty of kids who don't know who their fathers are or who are being raised by men who didn't father them. Loads of kids go through life not knowing they have half-siblings roaming the globe. What they don't know isn't hurting them in most cases."

I wanted to yell at her that Jennings' own sister didn't know who her father was. Alana didn't know hers. I didn't know mine. But I choked those words down. "You're not thinking of joining, are you?"

From her car seat, Alana started to fuss. Her whimpers barely permeated my awareness. The ringing in my ears peaked and plummeted in a chaotic clatter, shrill and angry.

"It's okay, sweetie," Lauren cooed, her gaze flashing to the rearview mirror with a consoling smile. She redirected her words to me. "Yeah, I am thinking of joining. I just have to provide a DNA test."

"I don't think I have those documents anymore," I snapped, grateful for an easy out.

"The old test wouldn't work anyway," she replied. "I have to take a new one through this online company. They are using it as a way to verify and link those of us who share paternity."

She kept talking, but I couldn't hear her words, couldn't hear Alana's anxious cries. Only the blaring siren in my own ears. I had to convince Lauren this group was the worst idea, and she should veer far from the notion. She should walk away, run, continue the life she was paving. I looked at her, my vision fading and sharpening again. Her jaw was set.

"Mind if I pop into the drugstore? Jennings said I could pick up a test kit there."

She'd already flipped her signal on and was slowing to make the turn into the pharmacy closest to our home. I had to stop her. While she searched for a parking spot, my mind spun. I felt dizzy, like I might pass out. My pulse strobed in my head, and sweat burst from every pore.

"You wanna stay in the car with the little monster?" Lauren asked, putting the car in park. She thumbed toward the backseat and flashed a wink in the rearview mirror.

Alana quieted.

"I shouldn't be long." She took her purse and reached for the door handle.

"Wait!" I yelled. My mind was overrun with thoughts of the damage this test could do; history blinded me. I grabbed her arm.

"Jeez! Go easy!" she barked, twisting from my grip. My tone set

Alana off. "If you want to go in, that's fine. It's just her feet and all. And now she's crying again."

"No, Lauren," I pleaded. "I think you need to think this through. Mull it over. Do you really want to dig up the past again? We're so happy."

"Happy?" Alana asked with a whimper.

Lauren peered over her shoulder and smiled at her daughter.

"Yes, honey. Happy," she said to Alana with a sing-song voice, before speaking to me. "We're all happy as can be right now. But I still have so many questions." She relaxed her hand on the door handle. "Look, Mom, I can't expect you to understand any of this. Fortunately, there aren't too many people who could understand…"

She trailed off, her eyes shifting as she searched for words. "But I think it might help. We all share a bond, even though it wasn't one we ever wanted. It is what it is. I really want to get to know these people. They're my family, Alana's family."

"Is this some twisted ploy to get back into Jennings' life?" I spat, straightening my back and fixing her with accusing eyes.

She was dumbstruck. Her mouth opened, her brow twisted.

"Because if it is, well…" I hoped the words were landing with the intended brunt. "It's just sick."

I watched the flush race from her neck to her hairline, igniting a fire in her eyes. She looked at me as if I were the monster. I hated the shifting look of anger gathering inside her. I hadn't seen it in fourteen years.

"How dare you!" she yelled, snatching her purse to her chest and fleeing the car. After she slammed the door, she glared at me through the window. I had to stop her.

I jumped out of the vehicle, not bothering to shut the door, and ran to her, blocking her movement. Alana's cries hit a crescendo.

"Please, Lauren," I begged. "I'm so sorry! I didn't mean those things!"

She crossed her arms and shifted her glance to the sales banners pasted inside the store's windows. She was giving me a chance!

"Please, honey. Just get back in the car. Think about the impact. Sleep on it." While I spoke, I approached her as if cornering a wild animal. Honey oozed from my words, which came gentle and low. My arms opened for an embrace, making it easier to grab her should she make the wrong move.

She was quiet, but I could see the thoughts churning through her mind. Her body softened as the seconds ticked by. I was certain I'd convinced her and dropped my arms, reaching for her wrist so I could guide her back to the car. From the backseat, Alana watched. Even the child sensed the storm calming as she looked at us with hopeful eyes.

"I'm sorry," Lauren said, shifting her weight to take a step closer to the doors. "You're wrong about this. Please stay with Alana. I'll be right back."

She moved to push past me, and my hand caught her wrist. I jerked her close. Our faces almost collided. Her breath felt hot as it confronted mine, and a mask of confusion fell over her face.

"Please don't!" I whispered as an elderly woman shuffled past us, throwing a glance over her shoulder. Her eyes were wary as she clutched the collar of her jacket and hurried to the door.

"Let go of me!" Lauren cried. Gaining control of her volume, she hissed, "This is absolutely crazy!" Her eyes darted around as she looked to see if anyone was witness to the scene.

"Lauren, I'm serious."

She made a move to turn toward the store, and I wrenched her back.

"Mom!" she yelled.

"Please," I whimpered.

It wasn't working. She twisted away again, but I spun her back to me. Rage flashed in her eyes. She was no longer concerned about onlookers, but I was, noticing cautious glances from others in the parking lot. In shame, I released her arm from my grip just as she yanked herself free. Her feet teetered on the edge of the curb, arms pinwheeling.

I watched her fall in slow motion. Her hair lifted forward and covered her face, erasing her wide eyes. Only her mouth, lips tightened into a perfect O, was visible. Her shoulders curved inward as her body reflexively tried to save itself. I reached out for her again.

Our fingers brushed, but momentum carried her backward. I didn't grab her. Her head hit the pavement with a dull *thwack*. Blood trickled out in a stream, drawing a red line through the faded yellow parking space line.

I stood fixed to the spot, unable to move. Not one muscle gave way. A young couple rushed to Lauren, and the man fumbled around in his pocket. The woman slid across the pavement as she reached for Lauren, securing her head in her hands and yelling for her companion to call nine-one-one.

TWENTY-SEVEN

PARTURITION

The accident devastated Lauren's brain. Three months later, after the hospital had done all it could for Lauren, I moved her to Coventry Springs. By request, she was given Shelby's former room. I was excited for her to be out of the hospital and in a place that wasn't so terrifying and sterile.

Alana was in the common room being fussed over by the grandmotherly residents of the care facility, while I fussed about in Lauren's new room. I taped Alana's drawings and cards from her students on all the walls to brighten the space. Jennings and his wife sent a stunning floral arrangement, and I watered it, picking off some browning leaves. The staff members assigned to care for Lauren's transfer tended to her, checking IV lines and adjusting her cannula. Lauren was in the best hands.

Dr. Hastings, Lauren's neurologist, entered the room.

"Good morning, Mrs. White," he said, taking in the space with his hands on his hips. He nodded. "This is a comfortable room. Bright, nicely appointed." He approached me, one hand outstretched. Machines beeped and pinged behind Lauren's bed, and a nurse pushed buttons on the maze of flashing lights and screens.

I shook his hand and moved to Lauren's side to take her hand. An ugly green bruise seeped out around a bandage on the back of her hand. Her skin was porcelain aside from the offending mar.

"She seems to have tolerated the move like the champ she is," I said. My smile landed on her sleeping face.

The doctor set his tablet on the high table next to Lauren's bed and waited for the screen to come to life. His lips twitched back and forth as he scanned the secret scrolls that outlined Lauren's condition. He nodded his head every so often. Her diagnosis was UWS; it stood for unresponsive wakefulness syndrome—the same fate that had befallen Shelby Addison all those years ago. I smoothed her hair and considered coloring it for her as soon as her wounds healed. She'd be embarrassed of the two-inch dark roots crowning the places where her head hadn't been shaved. Maybe I'd color it to match her natural color. She always had the prettiest hair.

"Yes, everything looks to be in good order here," the doctor said, snapping his folio shut. He tucked it under his arm. "Don't hesitate to call if you have any concerns. One of my colleagues or I will be by each day for the next few weeks. Then, if she's doing well, we can check in weekly, maybe even monthly, depending on how things are going."

"Dr. Hastings," I said, rounding the bed and standing by his side. "We can't thank you enough."

"You're very welcome. I wish there had been more we could have done."

"Well, she's here, and for me that is everything." I hugged the man. He wasn't prepared for it, and the moment soured from sentimental to awkward.

"All right, then. Call my office with any questions, and I'll be seeing you both soon. Have a good day."

I walked him to Lauren's door and peeked into the hall as he departed. Alana's squeals of laughter floated to me. I'd made the decision to vaccinate her. Lauren had been against it before the accident, but it was necessary to keep Lauren safe and allow Alana entry to the care facility. Alana was all laughs at the moment, but her lunch and nap time were closing in on us. I needed to get her home. Her routine had been hurled out the window after Lauren's accident, and we were still struggling to get her back on track.

I went to Lauren's bedside and watched her. Sunlight fell across her face when I opened the blinds. As horrific as the accident had been and as devastating as her prognosis was, at least she wasn't alone. She still had me. And Alana. And just as important, I had her. She was here. So was her family. I kissed her forehead.

"We'll be back after Alana's nap to check in on you, dear. Rest comfortably."

Back at home, with Alana fed and tucked in, I went to Lauren's room to gather some of her belongings. I had a box of photos to take to Coventry Springs and wanted to bring some other items— her favorite pillow, one of Alana's blankets, unwashed. I hoped the token, with its sentimental musk of Alana's shampoo, sweat, and slobber, would comfort Lauren while she slept.

I brought the small box to the entryway and fingered through the items, knowing there was something I was missing, when it hit me. I went to my room. Since my knees weren't as spry as they used to be, I'd relocated my keepsake trunk to the shelf that used to hold Roger's shoes. I brought the box down, took it to the bed, and opened it. The stuffed bunny sat atop the other items I kept secreted from the world. I stroked its pink, faded fur, the bare spots, its little paw tattered and frayed where Lauren had gripped it during play and sleep. All of it showed years of love.

I lifted the rabbit to my nose, breathing it in. Like a wave, the scent crashed upon me. My baby, my sweet, beautiful daughter, as she used to be. Full of life, full of hope, with a future. As I inhaled the essence, tears streamed from my eyes. I swiped at my face, reminding myself how lucky I was to still have her. I never had to fear her leaving me again. There would be no man to sweep her off her feet, carrying her and my precious Alana away.

Just below the treasured rabbit lay my pregnancy journal, the cover warped and cracked with time. I lifted it and let the book fall open in my hands, not surprised to see what page I landed on. It was one I'd revisited often during my pregnancy with Lauren. It held my most tightly kept secret. The one thing that would have laid waste to my relationship with my daughter. The reason she couldn't join the forsaken group of Dr. Addison's children.

Without further thought, I returned to the foyer with both items and tucked them into the box. I knew the time had come to reveal the thing I always believed I would take to my grave. Lauren could now know the truth. Perhaps it would set me free, allow me to move forward. Maybe I could be a better mother to Alana than I'd ever been to Lauren.

As I paced the kitchen, I convinced myself the time was right. Before I had a chance to talk myself out of it, Alana called to me from her bedroom.

———

"Do you ladies think Alana could be your lucky charm at bingo this afternoon?" I asked, plopping Alana in an empty plastic chair in the common room. A group of four hearty women sat with elbows on the table, chins resting in their bony hands. The completed corner of a puzzle made a tiny island in a sea of pieces laid out in front of them. They'd all survived Covid and were like family to me. Alana was just the distraction they needed from their impossible task. The puzzle was forgotten as they pawed for the child's attention.

"She's certainly the cutest good luck charm," gushed Betsy, perilously lifting the girl from the chair to her lap.

Across the table, Rhoda produced a sucker from her sweater pocket.

Alana took the treat, and Betsy helped her unwrap it.

I kissed Alana's forehead. "Thank you, ladies. I need some time to get Lauren settled in."

"Of course, dear," Sophia said. "Take all the time you need. We'll keep this little one entertained."

I thanked the women and retrieved my box from the floor,

leaving Alana's backpack behind. "There are snacks in her bag," I told the women as I headed down the hall.

The lights were turned off in Lauren's room, and someone had drawn the curtains. I made a mental note to request the room remain lit during daytime hours. Lauren wasn't fond of gloomy spaces. I opened the blinds and snapped on the light. Next, I swapped out one of the flat pillows with its scratchy case provided by the nursing home with one from Lauren's bed at home. I fluffed it and laid Alana's blanket next to her face, minding the wires and tubes that trailed in and out of her body. I placed the bunny on top of the blanket. It was such a peaceful image; I took my phone out and snapped a picture.

I went back to the box, retrieved a framed photo, and placed it by Lauren's bed. It was a portrait of Alana. One I had taken after the accident. Returning to the box, the journal stared up at me. I lifted it and held it to my chest. Disquiet fell over me like snow, piece by tiny piece melting into me. I absorbed the grief they held.

How could I ever expect her to forgive me when I'd never forgiven myself? Maybe now, if I spilled the poison I'd held inside all these years, we could both achieve a state of forgiveness. It wouldn't hurt to try.

I sat next to her and wished I could see her beautiful eyes again. Longing rattled around the empty shell I'd become. I'd been weak. I'd been powerless. I had no choice back then. But in the face of every choice since, I'd doubted myself. In the end, it had cost me almost everything. Again, I thanked the universe for sparing her life.

Cracking the book open, it fell to the page I needed to read to Lauren. I sat next to her bed and cleared my throat.

My dearest Lauren,

The doctor confirmed today what I've known all along. You are a girl. I couldn't contain my joy when he told me the news. I'd like to say your father was as happy as I, but, well, he had his heart set on a boy.

Too bad for him!

I believe your being a girl, the fulfillment of my lifelong dream, was a gift to me, a reward for all I've endured. I hope motherhood never eludes you. That you are not cursed with a forsaken womb and you never struggle to feel complete. That you are never forced to make the choices I've made.

I lied to your father. In a horrid act of desperation, I eliminated him from the process of making you. He didn't understand how strong my want was. He was denying me the one thing I needed most in life. If you think about it, really, it was his fault. He forced my hand.

The words on the page became fuzzy, distant, as my mind returned to that day. I set the journal on the bed and spoke from memory, the words spilling out of me as I relayed to Lauren the events of the day I returned to Dr. Addison's office alone.

I sat in the exam room. The shadows of my deceit lingered above me as I flipped through the pages of that horrible book. Statistics and photos spilled across each page. It was overwhelming. I hadn't a clue how I'd make such a momentous decision on my own. It wasn't like I could take the book home and peruse it at my leisure. The pressure to decide was immense.

I closed the catalog in complete panic and frustration just as Dr. Addison entered the room. He saw me crying.

"Now, Mrs. White," he began, leaving the door open for his nurse. "This is not a place for tears. This is a place for new beginnings, right, Nurse Carol?"

"You're absolutely right, Dr. Addison," the nurse chimed, looking at me with her disorienting smile.

"I know," I said, snatching a tissue from Nurse Carol's hand when she held it out to me. "It's just—" I couldn't make my mouth say anything more and shuddered with sobs.

Nurse Carol lifted the book out of my lap and placed it on the countertop. "Lie back, dear. Everything is going to be okay. You don't need to make a decision today. Take some deep breaths. I'll be right back. I forgot to pull a donor contract for you, Mrs. White." She left the room, leaving me alone with Dr. Addison.

"Nurse Carol is right. And if the decision is still too daunting for you, we have ways to help guide you through the process." He winked at me and disappeared behind the sheet that divided my body. "You're not alone," he said, his voice muffled by the barrier.

The nurse knocked gently on the door before reentering the

exam room. She held a folder and cleared her throat, her eyes darting to the doctor's as she placed the folder on top of the catalog, where it was in my direct line of sight if I rolled my eyes to the left. I rolled them to the right as I scooted my rear down to rest my feet in the stirrups. The only noises in the room for the next few minutes were the squeaking of his chair and the wrinkling of paper beneath me.

"Relax." His voice filled the space with a boom, making me jump. He didn't comment on my reaction, just proceeded to insert the ultrasound wand into me. I should have grown used to the intrusion by then, having accepted the vile tool inside me countless times. It still felt like a violation.

"Hmmm." His voice was quieter this time. "Well, this is an unexpected development." He fell silent as the wand explored my insides.

I struggled onto my elbows and strained to see the screen, which he kept directed at himself.

"What is it?" Panic swept me up in its current. Was there something wrong with me? Something that would keep me from becoming a mother? I squirmed but was forced back to the table when the probe struck a sensitive spot. The pain felt like a bolt of lightning.

"Please be still, Mrs. White," he said, not looking away from the screen. "I don't want to hurt you." He withdrew the profane tool and turned the monitor to face me. The image on the screen meant nothing. It was just a fuzzy jumble of black and white and gray, an alien landscape.

"You won't have to pick a donor after all," he said, pointing to a tightly bundled bean shape in the swarm of gray-scale. "This right here"—he tapped the bean-bundle—"is a perfectly developed embryo."

I fell back on the table and replayed his words in my mind until they took focus, made sense. I was already pregnant. We'd conceived unassisted. Roger and I had done it without Dr. Addison's help.

"Oh my!" Nurse Carol exclaimed, clapping her hands three times and driving the revelation deeper into me.

"I'm sorry, what?" I muttered.

"You're pregnant," he said. "I'd say roughly eight weeks, give or take a few days. You don't need me at this point. You can go home and tell the happy father to be. I'm sure he'll be over the moon!"

"I'm—" I couldn't say the word. It was far too big a word to utter. The room brightened and the air grew easier to breathe.

"Congratulations!" He removed his gloves and offered me his hand, and Nurse Carol simultaneously lifted the table until I was upright. My knees were cocked together, the sheet slipping away due to the motion. The nurse reached down and threw it back over me as I sat exposed and uncaring. Finally, a smile arched across my face.

I returned to the journal now. My fingers scanned the page, making sure I hadn't left anything out. I knew better. The day was etched on my memory clearer than even the day Lauren was born. I continued to read aloud.

So you see, I have no need to tell your father. Somehow, despite the steps I've taken to get to this point, I've been granted this gift. The gift of you. I've had moments of doubt, believing it all to be some great illusion. As if I wasn't worthy of such a perfect outcome. But I am!

Who knows how the conception happened? Maybe it was the weight I lost after Mother's death or the combination of vitamins I demanded your father take. Or maybe he was right and during the window when he'd denied me further treatments, my psyche relaxed enough to allow nature to take its course. Whatever the reason, I'll take it.

I used the extra money I hid from my mother's estate to hire a decorator for your nursery, one Nancy recommended. I've quickly learned that getting pregnant costs less than being pregnant. I couldn't afford much, but while your father was at work, the designer hung the wallpaper and helped me pick out the perfect crib and bedding. Yours is by far the nicest room in the house! Your dad thinks I did it all myself. Our little secret.

I can't tell you what a relief it was that the procedures were over. That I'd never have to subject myself to the injections and treatments. I wouldn't have to convince your father that you were his. I'd feared being able to look him in the eye as I handed you over to him. Surely he'd know immediately if you weren't his offspring. He'd never have believed I picked a stranger from a book. He would accuse me of cheating. Now, that fear is squelched. I have nothing to hide and everything to celebrate.

I'll say goodbye for now, my sweet, sweet girl. Growing you is an exhausting but exhilarating journey. As always, I can't wait to hold you!

All my love, Mommy

I sat down next to Lauren and closed the book, feeling lighter than I had in ages. As difficult as it had been to conceive, to raise a child, to do the things I'd done to achieve those dreams, keeping it all concealed had been almost impossible. But I'd succeeded. Roger never learned the truth, never knew I'd gone behind his back with the intent of selecting a better donor to create a child.

And Lauren never learned how I'd used the past to fashion an altered future for her, one that resulted in Alana being brought into the world. I knew if push had ever come to shove, she'd choose Alana over building a life with Jennings. Knowing a life with the Ellingtons would ultimately end badly, I risked everything to prevent her from experiencing that pain.

And now, the three of us would be together forever. My own little perfect family. Lauren's shoes would be hard to fill, and some might think me too old to mother a young child, but I knew I was up to the challenge. I'd grown so much since Lauren was born.

There was a knock on the door, and it whispered open. Alana darted from behind the nurse's aide and ran to me, jumping onto my lap.

"She was asking where her Nana was," the aide said.

"Here I am," I sang to the girl, lifting her up. "Your mommy has been waiting all day to get a kiss from you." I held the child over Lauren as she strained to land her lips on her mother's cheek.

"Mommy still sleepy?" Alana asked as we settled into the chair at Lauren's bedside.

"Yes, sweetie, Mommy is still sleepy." Alana wiggled in my arms. "I bet you're sleepy too," I said playfully.

"No, not sleepy, Nana," she whined.

"Well, in that case, maybe we should go to the cafeteria for some ice cream! Just let me fix your hair. You look like you've been in a pillow fight." I turned my granddaughter in my lap and braided her hair while my daughter slept next to us.

Also by Lisa Courtaway

Red Water - Shadows of Camelot Crossing, A Haunting in Stillwater, Book 1

Deep Water - Shadows of Camelot Crossing, A Haunting in Stillwater, Book 2

Muddy Water - Shadows of Camelot Crossing, A Haunting in Stillwater, Book 3

Nova and the Ghost - A Haunted Hallways Mystery

To learn more about the author, please visit her website at www.lisacourtaway.com